WEAPON UwU

VOL 1: GODKILLERS

SJ WHITBY

This is a work of fiction. Names, characters, places, and incidents either are the product of the author's imagination or are used fictitiously. Any resemblance to actual persons, living or dead, events, or locales is entirely coincidental.

Cover by Jenn Lee

Typesetting by Gladys Qin

ISBN: 978-0-473-57654-7 (paperback)

978-0-473-57655-4 (ePub)

978-0-473-57656-1 (Kindle)

For everyone who wanted more mutants

Content Warnings

This book contains subject matter that may be triggering for some readers. Please be aware that while Weapon UwU Vol 1 is a "cozy horror," it contains a number of disturbing scenes. It also includes: blood, gore, drowning, death, murder, cannibalism, haunted house, eldritch monsters, spiders/insects, psychological manipulation, mind-control and mention of non-consensual medical experimentation.

Previously on Cute Mutants

This book takes place after Cute Mutants Vol 1 - 4. While reading these books in full will give greater enjoyment, here's a brief summary of important events...

It all started in Christchurch, New Zealand at Emma Hall's party, where she kissed a group of other people from her school: Dylan, Dani, Alyse, Bianca and Lou. Every single one of those people got superpowers. It took a few false starts, but they eventually teamed up and became the Cute Mutants. It's a good story. You should read it!

During their various shenanigans, they came to the attention of the government, who attempted to wrangle them into corporate superhero training. This didn't go at all well, partly because certain corporations wanted nothing more than to figure out exactly how Emma worked and how she could make other superheroes. Things got dark, and the team lost someone very close to them, but they gained new members too and ended up running the corporation for themselves.

Their new success brought them unwanted attention from a right wing military/religious organization known as Quietus. As more mutants were appearing around the world, created by a mutant with a rainbow for a face, Quietus were dedicated to their eradication. A series of bloody battles later, Dylan executed a Quietus agent on live television and the Cute Mutants became instantly notorious.

Lying low in the secret mutant enclave of Westhaven, Dylan and the others didn't take well to being put in the corner. They continued to fight against anyone who oppressed mutants, even though this led them to clash with the Westhaven Council and the enigmatic mutant Amethyst. They also learned the chilling truth: that mutants had existed before. On the verge of extinction, Emma's mother—a mutant called Teen Spirit and the most powerful psychic in the world—had wiped the knowledge of mutants from every mind in the world. Emma's other parent, a reality warper called Heart of a Flower had twisted the act at the final moment, so Emma's mother had forgotten too. The secret within the secret—Emma was an incredibly powerful mutant who had the power to save the world.

As they continued to fight against the humans and their attempts to destroy mutantkind, there was one more truth to reveal—the Council member Amethyst was Emma's parent Heart of a Flower in disguise. Their plan was to use Emma and her friends as a powerful weapon to win one final, brutal war against humans and establish mutant supremacy.

The Cute Mutants refused, and Heart of a Flower took brutal revenge. Emma was killed, along with a number of other mutants. Desperate and grieving, Dylan and the survivors managed to use a particular mutant's power to send Heart of a Flower to a parallel universe. They were about to execute the villain when someone dragged them out—Emma, who had brought herself back from the dead and undone the deaths of the other mutants too.

With Heart of a Flower safely tucked away, everything seemed to be returned to normal—aside from the problem of having the world's most powerful mutant learning to control her new powers. And people weren't exactly happy with having such a powerful threat sitting idle. So Dylan and Dani, along with the mind-erasing mutant psychologist Ray, decided to send a team of mutants on a mission into a parallel universe with one goal: to kill a mutant as powerful as a god.

I

HEART OF A FLOWER

GLADDY

Everything sucks and this is why: I've been thrust into a scenario that's doomed to fail. I hate this at a bone-deep level. I want to succeed. I want to crush it. This is my first true command mission: travelling to a parallel universe with a group of misfit mutants.

Our goal: executing a god.

The catch: we'll have no powers there. Theoretically, neither will the god.

All this assumes I can believe everything I've been told. Which I do, I suppose. There are few people I trust, but Dylan Taylor is one of them. Part walking disaster and part revolutionary mutant firebrand, I can rely on Chatterbox to fight for us.

We're all mutants, with extraordinary abilities, some of us more surprising than others. My personal superpower is to look at someone and see their secret fears. Right now, I'm face to face with Dylan, who is blinking at me with a scowl. It's rude to look away, so I'm stuck looking at their ghosts. They're so clear—a series of figures presided over by a tall, strong girl with purple lips and unruly black hair. Behind their eyes, a beautiful Korean woman dies a thousand times in a thousand ways. Each time, Dylan is a second too late to save the day.

It's painful to look at her, because she's been forged by so much loss and struggle. He's an open wound of regret, furious over the people the world has taken from him. They'd burn a lot to the ground to secure safety for mutants. Or have burned, depending on what angle you're looking from.

"I'm sorry." I force my attention to Dylan's face and not the fears that play out there. "What were you saying?"

"I was only asking if you were done with the fucking coffee, Fetchy."

"Oh." I flinch as if they startled me. "Yes. I've had mine already."

"I hate it when you look at me like that." Dylan swipes the plunger off me and fills a cup. "Makes me feel haunted." His lips twist wryly. "Aren't you supposed to be off on some hush-hush mission for Farsight?"

Truthfully, it's a reckless mission for Chatterbox, but they remember none of this.

"It's a milk run," I tell them.

"You take your coffee black." Dylan leans against the bench and sips. I can't even tell if this is one of their jokes or not. There's too much intensity to look at him, so I pat her shoulder and leave the room.

My thoughts are on the mission. I can't see my own fears in the mirror, which I'm grateful for, but one of them is failure. The reason I inherited this awful job is because I'm on the very short list of reliable people stored in Dylan's tousled, worried head. In turn, that means all this falls on me. My burden, my responsibility. I cannot fuck this up. I won't be the person responsible for bringing this down on top of us.

It's complicated because our assassination target is Heart of a Flower, creepy reality-warping mutant and parent of Goddess. The Goddess in question is one of Dylan's best friends, Emma, who happens to be the most powerful mutant in existence. She doesn't want her parent taken off the board, still harbouring some hope of future reconciliation. The rest of us had a backroom meeting and agreed it was a Very Bad Idea to keep someone so powerful and dangerous alive. Hence the mission, hence the secrecy, hence me being thrown out of my comfort zone and into this cursed situation.

Dylan doesn't remember about the mission because it's been wiped from their brain. Emma has a habit of wandering through her best friends' heads. I am terrified of Goddess and so I keep her at arm's length. She would be among my fears too. There's such a thing as too powerful. I shiver at the thought she might be eavesdropping on me.

"Guess who?" Cool hands cover my eyes and I feel a body press against my back. I know exactly who it is, because there are very few people on this entire planet, human or mutant, who would take this liberty with me. Most are intimidated or wary, which is honestly how I like it.

"Alyse." To be fair, she's the other one who *might* try this.

"No." There's delight in her voice, even though she knows I know.

"Dylan, I'm tired of you doing this," I snap, and she giggles.

"It's Maddy. Sourpatch." She whisks her hands away and spins me around by the shoulders. Her blonde hair is in a lopsided pixie cut and her cheeks are pale, but her brown eyes sparkle when she looks at me.

"You're the last person I would have guessed," I tell her.

"That's because you're the worst." She links her arm through mine. "When are we going on our top secret mission?" She whispers the last words in a voice somehow louder than if she'd spoken them normally.

"I've explained the concept of secrecy to you multiple times."

"Fine, okay, I'll call it the tee-ess-emm. But I still want to know *when*." Maddy has fears too, like anyone, but she makes an effort to hide them from me. I pretend I don't notice, crossing my third eye so they blur out of focus. It doesn't entirely work.

"Soon, but first we need to round up the others," I tell her. "Assemble the team."

"Weapon UwU!" Maddy came up with the name for our new squad, and it genuinely irritates Dylan, which I find immensely pleasing.

"Yes. Weapon UwU." It is an incredibly ridiculous name, given that it's some emoticon happy face, but Maddy lights up when I say it. It's worth all the ridiculousness in the world, because she's been through a lot.

Together we make our way through the cave system where we live. Westhaven is the current mutant refuge, hidden away in a top secret location known to almost nobody. It's home to more than two hundred mutants, very few of whom I've made the effort to get to know. I don't see that changing.

Most of those I *do* know wait in a small antechamber, along with the slender figure of Ray. They're the local psychologist, as well as the mutant responsible for the delicate incision in Dylan's memories that cut out all the details of this mission.

I trust Ray, and I'm not entirely sure why. They dress like an assassin's blade, and speak even more sharply. If Dylan is currently playing roulette with pronouns, Ray is most definitely a they, someone exquisite for who there is no comparison. I wonder if this is what attraction feels like.

My attention drifts to a slim boy with very short hair and an angelic face. He smiles at me nervously. This is Lou, or Glowstick. His power involves heat and light, triggered by sexual arousal. I hate my power, but I'm still devoutly grateful I didn't get stuck with his. I make the poor boy nervous, apparently. What a shame. "Uh, hi Fetch. Ray says we've got a mission. An important one."

"We're the new badasses in town." The short girl with shaved hair is Katie, or Dragon, who rather predictably breathes fire.

"Quite," I say.

Katie doesn't like me very much, but is much less cowed by me. She and Maddy connect in a way that makes me feel left out, although I'd never admit it to anyone. Together, they can be very annoying.

Skye Prime is here too. She's tan with broad shoulders and a long braid, and her power is to generate a series of increasingly erratic clones. Rounding out the group is a muscular woman in her thirties called Ye Shou, who I know very little about. None of the others will tell me what her powers are. Even Maddy will only tell me it's a secret and then goes off into peals of laughter.

"Uh, Fetch. I've been meaning to ask you." Lou swallows hard. "Do you think I can bring my girlfriend? Her name is Jenna and—"

"The team is the team." My voice is cold and barking, leaning on authority too hard. Trying to control everything. "What's her power?"

"Invisibility," he says eagerly, which does seem like an excellent power for a group of potential assassins to have. "Except it's not entirely, um, reliable yet."

"She's the one who pops in and out of existence all the time," Maddy says helpfully. "I like her. I think she's awesome."

This is less helpful than it seems, because Maddy likes most people. She even likes me, the eternal grump, although the force of her regard can be overwhelming. If we're ever separated for any length of time, she'll send me strange warbly Snapchats of her singing along to sad songs.

"We can't take Jenna if her power isn't reliable." I don't intend for the words to come out so harshly, but Lou's face falls. Now he'll be even more skittish. I look away. Keeping eye contact with most people is too hard.

My gaze drifts back to Maddy instead.

"Don't worry, Glowboy. When we come back from this mission, we'll talk to Jenna, won't we?" Maddy says.

"Yes, of course." I glance quickly at Lou, and he brightens. Most of his fears are nothing to do with me. The same worries about the future, of losing more friends. And more intimate things too. It feels voyeuristic to watch the parade of his various transitioning selves. I want to tell him that *of course* he's boy enough, but that feels too intimate.

"We can help her with training and everything," Maddy burbles, crossing to Lou and patting his shoulder. "Invisibility is a super cool power."

I wonder idly what invisibility *means*. Dylan's girlfriend Dani has a theory on how everyone's mutant power matches some aspect of their personality. For example, Dylan's awkwardness and lack of social skills led her to be able to communicate with objects. Lou's confusion about his sexuality means he has great outpourings of energy when he's turned on. Dani's never given an opinion on Maddy, but my private joke is that she's so fundamentally and impossibly sweet, and acid spit is a way to balance that out.

The truth behind my power is less pleasant and less ironic. I've always been perceptive and cynical. I used to pride myself on being able to cut others down, on choosing the precise word to launch at someone's soft underbelly. It was a technique I learned from my father and cultivated well. Now my ability gives me too much information, every intricate detail of how to take someone apart.

I can use that, and I have.

Your fears make an excellent weapon, precisely forged. You barely feel it going in.

"Fetchy." Maddy crosses to me and pats my cheek lightly. "Stop staring. Haven't we got better things to do?"

"Yes." My gaze flashes from face to face. My team. Weapon UwU. I'm starting to agree with Dylan on the name. How can we possibly be taken seriously? Or perhaps that's the point. Who'd expect us to be a team of deadly mutant assassins with a moniker like that?

MADDY

I can see Gladdy's nervous, so I smile wider at everyone to put them all at ease. It's like my job, seriously. World's greatest Fetch-wrangler. It was a little mean of Dylan, honestly, to put her in this position. Gladdy was made to live in a boardroom and sleep under an expensive desk, dressed in astonishingly fabulous suits and giving commands with an airy wave of her beautiful hand.

Instead, here we are in a cave with a bunch of angsty teenage mutants, ready to do terrible things. As a leader, Gladdy needs to look people in the eye, which means all their fears are *right there*—the darknesses we tuck away every day and pretend aren't real. I try to hide mine from her: that I'm a real life monster, that I'm unlovable, that I'm always *too on* and *too much* and nobody could withstand the full intensity of Madelaide McLean without running screaming for the hills. She pretends not to see it, and I pretend that's real, and that's what a relationship is.

I know it's hard for her. I've been with her when the walls come down. So I let her look away, and smile wider. I clap my hands for attention, and feel the acid churn in my gut. "Listen up. We're being trusted with something important. *Dylan* has asked us to do this."

That gets Katie's attention, the ridiculous little dragon. As much as she likes to troll Dylan, she idolises them. If Dylan asked her to roast *me*, I think she would, and she likes me a lot. I poke my tongue out at her and she gives me the finger back.

"Yes, it's for Dylan, and it's important, but what are we actually *doing*?" Katie asks.

"We'll discuss it elsewhere. Away from Westhaven." Ray looks very sombre today, dressed all in immaculate shades of dark grey.

I like Ray, although everyone else is scared of them. They're just a therapist for God's sake! We have really cool chats, even when we're talking about death and resurrection, and how the person you love maybe doesn't love you back. They try to be all deadpan, but I totally see the corner of their mouth twitch all the time.

I know our team seems like we're the B team. Everyone thinks Dylan and Dani and Alyse are such hot shit, and maybe they are. But they've also got Feral—who is basically just Catra if she was bitten by some kind of werething—and Penance, who is stabby stabby murder princess. They're a bunch of weirdos, just like us.

And who are the ones Dylan trusts with interdimensional murder? He's not asking any randos to do it. No, they picked us, because we're all part of her found family of misfits that rivals any fictional one you can think of. They call us the Cute Mutants, because we're what it says on the tin.

"What are we waiting for?" Skye's fidgety and nervous. The air around her blurs, and a pair of clones pop into existence beside her. Each clone she generates is different—the further you go down the list, the more erratic you get, like a copy of a copy. There used to be nine Skyes, but now there are only seven. Every time I think about two of her dying, I want to close my eyes and wish really hard, as if the acid is my secondary mutation and my true power is to undo terrible things. Only I'm not very good at it. The clones stay gone, and we're left to carry on in the sadness.

"Honestly," Skye Two drawls to her original. "Perhaps you can chill. Stop embarrassing me into coming out and cleaning up your messes."

"Fuck Prime," Skye Three says. "If we could only pack *her* back inside and let someone competent drive."

"It's got to be you or me, Three." Two eyes Prime disdainfully. "The others are too fucking ratchet."

"Obviously. Six would last about five seconds before being arrested. Still, better than Prime."

Skye Prime retreats to the wall of the cave, looking at her feet.

"Skye." Ray's voice is gentle. "Remember the exercises we talked about?"

Prime nods, her eyes big and watery, but she takes a deep breath and murmurs to herself. Before long the two clones blur and disappear.

"Excellent."

I bug my eyes at Ray, because here I've been chatting away like they're my friend when I'm in therapy, and they're actually a little bit magic. "Now, to answer your original question, we're waiting for our ride out of here."

The location of Westhaven is a big secret because lots of people want to kill mutants. That's not me being dramatic even though I *am* that bish. In the few months since I became a mutant, a lot of people have tried to murder us all. Most of them are buried in unmarked graves, although some of them were too melted and needed to be hosed away. Yes, that is me, the badass acid-spitter. Anyway, not every mutant has cool attack powers, so we have to keep quiet and hide away from trouble. Otherwise this little baby nation of ours could be wiped out. It sounds like an exaggeration, but it's come scarily close. When I first met Dylan, they were a clumsy kid keeping everything in the air, running on reckless hopes and dreams. Now she's been honed into a blade poised at the throat of the universe, ready to spill cosmic blood for the mutant cause. Yes, I *told* you that dramatic bish is me.

Keepaway races into the chamber and skids to a halt. Gladdy and I know them from way back, because they came up in the same cages where we were created. They're a teleporter, so they'll be our ride this evening.

"Hey Maddy." A shy smile crosses their face. Then they see Ray and any further words die in their throat with a strangled sound. What is it with Ray? I see the way Gladdy looks at them too, like there's something appealing about being impossibly svelte and elegant, looking like an assassin's blade came to life.

"Are we leaving or not?" I ask instead. "Or are we standing around being emo?"

Ray gives me their sliver of a smile. "Yes, Sourpatch. We have a mission. Keepaway, if you would? The usual diner will do, I think."

Our teleporter presses the flat of their palm against Ray's left shoulderblade and they disappear. Lou goes next and then Skye and Ye Shou. Only Gladdy and I remain.

"You okay?" I ask Keepaway.

They smile wider than I've ever seen. "It's a good job. I like being useful. I took Dylan and Dani to the Greek Islands for a picnic this morning."

I snort. "Yeah, I bet there was a *picnic*, but they didn't take any food."

Keepaway blinks at me. "I'm confused."

"I'm not explaining the joke."

They frown, but place their hand on Gladdy's arm, and she vanishes too. "I could take you and Fetch somewhere nice if you wanted." Heartbeats pass. "And Dylan *did* bring food, although it was mostly terrible junk."

"I don't think picnics are in our future. Now hurry up and send me away."

"Sometimes a picnic is just a picnic." Keepaway pats me awkwardly on the arm, and the world shrinks to a dot.

~ UwU ~

When everything reappears, I'm on a quiet street, standing in the parking lot of a diner. The sign outside screeches quietly as it rotates. There's a single dirty car parked across the lines. The windows are covered in the same dust that coats everything. It's like stepping into a scene out of a movie: a lost diner, somewhere in the dark parts of America.

Gladdy leans in the doorway, holding it open. There's the slightest frown on her face, and I feel the same worn-out urge to touch her. I want to press my fingers into the creases and smooth them away. To have her look into my face and see nothing of my fear, but everything else that burns there.

I may as well wish for a world where mutants can be happy and unafraid. So I smile at Gladdy as if my fears are nothing more substantial than dust.

"Holding the door for me, my lady?" I sweep an elegant bow.

"Maddy, you're so annoying."

"I'm not the one letting all the dust in." I elbow her in the stomach as I duck past her and into the cool interior.

We're the only customers, but Ray has everyone clustered in a single large booth against the far wall. Gladdy lets the door bang closed and we walk over. There's a waitress taking orders, but her vowels are so heat-softened I find them hard to follow, so I let Gladdy order for me. I need a lot of food to keep this whole acid thing going, but since I died I've been really picky. I do like pancakes though. Hopefully they have pancakes.

Oh yeah, I died, and I did it before it was fashionable. I was resurrected through some mix of mad science and Goddess blood, a cocktail never since replicated. Aren't I just the specialest girl in town?

Of course, then Dani Kim the showoff got herself killed stopping someone from exploding and then got resurrected by a friendship circle. After that a whole other bunch of people got murdered by Emma's parent and brought back to life. I'm the trendsetter, really.

I tell you, our lives are impossible.

"Stop mumbling." Gladdy nudges me. "You're doing the narration thing."

"Bad habit." I look at Ray, who is not twitching the corner of their mouth at the moment. "Quiet now."

Everyone's attention is on Ray, which doesn't seem to faze them at all. They clear their throat and begin talking. "I'm not sure how much everyone knows. So let's sum up the barest facts, as that's all you need. One of the deadliest mutants alive is currently depowered. We need to carry out the execution while it's possible."

"Execution." Lou glances around at us, as if we wouldn't get it without his helpful interjection.

Skye trembles, and Ray reaches across the table and touches her wrist lightly.

"Yes, execution. Heart of a Flower's crimes are numerous. They are responsible for the nonconsensual creation of multiple mutants, as well as the formation of Quietus. They also performed long-term manipulation of the Westhaven council under their guise of Amethyst."

Ye Shou leans forward. "What the hell? *Our* Amethyst?"

"Do you want proof?" Ray asks. "Or do you trust me?"

"Completely."

"Then believe me this is a long time coming. Heart's aim was a war between humanity and mutantkind. One that humans would lose." Ray breaks off as the waitress returns to the table with various drinks, sundaes, and baked goods. This includes the largest chocolate chip cookie I've ever seen, which is laid in front of me with suitable reverence befitting a cookie of its stature.

"I thought you'd like it," Gladdy says.

"Thank you." It's been warmed and I pull off a piece and offer it to her. Gladdy dips her head and takes it with her mouth. There's a moment where her lips brush the tips of my fingers. If I was a fool, it would make my sluggish undead heart lurch to life in my chest like I'd run a race.

I have slightly more sense than that, so all I do is break off a chunk for myself.

GLADDY

Maddy insists on feeding me parts of this enormous cookie by hand, which is messy and makes her laugh. I realise Ray has paused their recital and is watching me with what feels like judgement. Their fears are complex and dizzying, to do with a web of possibilities feeling blindly into the future. They coalesce around Emma, and whether she offers hope or doom. Also whether a group of late-teen disasters can shepherd the mutant nation to safety, in amongst a human race that seems determined to drive off a cliff.

"Enjoying your cookie?" Ray asks.

"Why?" Maddy grins. "Do you want some?"

"I can eat and listen." I aim a smile of my own back at Ray. I wish it was a fraction as bladed, but all they do is incline their head and look down at their neatly folded hands.

"Many of you confronted Heart of a Flower. You know how powerful and dangerous they are. It would be impossible to kill them if they weren't currently in a place where, according to both Chatterbox and Marvellous, mutant powers are ineffectual." Ray finally unfolds their hands to wrap them around their coffee cup, although they don't drink. "Your task is to enter this place and kill Heart."

Nobody says anything for a moment. There's the faint scraping of knives on plates from Maddy and Katie, who are the only ones able to eat through this.

Katie swallows loudly. "No powers. That means us too."

"Yes. No fireballs, no acid."

"It'll be only me," Skye whispers.

"What does that mean for my powers?" Ye Shou asks.

Ray's eyelids flutter. "I'm not sure. Perhaps you should hold the door for this mission."

I try not to make an irritated huffing sound and only half-succeed. This game of not telling me about Ye Shou's power is annoying. There are no clues when I look in her direction. Her fears are all to do with her family who she hasn't seen in months, since she was abducted by Quietus soldiers.

Lou clears his throat. "So we have to kill Heart the, uh, the—"

"The way humans have been doing for a long time." Ray's lips make a subtle twist. It's almost a smile, but I can't find the joke in it.

"I'll do it," Maddy says.

I feel like my own fears are naked for the whole table to see. "We don't know about your powers over there either. You're alive because of Goddess, which means…?" My hand flutters in the air.

"It's a good point," Ray says. "Sourpatch can monitor the portal with Ye Shou."

"I'm staying with Gladdy." Maddy has her stubborn face on. "We go together."

"You've gone on missions without me," I remind her softly. "Dangerous ones. And I—" The sentence is too hard to finish. I want to tell her I couldn't bear it if she was gone, but it's the sort of sentence that comes with strings and barbs. She'll weave rocky pieces of truth and wishes together on a string and call it something whole.

"You what?" Maddy asks.

"It's too dangerous." I close that door in her face, even though I see the hurt there and the fears that flare behind it. The urge to reassure her is a knot in my larynx. I could tell her she can be safe with me, but that might be the worst lie of all.

"Fuck me, you goddamn babies." Katie shoves her empty plate into the middle of the table and splays her fingers on the surface. "I'll stab the fucking asshole. They tried to kill us all. I'm not going to cry for them."

"If you can't, I will." Everyone turns to look at Lou when he speaks. "If this is necessary, if this is what Dylan wants… They're not the only one who's changed."

"Mutant warrior." Katie grins and punches him in the arm. "I'll let you be my backup."

"Heart *hurt* people." Maddy's voice is suddenly hollow. "He killed people, and I know it was a game to him or whatever, but…" She gestures, her hand like a fluttering bird summing up so many words. Her face crumples, and behind it all her fears blossom in crystal-clear perfection.

I don't remember it, but Heart of a Flower killed me too. It's only because I've watched it replayed on the face of everyone who was there that I believe it. The hideous sculpture he made of me, and how Maddy wept.

When we came back and everything was allegedly fixed, Maddy slept—or an approximation of it. More correctly, she thrashed about in bed like something caught on a hook. I perched on a chair beside her like a creature out of a nightmare, craning over her and watching as she relived my death over and over again.

She's seen her love die. I don't know that I understand love, at least not as it's told in stories. I trace it through the afterimages of fears. The obsession people have with loss—Dylan in Dani's eyes and Dani in Dylan's—leaves a mess of complex contours. From that I can reconstruct what I think people mean.

I saw Maddy's love for me as she mourned my passing. A human shadow etched in her mind.

What I saw was a person who doesn't exist. It's a shell I built a long time ago—a beautiful, brittle mask. I peer out from inside, pulling the strings that make it go.

My greatest fear is the discovery that I'm fake.

I know how obsessed the others are with mapping what Maddy and I have. I extracted this truth from Dylan one night a while back, before we came to Westhaven. Our insomniac patterns synced up and we found ourselves on the roof of the Yaxley building, sipping whiskey and looking out over the city.

"You can fucking tell me, Fetch." Dylan rolls the shot glass between their fingers and raises it to their nose to inhale the smoky traces. "I'm entirely fucking one hundred percent goddamn take-it-to-the-bank reliable with secrets."

"Except for the part where you tell Dani."

"I do tell her everything, the messy guts of me and all. It's like a game of chicken. When will she swerve?" There's a flash of teeth under the streetlight. "She crashes into me every time."

"Maddy and me..." I join her at the edge of the building and look out over the city. The street below is quiet, aside from a couple walking past, heads down in coats. The alcohol warms me up, but it also fuzzes my words, makes them pliable. "We look after each other. I trust her. There are nuances."

"The nuances of bro." Dylan grins at me. The wind catches her tousled hair and whips it off her face.

"What the hell does that mean?"

"Your relationship. It's friends but it's more."

"We are not friends with benefits."

Dylan laughs and hurls the shot glass over his shoulder into the night. I don't hear it land. "That's your dirty mind, Fetch my love. Friends with tangled pieces all tied up in knots. You wade through shit, you hold each other up, and you come out bros."

"The nuances of bro." I whisper it like it's a secret. It feels truer than most.

"I'm adding it to Lovepool." Dylan fumbles with their phone.

"What the hell is that?"

"Shared doc." She winks. "Where we keep the odds on your relationship statuseses...es? I'm too drunk for this. Hey Siri! Remind me to update Lovepool in the morning. Remember this because it's very very important: the nuances of bro."

"I'll do it." My words scatter on the table like thrown coins. "I'm field leader. I'll take Heart's life."

"Ugh." Katie slumps in her seat. "Why do field leaders always get to take the fun jobs?"

"We're talking about taking a life. You don't need to call it fun." Ray bestows a rare frown. "Are you sure you're up to it, Fetch?"

"Plenty of backup if I'm not." I hold Ray's gaze.

"Excellent. I'll return to Westhaven. You can travel to Christchurch from here and I'll send Palimpsest and

Trang after you. It seems safest to open the portal in the precise place we did last time."

"Parallel universes." I finally touch my tea, but it's cold. I sip it anyway. "We're sure about this?"

"It depends how much credence you put in Marvellous," Ray says.

"More than most," I admit. "Although it seems—"

"Fantastical?" Ray smirks. "Given who we have sitting around this table, parallel universes seem to be rather traditional and mundane. Wouldn't you agree?"

"Bubble universes." Ye Shou brightens, tracing patterns on the table with her fingers. "Have you read up on Max Tegmark, Fetch? The science is far more credible than whatever happened to me when Spark bent reality to unlock my DNA."

I've actually read Tegmark, or at least articles about Tegmark, but it doesn't seem like the time to geek out about the levels of the multiverse.

"I'm sure Gladdy finds it very interesting and could talk about it all day." Maddy beams around the table. "Dani and Dylan went there and came back fine, so let's get this over with. Then we might get a mission where I can help more than holding the door for you lazy lumps."

She slides out of the booth and holds out her hand to me. There's a second or two of hesitation before I take it. The nuances of bro.

MADDY

Keepaway is leaning against the window of the diner as we come out. When they stand, there's a faint shadow of them left behind in the grimy window.

"Next stop?" They wave their hand towards me and I scurry out of the way, in case they accidentally send me to the moon or Texas.

"Christchurch. Same place we fought Heart."

"Scary." Keepaway shudders and I wonder what their fears are. I almost never ask Gladdy, even though I always want to know.

This time, I let them touch my arm so I'm the first one to go.

The day is overcast, a heavy layer of grey cloud with only an arch of clear sky to the northwest, glowing faintly golden. The trees whip in the breeze that carries dry heat with it, like opening an oven and having it roar at you.

Lou appears next, shortly followed by Skye, who still looks overwhelmed.

"Don't worry. You can hold the door with Ye Shou if you want. You don't have to come in and kill anyone."

"No. I suppose I don't." Her mouth flattens. "But I'm still going in with the team."

I don't bother hiding my eye roll, because it's not like Skye Prime is going to shout at me. I know it's mean, but it *might* be better to have a clone in charge. Dylan loves Six, because they're approximately as foul mouthed and aggressive as each other, which goes to show how many degrees separate Prime and regular Dylan.

"What the hell are you giggling about?" Lou asks me.

"I'm imagining Dylan Six."

"Oh God. I can't even. I think we'd all have been stabbed a long time ago."

"Imagine how they would talk. Fuck fuck fuckitty fuck."

Lou shakes his head solemnly. "That just sounds like normal Dylan to me."

We're both still laughing when Ye Shou appears with Gladdy right behind her.

"Something's funny," Gladdy says.

"Dylan Six apparently." Skye's nervous enough that Two has appeared and is talking for her. "I don't get it myself, or the crush Dylan has on Six."

"Let's all be glad Chatty has the weird power they do rather than clones," Gladdy says.

"Chatty." Ye Shou raises an eyebrow. "It is odd to me the way you're all so companionable with your leaders. When I first saw that footage of Chatterbox and the trial they held with Abigail Tanner, I thought I had found a person unafraid to fight for our people. There is someone I can follow."

There's an odd silence that falls because we all know Dylan, especially Lou who knew them before they were Chatterbox. And while Ye Shou is right, we've all seen Dylan standing barely-dressed in front of the fridge shouting about who ate the last piece of pizza. We've seen them become a sobbing wreck in their parent's arms, and be tipsily terrible at board games.

Dylan isn't so much a leader as the one in the family who keeps making the decisions.

But on the other hand, Ye Shou is right, because we all follow Chatterbox. We're here on this impossible errand, aren't we? That alone is proof.

The quiet is disturbed as Palimpsest and Trang appear one after the other. She's tall and muscly with tiny writing all over her skin and Trang is a slim and quiet guy. Their mutant power works together, which is super cool, and I wish mine and Gladdy's did. When Trang reads aloud the words written on Palimpsest's skin, they come true. Together, they're a living spell book who opened the door to the parallel universe where Heart is.

"We're really doing this?" Palimpsest shudders. She missed most of the chaos, but did turn up when—

My brain refuses to process it. It makes me seize up every time. You can't question miracles, because maybe they'll be snatched away. I want to reach out and take hold of Gladdy, to wrap my arms around her and press every part of myself against her, the pair of us unrolled into two dimensions to maximise surface area. I want to force her to stay in this world, to negate all reality of her possible death.

"You're looking at me weirdly," Gladdy says.

"I'm thinking about how hideous you are."

"Fuck off, you undead troll." Her mouth is soft and curved, and I think about how words like this are easier to say than proclamations of love, because you can accrete all those feelings in the in-jokes like layers until they mean so much more from the inside than you could ever tell.

"Field leader," Lou says loudly. "Stop making googly eyes at your girlfriend. You're as bad as Deezer."

Deezer is Dylan and Dani, as in "the D's are." Usually in sentences like *the D's are making out again* or *the D's are off doing God knows what, except then we're all God because we all know what.*

I wait for Gladdy to protest that I'm not her girlfriend, but she wraps her arms about herself and crosses to Palimpsest. It's not a signal. I'd be a fool to see that as a signal. Maybe it is.

"So you just read it aloud?" Gladdy asks Trang.

"That's how it works. Of course, we've never done one of these twice before, so we're in uncharted territory. It might fizzle." Usually when Trang recites one of Palimpsest's spells, it disappears from her skin. Emma borrowed another mutant's powers and bent them to perform a time-reversal trick and put the genie back in the bottle.

It's the same way she brought Gladdy and the others back from the dead, so I desperately hope this works. If it doesn't, then that means the resurrection might fail too and—

No. Gladdy is alive and I haven't noticed a single difference in her, no matter how hard I've looked. Emma died too, and she came back *better*, or at least far more powerful. I suppose that's what happens when you reassemble yourself from nothing.

"May as well find out." Palimpsest trails her fingers along the line of text in question.

Apparently it says something about opening a door to another world. I don't understand Vietnamese, but Trang reads it aloud in a firm, clear voice.

The instant he finishes, there's a sound like a door slamming. I look up to see one sitting a few metres from us. An ordinary wooden door that you might find in the hallway of an ordinary suburban house—like the one I grew up in before everything went wrong.

"Looks like the same door," Trang says. "Identical handle and everything."

"Do we open it?" Skye has four clones assembled around her now, which shows her level of worry at the situation.

"Yes we fucking open it," Five snaps. "I'll fucking kick it down. You watch."

"Prime, get them on a leash." Gladdy walks up to the door and puts the flat of her palm against the surface. "It feels like an ordinary door."

Lou wanders behind it. "There's nothing on the other side, like Dilly said. It's standing in the middle of nowhere, like something out of a story."

"For fuck's sake." Skye Five goes to nudge Gladdy out of the way. "Will someone just *open the fucking door* already?"

"Back off," I snap. "I've got powers on this side and I don't mind spitting at you."

Five's smart enough to fall back. Six might not have been. Behind me, Keepaway reappears to take Palimpsest and Trang away. Their job is done, while ours is just beginning.

"We're here to do a job." Gladdy twists the handle. "So let's do it."

Skye Five and I are jostling alongside her, just in case Heart of a Flower is lurking on the other side. Behind us, everyone else assembles. I'm willing to throw myself through the door to stop them no matter what. If Heart gets through, then we're all dead.

Maybe Emma can bring us back all over again, but it seems like a massive risk.

"No jump scares, please no fucking jump scares," Lou whispers behind me.

Gladdy pushes the door inwards in one sharp motion. If Heart is lurking there, it'll slam them right in the face.

The world beyond the door is quiet and dim.

There's no sign of Heart of a Flower.

There's no sign of *anyone.*

Gladdy steps across the threshold.

I don't even think about it. I step through the door.

Behind me, Lou lets out a screech. "Sourpatch, no!"

I look back over my shoulder with a grin. "I'm fine." I take a few steps further and spread my arms and look up at the sky. It's a dense, heavy grey that doesn't look natural. There are no stars or clouds that I can see. "Look, I'm totally fine."

"You." Gladdy grabs my shoulder. "You!"

"Me! If I'd collapsed or fallen down dead, you would have dragged me back through the door. It wasn't entirely stupid of me." This is a lie. I didn't even think. I followed Gladdy because that's what I do. Perhaps it's not what I *should* do.

Behind me, Skye Five strides through the door and promptly disappears.

"Five! What are you doing?" Four dives through after her disappeared clone, but the moment she crosses the threshold, she vanishes too. Two and Three are smart enough to hang back, but they vanish too once Prime joins us. Her powers are gone here, like everyone promised.

Katie practically skips through, dragging Lou after her. She peers around at the strange world on the other side. It looks like a street, but wider than the ones in our version of Christchurch. The buildings that line the way are very tall, made of a smooth grey material. I lose sight of the tops of them. They have doors and windows, but they don't look real, more like someone's scraped the shape of them into the buildings with a very large knife.

There are signs atop each door.

Enablement Potential Annex

Eldritch New Zealand Society for the Elderly

Christchurch Tumour Encyclopaedia

"This place is fucking weird," Katie breathes. "It's super creepy. I love it."

"I don't. I feel like something's lurking." Skye shudders and clasps her hands together. "I keep waiting for the others to come out and help me, but they're not there." She's on the verge of tears. "I don't like them being gone."

Katie growls like an angry puppy and makes a weird hissing sound in her throat. "I agree with that part. This no powers thing is bullshit. No fucking fire. All the rage."

Lou does a slow turn near the doorway and smirks. "Really wish you'd let me bring Jenna on this trip. Find a quiet spot amongst all these… creepy, creepy buildings and not worry about setting her on fire. Fetch, what's next?"

Gladdy takes me by the shoulders and stares into my eyes. "I can't see anything."

"You're blind?"

"Fears, Madelaide!" She crosses to Skye. "There's nothing here."

GLADDY

I look at Skye's face and can actually make out every detail. The strong nose, the nervous chapped lips, the startlingly long eyelashes that are surely fake, and the broken brown and gold pattern of her irises. I can't see her fears. They're usually an ever-changing chaotic froth, shifting on the whims of the world, teased out in strands by the sticky fingers of her anxiety. Now they're absent and her face is clear.

None of this is true. I'm merely blind to it.

I thought it was what I wanted, to be free of this curse that plagues me. Seeing the darkness and fear in people is objectively the worst superpower. Dani told me that once, a few drinks in, and it was a relief to hear that someone understood. There's no upside. And yet now that it's been taken away, I feel cut off. The fears are still inside each person. The darkness still exists. It's like losing a layer of reality from the world.

All these people are opaque to me.

I thought I was so unique hiding behind a mask, but every single person wears their own.

"You must be happy." Maddy takes my hand. "No fears."

"Yes." I look into her eyes, but her face is unfamiliar, stripped of context. "But we need to be searching for Heart. They could be anywhere."

"I'm in the doorway," Ye Shou says from behind me. "I'll warn if there's any incursion."

We have to stop Heart before they cross over. That's the only critical thing.

"I don't want to split up." Skye extends one hand to touch one of the nearby buildings and then recoils. "Who knows what else is here?"

"Had to fucking say that," Katie mutters. "Jinxer."

"These signs." Lou's standing a short distance up the road. "*Christchurch Lunarial-Agnostic Society*. What does that even mean?" He reaches out and pushes on the door. "Ah, fuck. It's spongy!"

When I brush my hand over the surface of the closest building, it's fibrous and slightly damp. I run my fingers around the edges. There's no handle. Gritty flakes come off and drift down onto my pants. They're far too expensive to ruin with greasy smears of otherworldly door.

I tentatively sniff my fingertips, which smell like crushed leaves. We should have come in here with test tubes and taken samples. This could be a technological advancement that could change the world. Or, with our luck, a toxic plague that would take us over. I look at the grey smudges on my clothing and hope I'm not going to infect our universe. I love these pants and don't want to leave them in—

"Wow," I whisper. "A parallel universe."

Growing up, my father had the Alice quote about six impossible things on the wall of his office. Since I got mutant powers, I've seen far more than that. Dylan likes to snark about handwaving the science, but I'm desperate to grasp at some fraction of understanding. Here I am, standing on a different version of Earth in another *universe*. Some laws of reality may have changed, but we can breathe the air and the language is the same. Which is astonishing on it's own because—

I'm lightheaded and my chest is tight. This can't be *real*.

We need to get this done and escape.

I take a moment to breathe. I glance at the others. None of them seem as disturbed by what they're seeing as me. I remind myself I can't see their fears. It's very possible they are, and we're all barely holding it together in this impossible place.

I need to calm down.

This is fine. The magical door between dimensions is right there. We can leave at any time. This is another world. Of course things will be different here. Get a goddamn grip on yourself, Gladiola.

"Katie?" I ask. "Do you want to try and get through one of these doors?"

She doesn't even ask a question. That's the advantage of someone like Dragon. They want to do all the crazy shit in the first place.

"Poke?" Dragon steps forward and scrapes enthusiastically at the strange material. It continues to crumble and flake, messy chunks of it falling to the ground. She inspects her fingers and gives a tiny shudder, flapping them in the air as if that'll get them clean. "It's super gross, like slimy and sticky at the same time."

I brush vigorously at my own pants. "Gross, but it's good news. If the buildings aren't accessible, Heart can't be hiding in any of them. So we don't have to search them all which would be…" My head tilts back as I gaze upwards, trying to make out the tops of them. Is the sky metal? They don't build Dyson spheres around planets, do they? What would be the point?

"Yes," Maddy says. "Positive thinking. That's what we need. And don't worry, Skye, we'll all stick—"

Except Katie's already gone ahead, and Maddy scurries to catch up with her.

"Wait up, Dragon. Do you not understand stick together? You'll get eaten by something and Dylan will never let me hear the end of it."

The street—for want of a better word—stretches into the distance. There doesn't appear to be anything to differentiate the buildings aside from the confusing signs. They're English but they make no coherent sense. If the buildings aren't real, what are the signs supposed to indicate? They read like they've been generated by a malfunctioning AI. Maybe in this version of our world, humanity is dead and nanotech is running wild, making a dead city under an artificial sky.

I peer between the buildings, but smooth, slightly curved fences run between them. The barriers seem as tall as the structures themselves, or at least I lose sight of them somewhere far above me.

I glance over my shoulder. Ye Shou is still framed in the doorway, shrunk by perspective. I have this superstitious feeling that if we lose sight of her, we'll be lost forever. My own fears, running wild because I can't be distracted by the nightmares of others. Why were we so foolish as to come here? Couldn't Dylan trust someone else on an errand to another world to kill a god?

Up ahead, Maddy and Katie are hand in hand, zigzagging from one side of the street to the other as they check out each building. This is the advantage of being a handwave the science person. You get to dance around a terrifying new world as if it's an amusement park.

"I wonder why our powers don't work here." Lou falls into step beside me. "Seems strange."

"Yes." I'm grateful for the distraction. "It means our powers aren't entirely tied up in ourselves or our DNA."

He shakes his head. "Some link to the planet. Emma and Dani might have theories. Dylan too."

"Comic book theories."

"Better than none. Perhaps there's something about Earth's magnetosphere, or solar radiation from our star. Maybe there really are cosmic rays that trigger it and this version of Earth doesn't have them."

The building we walk past says *Branching Reality Nexus (Abridged).*

"This place." I can't hold back a shudder.

"It's creepy feelin' for sure. Depending on what forms parallel universes, you have to wonder what happened here to make it so different to our world. How is it still called Christchurch?"

I glance at him, but he's watching the buildings. "Don't laugh, but I used to read a lot of science fiction stories. My Dad was obsessed. Makes sense given he was a bit of a mad scientist himself, right?"

"Pear's no mad scientist, but they read a lot of it too. I get the hand-me-downs when they're done," Lou says. "I loved the one about the robot who was part of the ship. One Esk."

"That's the worst summary of *Ancillary Justice* I've ever heard, but I love that book too."

"The problem is when I read something like *Christchurch Neural Maladaption Cathedral* I feel like we're in a story with a fucking terrifying ending. Something Lovecraftian with a horrible god slumbering in the deeps." Lou pauses and stares at a building saying *Little Shop of Night Terrors*. "Even though he was a racist asshole."

"Such a racist asshole." I laugh despite myself and the surroundings. "But yes—this is Cthulhu Christchurch if ever there was one."

"Don't say that." Lou grabs my arm and points with the other at a sign saying *Inalienable Temple of Vixx-Luqualatan*. "You're fucking encouraging it."

"It said that before, right?"

"I think so." His voice sounds a tiny bit hysterical, which is not what I need right now. "Could it be listening to us? Picking up on some vibe?"

At least we're still in sight of Ye Shou and the door. I need to focus on the mission. We're here for a reason, and that's more important than deducing what this place might be. I take a deep breath, ready to move on, and that's when the screaming starts.

MADDY

Gladdy is being odd again. Perhaps I should pay more attention to the moments where she's *not* being odd. I love her, and that's something I can't deny. It's not a fact I feel needs to be hidden away from others, or dressed up in other words to pretend it's somehow categorically different. Dylan can shove the nuances of bro. I want to talk to Gladdy, to break the oddness down into pieces that make sense. But from painful experience I know the best thing to do when Fetch is in her feelings like Aubrey is to give her space.

Katie's a few buildings ahead. I bet she's forgotten she has no powers.

"Wait up, Dragon. Do you not understand *stick together*? You'll get eaten by something and Dylan will never let me hear the end of it."

She sticks her hands on her hips and glares at me as if I'm being unnecessarily boring. At least she does stop, so it doesn't take me long to catch up.

"We should at least pretend to wait for the others."

My breath is coming fast.

"What's the big deal? If anything happens I'll just—"

I raise my eyebrows at her.

"Pummel them into submission," she says with a laugh. "Then drag them through the door and roast them."

"I knew you'd forgotten."

"Whatever. I'm offended you underestimate my pummelling skillz. Yes, I said that with a zed." She grabs my hand and tugs me towards the nearest building up ahead. "Look. *Oceania Vulgar Complacency Sphere.* This place is *weird.* And the doors don't even work." She kicks it and the toe of her boot sinks a little way into the surface.

"Gross." I wrinkle my nose and we cross to the building on the other side. "*Christchurch Invalid Invalid Invalid Domicile.* It's totally wrecked here. No wonder our powers don't work."

"Where is this stupid Heart of a Flower anyway? Maybe they've been walking down this same street since they got here and they're miles away."

"Oh God." I squint into the distance but the street seems to carry on in the same direction forever. "I think everyone assumed they'd be waiting around by the door in case we came back."

"You're both right." A person steps out of a shallow

alcove between two buildings just ahead of us. They're rumpled and exhausted. Their clothes hang loose on their body and their face is hollow. "I walked for a long time in one direction but it never changed." They wave one hand limply. "Then I turned around and came back. There's no day or night here, although some-times it rains. I think it's on a timer. That water's the only reason I'm alive, although there's no food of any kind, so I wouldn't have lasted much longer." There's a very awkward pause. "Who sent you in here?"

Katie and I both stare at Heart of a Flower. We came in here to hunt a monster, and we've stumbled across a shell of a person. I'm *supposed* to be terrified, but I'm not at all. It's sort of sad, really. We could have left them here and they would have died without any intervention. I don't know if that's better or worse than coming here to kill them. It feels worse to me.

"Why does it matter who sent us?"

"Was it Chatterbox? Revenge for my daughter?"

I smile at them. "Your daughter's fine."

"Really? That's very—" Heart lunges at Katie and I let out an incoherent screech. Even though they're weak from hunger, they bear her to the ground. Katie tries to spit flame, because it's always her go-to move.

I scream, but I'm frozen as Heart bangs her head on the ground. As much as I mocked Dragon and her fire fetish, my first urge is to spit acid. I even try and cough it up, but it dribbles down my chin—saliva that doesn't burn. Is there really nothing brewing in the cauldron of my stomach?

The sound of Katie's head hitting the ground and the high-pitched animal sound she makes startles me to delayed action.

"Get off her!" I barrel into Heart, but they swipe me away with one arm. I sprawl on my hands and knees. I never learned to fight. I didn't think it would matter. But I still get to my feet and launch myself back at them, just as they take Katie's neck in their hands and start applying pressure.

I rake my fingernails at their wrists, because that doesn't need powers at all, and gouge white lines in their flesh, with fat beads of blood welling up.

Heart doesn't relax their grip. Katie is making horrible noises, and I can't understand the words. Her eyes bulge and her hands flail.

"Haven't you killed enough people?" I wrap my hands around Heart's head and jab my thumbs into their eyes. They finally let go of Katie, who coughs and splutters. My shoulders sag in relief, but their fist hits me hard across the face. It jars my whole head. I fall backwards, and sit on the ground blinking. I know I'm supposed to get up and do something, but my limbs are on a delayed timer. My default option can't be watching my friend get strangled.

Lou rushes past me, and one foot connects hard with Heart's shoulder. He slides to the ground, manoeuvring himself around to wrap both arms around Heart's neck, legs bracing. I've seen him do this sort of thing in practice with the others, laughing and shouting and calling each other names.

It's very different to see it in reality. It's faster and more brutal, on the edge of savagery, bone and meat impacting each other.

Heart flails one hand around, reaching back like a wild claw.

"Grab the arm," Lou grunts. "That'd help. Break a fucking finger or two."

Katie is back on her feet. She kicks Heart right in the face. Something breaks, either their nose or their teeth. It's hard to tell from the blood.

"Easy, little Dragon," Lou says. "We've got him."

"Fuck them," Katie rasps. "They tried to kill me." She puts Heart's arm into a hold of her own, bracing one boot against their midsection.

"Bloody hell." Gladdy approaches with confident strides. She's wearing a jacket that fans out around her just a little, to give her that military commander look. It suits her. "That happened fast. Glad you were onto it, Glowstick."

"It's called training." He smirks. "You two never liked it. Relied on your powers too much."

Heart of a Flower tries to speak, but Lou has their neck clamped tight. Skye Prime is hanging back, both hands pressed to her lips as if she has to manually stop herself from screaming.

"Let them loose," Gladdy reaches into the pocket of her combat jacket and pulls out a long knife.

"You sure?" Lou doesn't look at all convinced.

"If they try anything, you'll deal with it. I trust you."

Lou releases Heart of a Flower and retrieves a blade of his own. I didn't realise he brought one through. Maybe secret orders from Dylan.

Heart doesn't bother getting up. They lie on the ground while we cluster around.

"Fuck you." Katie huffs air as if she wishes it was fire.

"So my daughter lives. Did she send you in here to fetch me back, or to see me dead?"

"She doesn't know we're here," Gladdy says.

"If you think that, you're a fool. If she's alive, she is in full command of her powers and will at the very least register your disappearance to this reality." Their gaze travels across us all. "Does she rule the world yet?"

"What the fuck are you *talking* about?" Katie asks. "Does Emma rule the world? Of course she bloody well doesn't."

"Such a waste." Heart sighs. "It's a lesson in humility, learned late and bitterly. No matter how smart and powerful you are, you cannot order the world to your taste."

"We're not here to listen to you pontificate," Gladdy says.

"You're here to sentence me to death."

"No." There's a pause. "We're here to carry out the sentence."

"Ah. Not to bring me back before your Goddess in chains? Marvellously ironic nickname, I have to say."

Gladdy clutches the knife, and her knuckles are white. "There's no way we're letting you cross the threshold back to our world."

Heart laughs, but there's no humour in it. "You realise she's more powerful than me? More powerful than all of you. She could limit my abilities quite easily."

"Nice try," Katie sneers. "I'm sixteen years old, and I'm not naive enough to fall for that shit."

"It's true. You'll find out soon enough." They get to their knees, slowly and awkwardly. "Which one of you has it in you to kill me? You left the most dangerous ones at home, it seems."

"We had no shortage of volunteers." Gladdy doesn't do anything fancy like twirl the knife. She just points it straight at Heart. "But I'll do it."

"Ah yes. The one who saw the darkness in me." They smile, and I can see the resemblance to Emma in their face. It makes the thought of killing them too hard. Makes it too real, turns them from a monster into a person. I don't think I could do the knife thing looking at that face.

"We all saw the darkness." Gladdy is wavering too, I think, and I hope Lou or Katie can do the stabbing if it comes down to it.

"Yes, it's all very dramatic. I am the monster. Kill me and get it over with. I only ask one thing." They fish around their neck and pull out a ring on a slim silver chain. It has a large chunk of amethyst set into it. "I'd like you to give this to Emma."

"The ring stays here," Lou says.

"Don't be ridiculous," Heart snaps. "It's obviously nothing to do with my powers or it wouldn't exist here, would it? It has sentimental value. Believe it or not, I loved Lan Jing. That love was something I sacrificed on the altar of the mutant future. Yes, sacrifice. I am not so far from you and your friends as you would believe."

"You'll be dead." Gladdy takes a single step towards Heart. "Why do you care what happens to an ugly ring?"

"It's nostalgia and nothing more." They seem tired now, like all the adrenaline has ebbed away. "The last link in a chain. Leave it here with my corpse if you will. It was one final dignity, that's all. Now cut my fucking throat and be done." They throw their head back, exposing the line of their neck, the skin taut.

"The sentence has been pronounced, and it is death. You're too dangerous to live." Gladdy moves closer. Her hand is shaking. I can see it, and Heart can too.

They reach up and tug the ring from around their neck and toss it to Gladdy. She catches it in her right hand and thrusts it into her coat pocket, almost on autopilot. I hope she knows what she's doing.

"Go on then. Slay the beast," Heart whispers.

Gladdy takes a final step forward.

GLADDY

It disturbs me how much Heart looks like Emma. The curve of their smile traces the same line, and there's a similar watchfulness in the eyes. Overall Emma looks more like her mother, but I can still *see* that lineage written here. Heart's her parent in that they contributed some of her genes, but they never had a hand in raising her. Unless you count manipulation behind the scenes, in which they had their meddling touch in all our lives, drawing the strands together to weave a war.

They throw the chunky ring at me. It's gaudy, almost like costume jewellery, although the stone is remarkably beautiful, rugged purple shot through with veins of white. I wonder if it means something to Emma. I snatch it out of the air and shove it into my pocket. Perhaps the sight of it will trigger something in her mother to unlock memories. Or I should dump it the moment Heart is dead.

This is why we're here—to end a life. It makes me nauseated, but this isn't supposed to be easy. My other hand is on the knife. I can't remember why I chose to be the one to do this. Possibly in the foolish belief I can save the others from more fear or pain.

"Hold him," I say to Lou.

"Seems uglier the human way, doesn't it?" He grips Heart by the shoulders, one knee braced in the small of their back, arms held firmly.

"I'm not going to fight you," Heart says. "It'll only be ugly and messy and we've had enough of that. I don't want to die in some godawful wrestling match with teenagers."

"Last words." I adjust the grip on my knife.

They raise an eyebrow and regard me placidly. Every part of me feels tense.

I'm not sure what I'm waiting for.

"Screw posterity then." I draw the blade across Heart's neck. I lean into it, because I have no idea of the pressure required, but it's frighteningly sharp and sinks easily into their skin. Something pops or ruptures and blood gushes out.

And here I thought fragments of the door on my pants would ruin them. Blood spatters my jacket and all down my legs. The warmth of it soaks through the fabric. I take a long step backwards and Lou releases Heart's body.

Skye makes a high pitched sound, like someone's hurt her.

Heart topples forward, landing face first on the hard grey surface. Blood pools and spreads, moving quickly, coming out in spurts.

I look over my shoulder once again. The door is very small in the distance.

"It's done."

Katie crouches beside the body. She touches the head, lifts it, making the gash in the neck gape, and blood pulse faster.

"Good work." Maddy touches my arm. "You did it."

I almost laugh aloud, because it's like she's been out here *believing in me*, when all I was doing was killing someone. I do feel extraordinarily relaxed now it's done, as if I've been carrying tension in my shoulders since the moment I volunteered for this task, or even longer, since I agreed to this madness in Ray's office. I'd like to relax, to bask in this moment of completion. Probably not the best time or place for it.

"We should go," I say. "There's nothing else we need to do in here."

Heart's blood makes traceries on the ground, spider-webbing out in a complex pattern. It trickles into almost-undetectable grooves that run into wider channels along the edges of the buildings.

Skye's fidgeting, looking around herself as if she's trying to find her clones. "I know I get anxious a lot, but I can't help feeling this doesn't look good."

"It's like this place is hungry," Katie says.

"They're buildings." Lou's staring right at me, and I remember our conversation about Cthulhu. "Creepy fucking buildings."

"The door." I dredge some urgency up from the hollow at my center. "Everyone. Let's go."

People are staring at me, still standing in a loose group around Heart's body.

"Go," I shout.

Katie's the first to obey, with Maddy scrambling after her. Skye lopes along in their wake, but her legs are longer and she soon overtakes them. Lou crouches down beside Heart, feeling for a pulse. His fingers are bloody.

"Glowstick." I stare down at him. "We need to get out of here. Now."

He nods, then springs to his feet and begins running for the exit.

I go last. I'm field leader and I'm not leaving anyone behind. Except Heart, but they're not—

The urge to look behind me is overwhelming. I pause and spin around, expecting to see them staggering after me, their neck a ruin, and hand outstretched.

They haven't moved. Their body lies where it fell. Their blood flows ever outwards. How do people have so much fucking blood in them, and why do we keep running into scenarios where we find out what approximately five litres of blood looks like?

"Gladdy!"

I shouldn't have been looking behind me for trouble. It's almost inevitable that disaster lies between us and the door. It's like a shitty horror movie. Don't feed the buildings blood, children. It's a fucking no-brainer. God, give me a fright and I sound like Dylan.

The building frontages bulge outwards. It's like they're balloons full of liquid, and it's sinking down to pool in the lower part of the structures.

The first one to burst is *Christchurch Neural Maladaption Cathedral.* The facade explodes, the fibrous shell of it coming apart in thick, twisted strands. Creatures swarm from the broken husk—the same slightly luminous grey as the buildings. They're humanoid, but drift through the air like blown dandelion seeds. Their heads are bulbous and too large, bobbing on thin necks like stalks. The vacant holes of their eyes flare with virulent purple light. They're each about a meter long and there are so goddamn many of them.

"Fhtagn fucking Cthulhu," Lou says from beside me.

"Many greetings, much adaptation." Their voices are blown-speaker distorted even at a whisper. "Hive greets, hive sings. Kneel and pray, every cell alight for the ichorian god."

Everyone's stopped running in the face of this, even me. Not your best move, Fetch.

"Door," I scream, loud enough to hurt my throat.

Skye starts running first, and the creatures swarm her. They plummet from the air as if gravity has deigned to take hold of them. Her figure is blotted out. I'm too far away to take action, but I hold my knife and scream anyway.

Katie is closer. She's produced a pair of knives she wasn't supposed to have, but I'm profoundly grateful for. With a strangled cry, she throws herself among the monsters. There are wet popping sounds, like she's bursting balloons full of fluid. I don't get a chance to see anything else, because the creatures are descending upon Lou and I too.

"Church," they buzz in distorted chorus. "Embrace life. Embrace feed."

They have no mouths. The holes I thought were eyes are misshapen puncture wounds, and the light inside pulses rhythmically. They're not humanoid, not really. Too many pointed limbs, beating the air frantically as if they're wings. I reel backwards, but one attaches itself to me, shredding the sleeve of my jacket and clamping itself to my forearm. The limbs stop flailing and attach eagerly to my flesh, a forest of IV lines clamping down simultaneously.

"Ecstacy and transformation," it says. "The glory of the hive." The light from the creature blazes, as if the reaction inside is spurred to a furious crescendo at the taste of me. I stare at its face as if there's understanding there. Meaning behind the words. It wants something. We all want something. I wonder what the light tastes of.

Another creature hovers in front of me, limbs gently beckoning. Its light is warmer, welcoming.

"Change is growth," it tells me. "To evolve is to die. Death brings life and change brings more death. In dcath, we decay, and in decay we become."

There's a gentle pinch at my neck and one at my lower back. The purple floods me with warmth. The world is awash with it and it is luxurious. The creature, or the mind it speaks on behalf of, is correct—to evolve is to die. When we changed, we shed our old lives. They're not codenames that we have, but mutant names that represent our rebirth. Death is simply another tool of evolution, and we have been gifted in that we get to ride the wheel rather than being crushed by it. I have stood trembling at the peak as I descend into death and been reborn.

Each time I am refined further. This death will be yet another rotation on the wheel.

Something bursts in my face and the light dies. I'm drenched in fluid. It's cool and stings against my exposed skin. Numerous welts run along my arm. My back is soaking, my clothes heavy.

There's more sharp pops behind me. I whirl to see a figure marbled in rivulets of black and purple and red. Human eyes blink in a dripping face.

"Try not to die, Fetch." Lou's arms flash out and two more of the creatures burst in the air between us. When his knives vent their stomachs, more fluid jets out. "The trick is not to let them land on you. You've got a fucking knife. Use it."

I do have a fucking knife. I used it to kill a person a short time ago. I don't want it anymore.

"Change." A creature buzzes in front of me, a single proboscis extended. "Decay."

I punch my knife into one gaping eye hole, dragging the blade down. A flash of purple light makes spots dance in front of my vision. There are more creatures behind it, and I swing wildly through them.

Lou runs past me towards the others, as the creatures flock to him. He looks elegant and violent, like he's moving across some bloody Broadway stage, unleashing death in an intricate dance. When we get back—*if* we get back—I need to start taking training seriously. Beyond him, Katie and Maddy are standing back to back in front of Skye. Maddy has a knife now too and they're both lashing out wildly. Katie has a look of grim satisfaction on her face, while Maddy is panting with exertion.

Lou reaches them while I'm still wading through the deflated corpses of the creatures. The world strobes purple, the dimness of the place turned garish. With each flash of light I see more creatures spiralling above us, a vortex that won't be satisfied until we're drained.

I finally make it to the rest of the group. We make a bladed square above the collapsed form of Skye. "We need to reach the door. There are too many to kill."

At least the creatures hesitate now. "Refusal to embrace death is illogical. All die. All decay. All change."

"Not today." Fluid coats my tongue. I can taste crushed leaves at the back of my throat, along with something sour. "Listen up, Weapon UwU. We're all going to move for the door. All together, knives out. Skye, are you alive down there?"

"I need Two," Skye sobs. "I need Six."

"You need to get to the fucking exit," Katie says. "Then we'll have your friends back. But fuck, what I'd give for my powers right now."

It almost makes me cry to think about her lighting the world up with a blast of flame, which shows I am not coping well with all this. I'm not a crier, even at the worst of times.

I crouch over her, blade extended. "Crawl, Skye. We'll cover you."

"I can't." She's curled in on herself.

Katie prods her with one foot. "You can or I'll kick you to the door. You know I will."

Skye drags herself along the ground. She's drenched in blood and she's been fed on far worse than I have. Her arms are dotted with pyramids of flesh and the tops are split open like crude skin petals. At least she's moving.

The four of us shuffle with her, stabbing and slashing wildly as the creatures hover around us, occasionally darting in when they sense a spot to feed.

"Life plus, life advance. Little frozen things. Taste change's edge. Fear more. Embrace death."

My arm aches. Maddy is crying and I can't comfort her. Lou moves with grim satisfaction and I'm sure Katie is actually enjoying herself. I'm tiring, I know I am, and one gets close enough to reach my other arm. The warmth of it feels good against the ache and the cold. Purple light floods my eyes again, painting the world in violet.

The relief is so intense I want to cry.

I want to fall to my knees in this blighted world and let them all feed.

"Nearly there, Fetch." Lou's lips are touching my ear as he reaches past and knocks the thing from my arm with one slice of his blade. "A few more steps and we'll make it."

I raise my eyes to see different light spilling from the doorway. The light of home. It's so close now, a bright rectangle of grass and trees and pale sky. A painting of our world, in the midst of all this purple and grey.

Skye's on hands and knees and hauls herself over the lip of it. The instant she crosses, her clones appear—the full set of them. Of course, most of them throw themselves back across the threshold towards us and disappear because they're all fucking reckless. At least they're trying to help.

The last few meters seem longer than the rest. When Maddy makes the door, I almost give up. At least she's safe. Now I can collapse and let these things grant me mercy. The peace when they drain me isn't waiting on the other side of the door. There, it's only burdens and trouble and more fights to come.

"Gladdy, hurry up and get through," Maddy screams. "Please come back to me."

Katie grins, or at least I think it's her. All I can see is a short and furious creature, wielding knives and showing a smile that's smeared with blood.

"Get in there. Glowboy and me have got this."

I throw myself bodily across the threshold. It's warm on the other side, and I can feel all the aches and pains, as well as my heartbeat. All taken together, it means I'm alive.

Maddy crouches over me. She's a fucking mess. There are cuts all over her face, and she's drenched in a gory mess of fluid. She looks like she's been swimming in it, but her smile is as beautiful as ever.

Her fears are there too. I watch myself die and worse, I watch myself leave her. She approaches me, her heart cradled gently in her hands, and the Gladiola in her eyes knocks it carelessly to the ground to burst like one of the creatures, spilling all her goodness and warmth.

I turn away.

"Yes please. That's more fucking like it." Katie stands on this side of the doorway and screams. An enormous tongue of fire leaps from her mouth, a funeral plume that incinerates everything it touches. For a moment, we can only see swirling flakes of ash in the dimness of the parallel Earth.

Lou slams the door shut. It shakes the entire frame, but then it's gone, as if it never existed.

"Holy fucking goddamn shit." Katie throws her head back and sends another blast of flame up to scorch the sky. "We did it."

That's when my pocket starts making a loud and irritating high-pitched sound, a shrill siren of warning.

Everyone stares at me.

"Oh shit," I say.

MADDY

I totally understand why Gladdy did it. She caught the ring when Heart threw it to her, because she was distracted by preparing to murder a person in cold blood. And she did *that* because she wanted to save us from the burden of doing it ourselves. It's not her fault that everything fell apart so spectacularly afterwards, with demon mosquitos or whatever they were. *Of course* she forgot about the ring. We all did. It's completely understandable.

Except I think I'm the only one who follows this sequence of events. Everyone else is staring at Gladdy like she's broken the world.

Which, you know, she possibly has.

We're all soaked in the gross outpourings from stabbing a whole bunch of creepy floating alien vampires. Most of us have multiple wounds, scratches and cuts and the horrible pyramid feeding marks. I have a particularly bad ring of welts around my right wrist that's itchy and oozing with sluggish blood.

Despite all this, everyone's attention is on the ring in the palm of Gladdy's hand.

She's staring at it. It keeps screaming.

"Throw it away," Katie says. "I'll roast it before Heart can pop out through it."

"It can't be powered." Gladdy lifts the ring closer to her face and peers at it. "Otherwise it wouldn't have existed over there. Heart was right about that."

"They bent the rules somehow." Lou looks furious. "It's a trick. It's a trap. Why the fuck did you bring it through at all? I mean it's like the worst idea you could possibly—"

The ring stops screaming abruptly. Gladdy taps it with a manicured fingernail.

"Why did it stop?" Lou's still scowling. "And how does that seem *worse*?"

Ye Shou has joined us. "May I?" At Gladdy's nod, she picks up the ring and rotates it slowly. "Look, circuitry. I don't believe this is anything mutant-related at all. It's technological, programmed to emit a signal. This is why Heart wanted it brought through the doorway. Presumably it wouldn't function in the other world, much like our powers. Which raises interesting conclusions on its own, such as—" She breaks off and blushes. "Apologies. I'm rambling. Our primary concern should be what Heart signalled, and why they wanted it broadcast."

"Give it." It's Skye Four who snatches it from Ye Shou's hand. "Let's break the goddamn thing."

"I wouldn't," Ye Shou says. "Breaking it may cause a different kind of signal."

"Or stop it from making another one." Four squares up as if she wants to start a fight.

"Enough." Gladdy squares up to everyone, eyes clear and mouth in a flat line. "I'm taking responsibility for this. I was the one who brought it back."

"Amongst all that chaos," I squeak. I'll stick up for her, even if nobody else will.

"Four, give me the ring." Gladdy takes it before the clone can do anything else. "Whatever the circumstances over there, it's here now. We need to get this back to Westhaven and have someone analyse it before I do anything else foolish."

"Foolish?" The voice is melodic and sounds European. "Hardly, my darling."

We all look around to find the speaker. A tiny metal woman only a few centimetres tall hangs in the air. She's suspended in an ornate contraption that looks like butterfly wings, built from delicate traceries of metal and gleaming cogs.

"Hello?" Gladdy squints up at her.

"Yes, greetings to you all. I'm A Single Petal Floating on the Water. I know, the name is a mouthful, but you can call me Petal. And don't worry, dearest, you've done a wonderful kindness by waking me up. Heart had us all packed away neatly or standing carefully off to the side, preparing for the final days. Now we have received the emergency signal and everything will change."

"Wow." This sounds very terrible, but I have nothing more intelligent to say.

"I know!" The tiny woman flutters in front of me. It looks as if she has been carved from bronze, a figure with subtle curves and strong limbs. Her face is a simple metal mask, but she puts enough expression in her voice to make up for it. "Has Heart spoken of us to you? I believe you know my little sister, but I don't sense her in the proximity."

"Sister?" Gladdy asks.

"Yes, we shall get to that. First, it looks as if you have been through some dreadful ordeal. Perhaps I can do something about your injuries."

The cogs on her wings whir, making each other rotate in complex and hypnotic patterns. My wrist tingles and gets briefly hot. When I glance down, the welts are gone and my skin is smooth and pale again.

"Oh look." Petal sounds delighted. "I rather thought that might work. Now let's have some answers, shall we? There are so many things I can do with my machine." Despite the burbling cheer in her voice, this is clearly a threat.

"Why are you here?" I ask, since nobody else seems willing to speak. They're all gazing at her as if she's the second coming of Heart of a Flower.

"Okay, so we're starting with a question, and a rather obvious one too. The signal, silly. When they made me, my parent told me that one day a storm will come. We are insurance against that day. So now it's my turn to ask. Where *is* my creator and parent?"

"They're not here. I'm not sure where in the world they are." I feel like this is a very clever answer, and I'm thankful that Katie or someone didn't jump in and spill the whole truth. This little creature might not be too happy to hear about Heart's death.

"Yes." The wings flutter. "I'm also unsure. It's rather unexpected. And how did you happen to come across their ring?"

"They asked us to bring it here for them."

"And why did they not bring it themselves?"

I choose my words carefully. The truth is dangerous, but I don't want to be caught in a lie either. "We were in a strange place we entered through a door. I'm not sure precisely where it was. Heart gave us the ring and then they were gone."

"Humph." The figure flits back and forth. "This has the feel of a riddle. Yet the ring is here and they are not, and I cannot sense any form of them. So it appears you speak the truth, although you do so strangely. Let us trade question for question, in the hope we both find the information we seek."

"What do you want?" Katie asks, a tiny curl of flame ebbing from her lips.

"I'm not going to answer you, talking in that nasty fire-voice. I like the other girl better. I'm here for answers, which you already knew, so it was a terrible waste of a question. My turn again. Where's my sister?"

"I have no idea who your sister is," I tell her. "So I can't answer your question. My turn."

"No no no." The voice has lost all its charm. "That won't do. You know my sister very well. Her true name is Yǔzhòu, but you call her Goddess."

"Emma," Lou breathes.

"That is the human name given to her, once her mother was depowered and had chosen a subsequent mate. The truth is that she was the last of Heart's children—the only created in the organic method with another's contribution." Petal huffs. "Although that matters little. She is the most powerful of us, and so I ask my question again. Where is my sister?"

"In Westhaven." I don't think I can lie about this, even though things are spiralling out of control. "With the others of our kind."

"My kind too." Petal sighs. "For while I look like a machine, I am a mutant like you. Where precisely is Westhaven, so I can rejoin my sister?"

"Isn't it my turn for a question?" I ask.

"Westhaven is a half-answer, since it is only a name and not a location." Tiny bronzed arms fold across a delicately carved chest. "But I suppose I did not phrase it as correctly as I could have. Ask your question."

"How many children does Heart have?" I ask. Gladdy's trying to signal me with her eyebrows, but I have no idea what she's trying to say.

"I know of three more, Goddess and myself aside. There is my brother Two Thorns Twisted on a Stem, who took up residence in northern Canada before Heart put him to sleep. My sister, Delicately Drooping Stamen, who has never liked me and is gone from my awareness. And then Water Nourishing the Roots, who is floating off in the depths somewhere. I do not care to enquire further, as he is quite simply unpleasant. I should recommend staying far away from him, although that may not be possible. So here we are. Doom and disaster for all!" She claps her tiny hands together.

"Doom and disaster?" Lou's fingers glow. "What are you talking about?"

"An enormous waste of a question." Petal shivers. "If you've been paying attention, it should be *obvious*. My siblings. They'll be awake, and ill-tempered, and it's not going to end well." She flits through the air and hovers in front of my face. "Now back to my question. Where is Westhaven?"

"I do want to answer you but I don't actually know. It's a secret."

"Oh, I don't like that at all." She shakes her little metal head. "A secret. Perhaps I have a way of digging it out of your brain. Let me see."

"There's no need for that." Gladdy finally speaks up, sharp-voiced and leaderlike. "All you need to do is wait and they'll come to bring us back. Then you can accompany us."

"Yes." I look up at Petal. "It's true. You can ride with one of us."

"I'm not sure I believe you." She flits across to Katie. "You, angry girl. You will speak the truth in your furious eyes at least. Would you really take a creature like me back to your home?"

"Creature? We're all creatures." Katie lets smoke gush from her nostrils and squirts flame from the little gap between her front teeth. "Why wouldn't we bring you home? Are you untrustworthy or some shit?"

"I'm very powerful." The cogs in Petal's wings rotate. "Watch over there." She extends one little arm and a tree in the distance explodes in a shower of leaves and twigs. "There are so many things I can do."

Lou winces. "The healing was a good demonstration of your powers, so you don't need to—"

Katie whips around and lets out an enormous plume of fire that incinerates a patch of grass and sets another tree alight.

"Fuck's sake!" Lou rounds on Katie. "The tree didn't do anything to you, did it?"

Petal watches the tree burn like a crackling torch. "You are very impressive. I wonder if I can emulate your power. Perhaps if I—"

Dragon looks chastened, which is a near-miracle, but then she does look to Lou as an older brother. "Sorry, Petal. Can you heal the tree instead? They did nothing wrong and we need them."

"It is alive I suppose," Petal sighs. "All things are connected, and it does little to incur the ire of one so powerful." She flexes her wings and the cogs blur. The fire is extinguished, and the tree Katie burned returns mostly back to normal. The one Petal blew up looks like it's been stuck clumsily back together.

"Thank you." Lou gives a little bow.

"I tried." A faint pink light flares in Petal's mask like a blush. She flickers back over to me. "I cannot remember whose turn it is to answer questions, but I think I would like to return to Westhaven to speak with my sister."

"Of course. Let's make a plan to do that." Gladdy looks helpless, like she's stuck in the middle of a swirling current of events and is trying not to drown. It makes me wonder if Dylan made the right choice putting her in charge, and there's an immediate pang of guilt at my unfaithfulness. She's my best friend and I love her, in ways too complicated and various to count. Either way, it means I have to support her, even when everything is going from bad to worse.

"What in the actual fuck have you been up to?" I can hear Dylan's voice so vividly in my head that I almost laugh aloud.

"Dilly!" Katie shouts in delight. "You're here. Omigod, it was wild. Oh shit."

I turn around and it's really Chatterbox, and not my overactive imagination at all. Wearing his usual outfit of jeans and a hoodie, with that lopsided smile and their overgrown mohawk falling down over one eye. And behind her, a far more unexpected figure—someone beautiful and fine-boned, with long black hair whipping in the breeze.

"Oh god," Gladdy flushes deeply. "Hi, Emma."

GLADDY

This has been a series of disasters from the moment I caught that hideous ring of Heart's and put it in my pocket. I was too focused on steeling myself to murder. It's not like there isn't blood on my hands, but previously it was always at a remove. I could convince myself that my victims were swallowed by their own darkness. Katie would have done it in a heartbeat, but I can't shift this idea I should protect her because she's a sixteen year old girl. So I slit Heart's throat, and it was ghastly, and it's going to stick in my brain forever. The bigger problem is that somewhere in all that mess, I've made a huge mistake.

And now Emma is here, which means we have far bigger problems. I shove my left hand into my pocket because I don't want Dylan fucking Taylor to see the damn ring and know it was me that caused all this.

"You okay there, Fetchy?" Of course, they already have.

"It's done, if that's what you mean." I can hold their gaze without flinching, despite the fears that flock there.

"What's done?" She gives me a broad wink. "It's fine. Emma knows. The secret is well and truly out. Ray explained everything and now everyone's up to speed. We've had the shouting match. I lost."

"Shouting match." Emma links her arm through Dylan's. "That's what they call it. There was one person shouting, and it wasn't me."

"I have a loud voice, that's all."

"Thank you, Fetch. Genuinely." Emma reaches out and touches my wrist lightly. "It must have been hard to go in there without powers. Thank you for doing it so I didn't have to."

"See." Dylan claps me on the shoulder and puts a casual arm around my neck. "Everyone's friends again. We all remember what we *forgot*." They do exaggerated quote marks with their fingers. "Ray and Emma have had a very smouldering conversation. You've been to another world, killed someone, and bathed in the blood of something disgusting. One more tick in the win column for the Cute Mutants."

"Weapon UwU you mean." Maddy sidles up on Dylan's other side. "There is one little weird detail that you might want to know about."

Dylan's mouth twists. "Yeah, that shit always fucking happens, doesn't it? What appalling disaster are we facing now? Am I telling Dani I won't be home for dinner?"

"My sister," a small voice rings out. "Is this truly you?" Petal flutters down out of the sky. She has her wings pulled in tight around herself, and her mask-face tilts curiously. "My name is A Single Petal Floating on the Water, and I was created by Heart of a Flower as you were."

"The fuck is this now?" Dylan scowls, and I see her fingers flex open to reach for Oni. Their body language shifts towards Emma, and most of the fears that flare in his face are for her. Some flickers are *of* Emma too, and those are the ones that chill me most of all. I understand what it's like to drag your destiny out from under a domineering parent, but Emma has Heart of a Flower woven through her DNA. The potential for disaster is enormous.

"Sister?" Emma's voice cracks. She tilts her head back, gazing at the tiny figure.

I've barely seen Goddess since we all returned from the battle with Heart. She's kept herself away with only the inner circle allowed access. That sounds more bitter than I intend. I've heard rumours about the new extent of her incredible powers, but I've seen no evidence of it since we were all brought back from being unmade by Heart. There's no sign of it now either.

"I am." Petal spirals down and hovers above us. Her face gleams.

"I always thought of myself as an only child." Emma's fears are opaque to me, as if she's hidden herself away beneath a delicate mask, so I can only read her nervousness from the slight tremble in her voice. I can't even tell if the appearance of this mutant is a surprise to her.

"Sister as in?" Dylan's still wreathed in frowns.

"As in we are all Heart's creations. Although you have never met any of us, you are the baby of the family."

Emma holds out one hand, palm up. "I am happy to meet you. When did Heart create you?"

Petal flutters down but hovers fractionally above Emma's skin, as if she's too timid to alight there. "I only predate your conception by a small number of years. Some of my siblings are far older. We have fought in various skirmishes against humanity, but once you were born, all the plans were upended. The group of us have never been friends, each one of us a monster of Heart's specific creation, and once they had a more powerful option, we were secreted away in one form or another."

"And now you're back." Emma's voice is still soft.

"We were to ally with you in your final war against humanity, once you came into your powers and Heart's plan saw fruition. However, the emergency signal has been triggered, and this announces a drastic change in the order of things."

Dylan has shooed the others away, presumably to stop any of them jamming their conversational oar into whatever's going on with Emma and Petal. I'm surprised they let me join, given I was the one who brought the damn ring through.

Emma shivers. Wings erupt from her back, a larger version of Petal's with a vastly more complex array of cogs connected inside. They rotate and swirl while the metal rods that hold them flex in the wind. "As you can see, I have come into my power."

"Magnificent." Petal spins in the air. "Then the days of humanity are truly numbered."

"Vicious little thing, aren't you?" Dylan points one finger at the tiny mutant. "Sadly for you, we're not working to Heart's timetable anymore, and the extermination of humanity is on hold."

"What manner of wicked creature are you to speak so confidently and brashly?" Petal whirls to face Dylan. "I think I shall stop that messy thing pumping blood in your chest, and then you shall not speak like this to Heart's children any longer." The cogs spin inside her wings.

"No." Emma's voice is clear and strong, and I see the shadows cross Petal's face as her machine slows to a halt. In there, I can see the tiny mutant's fears—primarily her monstrous parent, of her construction and the threat of deconstruction.

I lean in close to her. "Still your workings, Petal. If I see a single cog turn, we will take you apart piece by piece. We have a telekinetic who could do that, stack each tiny component in the palm of her hand as punishment for hurting her love."

"You would not," Petal hisses. "You think you are heroes."

"Oh but we would. You say you have family, but you don't understand the word. We may not share blood, but we share everything else. When someone comes for one of ours, we will fight regardless of the cost. Unlike you and Heart's other children."

Petal both fears and hates her siblings, although in her mind it is hard to make out exactly what they are. I can only see vague outlines. She wants them dead, I see that, but she feels no remorse for it.

"Where is this monster who would take me apart?" Petal asks.

Emma smiles. "A breath away. But we wish you no harm. I would rather get to know my sister, not be at each other's throats because Heart wished it so."

"Threats," Petal spits. "You feign kindness, but you have your own pet monsters to threaten me. You are no better than our parent."

"Oh, she's slightly better." I stare into the metal mask. "Heart would have killed you for your weakness already, wouldn't he? You have already capitulated to us by your indecision."

Petal spins into the air, whirling violently though the cogs in her wings are still. "Get away from me, nasty mutant. I hate you, staring into my soul like that. ”

“Join the queue.” Exhaustion sweeps over me, scatters me like dust.

“Do not think your task is simple.” Petal flutters down to nestle in Emma’s palm, curling her wings about herself. “My siblings will not be deterred so easily from chaos. I am the most pleasant member of my family by far. Everyone agrees, although most see it as to my detriment.”

In her face, I see that she is the outcast. She expects to be hunted down by her older siblings, to be torn apart for merely existing. Most of this appears to be the result of stories told to her by Heart, rather than anything specific that she has endured.

“Perhaps you can help us find your siblings,” I suggest. There’s an aversion in the other direction that will be hard to shift, so I cannot manipulate her into this with fear alone.

“You won’t need my help.” Petal shifts as if seeking a comfortable position. “Watch the stories they tell you on your magic screens. They will make themselves known.”

It’s an ominous statement, and Dylan and I trade glances. It appears that by stopping Heart, we’ve exchanged one problem for another. We could have left them to starve in that parallel world, although these strange children of theirs would still be lurking.

"Let's get back to Westhaven." Emma's wings droop, and then fade entirely. She staggers slightly and rights herself.

"You can't do it?" Dylan is at her side in an instant, as Petal launches herself back into the air.

"Too much. Can't regulate it." Emma gasps. "The power flow is so… difficult. Gates and rivers, and I can't fathom the trick of it."

"It's okay. We'll get there. Sit and rest."

"What's wrong?" Petal asks. "Are you dying?"

"No," Dylan swings Emma up into their arms. "She'll be fine. And don't you dare try anything or my friend here will carve you up a lot more messily than Dani will."

A slender silver shape rises up out of the grass to bat almost playfully at the figure of Petal, who twists in the air and dances lightly along the blade.

"Hello, Onimaru," I say. It's an odd thing, Dylan and their objects, but the other Cute Mutants talk to them even though they hear nothing back, and it seems only polite. The sword hovers, seemingly content for Petal to play on it.

"I think this sword likes me," Petal says. "I don't think it would—"

Onimaru blurs through the air. He's frighteningly fast when he wants to be. He pauses with his tip pressed between Petal's wings.

Dylan looks up at him with a slight shake of her head. "Oni, don't show off. And where the fuck is Keepsy? I told them to be here."

The slender figure appears out of the air as if summoned. "Waiting, being polite, you know."

"Everyone home." Dylan's voice is firm. "Goddess first, then the others."

Keepaway touches Emma's arm lightly and she disappears. Then they jog over to where the others are standing in a large circle.

"It was bad in there, wasn't it?" Dylan's eyes are large and dark and focused on me.

"Pretty bad, yeah."

"Way I see it, you came out with everyone you went in with. Could've been a hell of a lot worse. Nice job, Fetchy. I think I'll keep you around." They give me the crooked smile as Keepaway comes back over. "Petal, hop in my hood and come back with me. And no fucking funny business, cos Oni rides with us too."

MADDY

It's a tiny bit annoying to see Gladdy magically included in the inner circle. It was sometimes like that when we were running our operation in Christchurch, but I got to elbow my way in there. Because it was Gladdy-and-Maddy and we didn't get separated.

Now I'm standing off to the side, while Lou and Katie talk shit. Skye laughs at their jokes and Ye Shou taps at her phone. It's frustrating that Fetch looks so comfortable next to delicate Emma and slouched, rumpled Dylan. Gladdy is so beautiful, and although I can conjure her face in my mind so easily, I still find my gaze drawn toward her. It's not just love, it's comfort too. I remember back in the cages at Jinteki, she would sit against the wall in the cage opposite mine. The light would shine through the window onto her face. From where I lay curled on my mattress, I could watch her as my stomach churned. My lips were always chapped and dry. Whenever I wet them with my tongue, the traces of acid in my saliva would burn. Her face, lit by that single sliver of light, was the only good thing in my world. I have so many more now, an embarrassment of riches, yet the memory of that time is still one of the brightest stars in my sky.

"Back to Westhaven." Lost in my thoughts, I don't notice Keepaway approaching until they've sent the others away and it's only me, watching Gladdy speak to Petal.

"Home," I say, and Gladdy and the others all disappear.

Westhaven is loud and crowded as it often is these days. Katie tries to drag me off when I first appear, but I wave her away. I lean against the cave wall while I wait for Gladdy to turn up. When she finally does, I link my arm through hers and tow her off to the dining hall.

"Feeling good?" I keep my voice light, because I always try to. She sees enough darkness in her life.

"Yes." She shakes her head with a little frown. "Dylan was complimentary. Almost sweet?"

"They want something." My voice is too sharp.

"Or they think we did a good job." She smiles at me. "Or both, perhaps."

"Why not both?" I nudge her and she laughs. It's always good when she laughs.

We line up for dinner, which is lasagna and roast vegetables. I'm starving. My body gets cranky if I'm not generating enough acid to keep my tank full. My power's not as bad as Gladdy's, but it's hardly one of the good ones. Dani has a lot of fancy theories about the underlying psychological causes of different people's powers. She's never come out with one about me, except to say sweet and sour.

I'm the only one who knows.

Back before the cages, when I was Madelaide—never Maddy, no not ever—I was a horrible person. I was the selfish and cruel child of selfish and cruel parents. Indulged and pampered, my favourite thing was to pour scorn on others. My heart was full of bile and I took a vicious joy in dripping it on all who crossed my path.

Of course, I was desperately unhappy, but that would have been little comfort to my victims.

After I died and awoke in a Jinteki cell, retching thin strings of acid that made the stone floor smoke and left pitted scars on my hands, I understood what people meant by karma. The toxic child had become literally toxic. Not only could I burn others, now I could burn myself.

Except there was a girl in the cell opposite, who saw terrible things in the faces of the guards. She whispered to me in the dark about being strong, about evolution and change, about reaching for the next branch.

Rebirth is opportunity.

I would make myself over again, be someone bright and shining. When people saw me, they'd see a face lit up by a shaft of sunlight, someone bringing hope and comfort. I would take the toxic stew of my soul and make something better from it.

Evolve into Maddy.

"Eat," Gladdy says. "You're talking to yourself in your head again."

"Did I ever tell you that you're horribly annoying?" I give her a dazzling smile.

"All the time."

"The dynamic duo." Dani slides into the seat opposite us, flicking platinum blonde hair out of her face. She pauses as she watches Dylan, who makes clambering in beside her look like a contortionist's feat. "Dilly says you had a wild ride today."

"Never feed the buildings blood," Gladdy says in the dry voice she uses with them.

"I told you we should've put that in the fucking briefing notes." Dylan grins and helps himself to food off Dani's plate.

"And I told *you* to get yams," Dani says.

"I don't like yams."

"That's a yam."

"Is it?" Dylan inspects it suspiciously and pops it into their mouth. "I don't think so. It's swede or something. Anyway, we're not here to debrief shit or eat your fucking yams. We're here to beg a horrible favour off you."

"I told you they wanted something," I say to Gladdy.

"Yes, it's me, nasty old Dylan, always wanting other people to do their dirty work. The thing is we've got the Emma..."

"Situation," Dani suggests.

"Is that what it is? I would call it a clusterfuck." They tug on the curls at the back of their mohawk. "Termifuckingnology aside, I don't want to leave her. There's definite bomb potential until we figure out how to get this under control. Fingers crossed it'll all work out, but I'm not willing to leave her while I bounce around the world hunting down Heart's leftover monsters." Dylan drops their fork and waggles their eyebrows at us.

I stare at them with no expression. "You want us to do it."

"I was actually hoping you'd offer, but I'll beg if I have to."

I'm not entirely surprised. It makes sense, but it's still terrifying. To be out there investigating horror after horror, mutants made by a reality-warping monster to cause trouble in the world like—

"Of course we'll do it." I'm annoyed Gladdy says it without consultation, but going to a vote wouldn't matter. Neither Lou or Katie will ever say no to anything precious Dylan asks of them. Skye will go along because she doesn't want to be left behind, and who fucking knows what Ye Shou thinks. It's not that I dislike Dylan, but she does have a way of acting and expecting the universe to fall into line. I'd kill for a fraction of that confidence.

"Thank you." Dani smiles at me, like she knows what I'm thinking.

"Any ideas of where to start? Petal mentioned something about northern Canada," Gladdy offers.

Dani laughs. "Northern Canada isn't exactly small."

"'Took up residence,'" I chime in. "Those were her specific words. She also implied that we'd hear about things happening."

Dylan grunts. "Yeah, mysterious fucking events. Little brat sat in my hood and kept chattering once she'd started. Talking about signs of the apocalypse and blood cults. Emma's going to keep an eye out for suspicious things." She grins at my expression, which is probably far too sour. "Look on the bright side, little Patch. This time you should have your powers."

"Little Patch?"

"Oh, terribly sorry. *Madelaide*." They tangle their hands in their hair again and tug. "What would be really fucking good actually is if this was one less thing to worry about. Dan keeps telling me to delegate."

Dani leans her head against Dylan's shoulder briefly. "I do. All the time."

"So be my trustworthy assassins. The best there is at the not very nice."

Gladdy looks up from her plate directly into Dylan's face. "You can trust us."

"That's right. Get a good look at all these fears." They haul themselves out of their seat just as clumsily as they got into it, and flash us a smile that looks genuine. "But you're free for tonight at least, so relax. Apparently the stars are pretty."

"Thanks, you two. It means a lot." Dani scoots out from her own seat carrying the dishes.

"What fears?" I ask, as the two of them walk away.

"Death." Gladdy looks back down at the table rather than facing me. "Lots of death. The end of the world. Emma going mad. These monsters of Heart's rampaging across the planet. Humanity going extinct. Mutant bodies in the streets. It's a wonder they can stand, let alone smile like that. It breaks my heart."

I feel an entirely irrational surge of jealousy. I want to be the one who breaks her heart. When she looks into my face, I want to see that mix of wistfulness and affection and bruised care. Instead I'm faithful and sweet Maddy who's always there, padding along with a smile and a gentle hand. Sometimes I think I'm little more than a—

No. I'm not that girl anymore. I've evolved.

I link my fingers with hers. "Look at me. There's nothing to be afraid of."

And I push all my bad feelings down into the toxic sour stew at the heart of me.

GLADDY

Looking at Dylan is like staring into an open wound. They care far too much. I don't see how it's sustainable. Dani's not much better. I wish my powers extended to fully seeing the comfort they provide each other. They're so beautiful together.

Worse than looking at Dylan is staring into Maddy's face, her fears printed neatly for me to read in excruciating detail. I see who she was, the person she worries is still inside her. I'm not sure she was ever as awful as she believes. What impresses me the most is how she rebuilt herself. She gives me far too much credit for my part in this. I was a lost girl in the dark, the same as she was. We reached out to each other, and through some magic beyond mutant power we hauled each other up. The bravest thing is to see your own flaws and evolve beyond them. She tries so hard to be strong and bright and perfect.

I want to tell her it's not needed, that she's amazing as she is, but then it would be diminishing her. She'd also know I see so much of her heart, and I think that would hurt worse. I'm not capable of giving her what she needs. She is a river of love, and I am a thin, brackish trickle. If I was to ever discard the mask, her love would evaporate. I'm not sure how I would breathe in that world, so I cling to her and hope she doesn't notice.

"Now whose turn is it to stare into space?" Maddy leans her blonde head on my shoulder and I tilt my head towards hers and I'd happily freeze this moment. I know she wants more, but this is so perfect and pure and unentangled. You could render us in a pencil sketch and see the beauty in it.

"Tired," I whisper. "It's been a day."

"I can still taste that mosquito stuff in my throat."

"Ugh, so can I." I scrape my tongue across the roof of my mouth. "It's this bitter aftertaste I can't get rid of."

"I could spit a tiny bit of acid into your mouth and maybe burn it out of your oesophagus."

I give a snort of laughter. "That is the grossest thing."

"Hold on, let me see if it works." She sits in her seat retching, and I watch her with this mix of disgust and fondness. Her tongue is hanging out of her mouth, and her eyes are squinting. "It does, Gladdy, honestly. I've burned the taste right out and it only hurts a tiny bit. Now come here and let me put some in your mouth."

My breath hitches and I don't know why.

She lunges toward me. I think she expected me to move away, but I'm frozen and now her lips are pressed to mine. Her tongue runs tentatively along the line of my bottom lip, and it parts wider in automatic response. I am not in control of my reactions. My throat stings faintly and I feel her lips drag themselves closed across mine.

She pulls back and I'm frozen in place. Her eyes flutter open.

The strange taste in my throat is gone. I want to tell her it works, but the words are burned away as well.

My lips are still parted. I feel the tingling left behind by hers.

The fears I see are too intense and I close my eyes against them. I need to choose my words carefully, because I cannot bear to shatter her. Except my thoughts are scattered like gaseous particles and my lips still sting.

This is all too much. None of this can be connected to anything, because I don't have the responses she longs for. Whatever I say, she will attach so many things to my words, so gently and carefully, weaving a beautiful lie from her wishes.

I open my eyes, because this is too awkward, and I catch sight of her disappearing, pushing her way through the crowds. Does this really count as a kiss?

"I'm not saying anything." Alyse takes a seat opposite me. "I haven't even updated Lovepool."

"What?"

"The kiss."

"What kiss?"

Alyse laughs. "Fine. Have it your way. But if you're going to be surreptitious, try not to make out at the dinner table surrounded by half the world's mutant population."

I don't know how to explain what the not-a-kiss was, because I can't even define it. "It's none of your goddamn business, Moodring."

"No, but when has that stopped me?" She arches her eyebrows and gives me a mischievous smile. Alyse is one of those people you can't help but like. Even I find myself comfortable with her, but I still can't explain what happened. It means something completely different to both of us, except the weight of it on Maddy's end makes me feel off-balance. It should have been like a friend scratching a hard to reach place on your back, but I can still feel the connection between us, tugging on me as Maddy walks further away.

"Is Emma okay?" I ask as a distraction.

"Oh God." Alyse transforms, mostly based on her moods, and now sitting across from me is a shadow creature with flashes of lightning for eyes. "It'll be fine. That's what she says."

Why did I choose this topic of conversation, given I can see her fears right there? Why am I such a goddamn mess? Why is it so hard to navigate these situations where love is involved? "We can talk about something else."

"I have to trust her. It's a lot for her to process, but if anyone can do it, Ems can." The shadow takes a deep breath. "But yes, let's talk about something else. Your love life is off the table, and so is mine."

"Shall we talk about Deezer?"

"The D's are fine, but that touches on that topic we're not going near. They're both with Emma now. Wow, when she found out about this black ops thing of yours."

I grimace. "Black ops is slightly overstating it."

Alyse is back in her regular human form now. "That's what Dilly calls it. And the name wasn't the part Emma took offence at." Alyse fidgets with her fork. "I told her it wasn't a good idea. Holding out for a reunion with… that person wasn't ever going to give her the happy ending she wanted."

"Her friends sneaking behind her back to kill her parent is a long way from that ending."

Alyse nods and see-saws her hand. "It wasn't supposed to work that way. Emma's powers extend further than anyone realised. But Dylan intended the Heart thing as kindness, and Emma understands that. Also that you were the one who, you know…" She makes a slashing motion at her throat. "…and what it must have meant for you."

Heart is not the first parent I've killed. When I looked into my father's eyes after I changed, I saw many things there, but not what he should have been most afraid of: me. I understand more than most the complexity of discovering your parent is a monster. My sympathy for Emma is real, but I'm glad that both of these people are gone from the world.

I understand you can become a monster yourself when trying to rid the world of evil, but it's a risk I'm willing to take.

"It's done now anyway." I push the rest of my food away. "Same with the ring. God, I feel so stupid about that." It's annoying being so comfortable with Alyse. Things slip out of my mouth that shouldn't.

"Eh, it happens. Heart seems like the exact kind of asshole who'd have plans inside of plans. The sort to scatter a bunch of monsters around the world. And you're the ones doing the hero business. Weapon UwU." She makes heart hands in front of her face and winks at me through them, back to her regular dazzling self.

"That's us." I shrug.

"Can you actually say it?" Alyse wrinkles her nose in delight.

"Say what?"

"You know what. Please?"

"You're very annoying," I tell her.

"That's what Dilly says, and I'm her bestest friend in all the world."

The pause stretches on while Alyse sits there batting her eyelashes at me.

"Fine. Weapon UwU."

She throws her head back and laughs. "You smile when you say it. Even you."

"Hey, I smile."

"Barely." She reaches across the table and pats my hand. "Make sure you take care of yourself out there, Fetch. Let the whole team look after you, not just Maddy. I know you think the family thing is cheesy, but it helps."

There are a lot of things I want to throw up as defence, but I let them fall. "Okay."

"There you go. Do the occasional big internet hug. Smile a couple of times a day. Listen to sad music. Or happy music, whichever one makes you feel better." Her smile is like having heavenly light slice through the clouds. The sort of thing to bask in. "The Alyse Sefo guide to life."

I hardly think this is the simple recipe that makes Alyse work. She has fears, like anyone, of failure and abandonment and rejection, but she shines anyway. I don't know how to do that. I'm missing the part of me that can.

"Thanks." I force a smile to prove it's possible. "I'll try." I grab my plate and get up from the table.

"Do or do not, bitch," Alyse calls over her shoulder as I walk away.

I go back to our sleeping quarters. Maddy and I have separate rooms, but sometimes we share one because Maddy needs the comfort. I like to sleep alone, because I don't need the overstimulation of another person's fears. My own whirling thoughts are enough, without constantly adjusting for someone else.

Still, I stand by her closed door for almost two full minutes, paused on the verge of knocking. There's no sound of movement from inside, so I finally walk away and climb into my own empty bed.

II

WATER NOURISHING THE ROOTS

MADDY

I spend a lot of time pondering the kiss, what it might mean, and who's to blame. Mostly, I'm mad at myself. Not with Gladdy, who behaved exactly how I would expect in a situation like that. I thought she'd flinch away from contact, but I shouldn't have even played at that. When our lips met, I was so startled that I reacted on instinct. Which, because I am a lovesick fool, involved actually putting my tongue in her mouth.

Then afterwards, she sat there with her eyes closed. No words, no response, not even any shift in body language for me to over-analyse. I may as well have kissed a statue. One with a beautiful mouth that trembled under mine.

We don't speak about it. It is as if we have both eradicated it from our minds. In reality, I am furiously fretting at it, shredding it into pieces with mental fingers and reassembling it in a thousand different contexts.

I am sure it hasn't even replayed in her mind a single time.

In the rest of Westhaven, life carries on. Emma is nowhere to be seen, still recuperating. The little mechanical figure of Petal becomes a common sight, flitting down the corridors after Dylan like a pet butterfly. Mutants scour the globe and monitor the news for any sign of Heart's other children. Despite Petal's ominous words, these mysterious threatening figures remain stubbornly quiet. I wish they wouldn't, because I need something to take my mind off everything else.

I hang out with Katie, and almost tell her fifty different times about the kiss. She'll pour scorn on it, which is what I need. Gladdy sleeps in her own bed each night. She claims she dreams of Heart too often, that I'd be disturbed by her thrashing about. Bad dreams have never stopped us before. I try not to read too much into this either.

It's almost a relief when I'm woken early one morning by my door slamming open. A figure is silhouetted in the warm light from outside.

Almost a relief. "Go away," I whimper.

"Don't fucking whine at me, because I'm pissed that I'm up too, and I've been up a lot fucking longer than you. Get your acidic ass out of bed, put some clothes on, and come find me."

There's no need to see anything to know who it is. Only one person talks like that. I manage to find my Yaxley combat uniform, and come out into the hallway to find Gladdy there, dressed in a t-shirt that barely covers her ass.

"I'm so sleepy," she mews, and if I wasn't still mad about the kiss, I would be melting at how adorable she is.

"Put them on." I hold pants out to her, but my voice is flat. I can't even be bothered trying to figure out what hurt she might see in my face. It's an endless spiral and I'm exhausted by it.

"Nice, Fetchy. Welcome to no pants gang." Dylan is in a hoodie that comes down to mid-thigh with the hood up and drawstrings tight so only their eyes are visible.

"We love no pants gang." Dani's in a man's shirt that is definitely indecent. I can't even look at her. "Maddy, I love the enthusiasm, but why are you in uniform?"

"Aren't we going to fight something?" I blink at them, still dazed from sleep.

"Not quite yet." Dylan yawns. "Fuck, I need caffeine. It's too early for my coffee kid to be up, isn't it?"

"There's a coffee mutant?" This is the first news that perks Gladdy up.

"No, he's got some weird power. I can't even remember. He gets me coffee though."

"Power's gone to their head." Dani grins. "Never thought my darling Dilly would have someone running around after them getting coffee."

"Hey, if someone offers me coffee, I am not saying no." Dylan covers their mouth. "Stop making me yawn. We're up at this horrible hour because we've got a ping from Emma's little search bots. The promised spookiness is afoot." They frown. "Afoot? Is that the right word?"

"Yes, although I've never heard a real person use it," Dani says.

"I'm pretty sure Pear says it. Or maybe it's from Scooby-Doo. Shall I call them?"

"At four am?"

"They won't mind."

Gladdy and I are blinking at each other, because if we're not careful this will become the Deezer show.

"The spookiness seems more important than the afoot." This feels like a controversial statement at this time of the morning, but Dylan only smiles.

"Probably, yes. Let's go find the briefing room."

I follow the no pants gang as we make our way through the silent passageways of Westhaven. The caves seem too perfect to be naturally occurring, and I wonder if a mutant created it back in the previous history of the world. That's a secret we've kept mostly under wraps—that mutants have existed before and were almost wiped out multiple times. Emma's mother erased that knowledge from the memory of every person on the planet, and so all of the stories about what went before are gone. It haunts me sometimes, thinking about all those mutants who we've never heard about, and all the things they might have done.

We end up in a small chamber packed full of computers. This is where Emma could usually be found, at least before the whole full-Goddess thing happened. Dani sits at one, clicking away furiously.

"It's so confusing. She's got so many of these damn crawlers." Dani pushes hair off her face, lips pursed. "But this must be the one. Three separate reports of strange happenings in a place with a weird name. Oh, look, it's pretty though." Images of a seaside town pop up on the screen. "It's in Maine which I think is kinda top-right in America, up near Canada. Anyway, someone got eaten by a blowhole and then a dude got snatched off a dock—apparently there were tentacles. Someone was also reported missing from a forest near an old monastery. That one sounds less likely."

Dylan nudges their way onto the seat beside Dani and peers at the screen. "Monsters sound fun. I'm jealous."

"That seems about right." Dani tangles her fingers in Dylan's hair. "You want to go fight monsters instead of leading the mutant nation."

"You said tentacles! It'll be fun. A lot more than council meetings and worrying about the likelihood of war."

"Fine." Dani shrugs, which makes her shirt rise up even higher. "Go then. I'm not your Mum."

"Don't be weird."

"I'm serious. If you want to run off and fight tentacle monsters instead of doing the hard work here, go have fun. I'll be waiting when you get back."

Dylan slumps in his chair. "You're ruining my display of petulance."

"That's the idea." Dani leans in and plants a kiss on Dylan's mouth, which perks her up noticeably. They manage to haul themself upright again.

"So how's about it, Fetchy? Sound like fun?"

"Far less fun than you seem to think it is."

Sometimes Gladdy can't help but get herself in a pissing contest with Dylan. They both like to run things. I think she also disapproves of Dylan, who acts like everything is so *difficult* and such an imposition, and then runs around like fortune's favoured child.

It's a little bit funny, but it's a sore spot and I usually don't prod it. Right now, I'm tired. I'm also still pissed off about the stupid goddamn kiss and the way it's not being talked about, so it's hard to hold back.

"I wish you *would* come, Dilly." I sigh and angle myself away from Gladdy. "You always get things done. There's a lot of flair when you're around."

"Flair," Dani snorts. "That's a word for it." Her fingertips brush the nape of Dylan's neck and the look in her eyes has such fondness that it splits my heart down the middle.

"I am the flairiest." Dylan's barely paying attention, peering at the screen. They take this love for granted, and it stings. "Ooh, look, shitty cellphone footage." They tap and then sit back as it pops up.

A small child toddles down a dock, a mother crouching along beside with arms outstretched to keep them from straying too far. In the background, a dude stands with a camera, looking out over the myriad blues of water and sky. He's dressed in a fancy peacoat with expensive boots.

"I hope the baby's not the one who gets eaten." Dani leans forward with a frown.

"The victim was Charles Bartholomew Randall Bartlett the Fourth," Dylan reads off her phone. "I hope that poor kid isn't saddled with that fucking name. Tentacles might be kinder. Poor taste, sorry. This is my brain without coffee."

The kid waves at the world, trying to grab at some fraction of its beauty. Their mother laughs, delighted.

The woman holding the phone laughs too. "So happy!"

The camera jerks. "What the hell? Becks, what was that?"

"The water." The mother gathers her child into her arms and peers over the edge. Around the dock, the ocean glows blue, as if it's drenched in something bioluminescent. A high-pitched sound emanates from it. "What's wrong with it? Is it polluted or something?"

"There's no pollution that sings," the camerawoman drawls. "This is some sea witch shit."

"Language."

"Shit, sorry. I mean sorry. Whoa."

The footage spins as a figure appears on the dock at the far end. It looks like a man who's fully clothed, water streaming off him. The camera zooms in jerkily. He's kinda hot, but I don't think he's really a man. It's more like some of the water climbed out of the ocean, assembled itself into a person shape, and is now taking its first tentative steps on land.

"Odd," the figure says. "Remarkably odd indeed. Water and land is an arbitrary division, yet why do I feel so transgressive? Excuse me, good sir?"

The peacoat man taking the photos finally notices that something's changed. He gives a whole full-body flinch and drops the camera. He crouches to pick it up and fumbles, nearly knocking it into the ocean.

"Dee, we need to get out of here," the mother hisses.

"This could be news," the voice behind the camera says. "Maybe an extrahuman thing."

"I am not having your fascination with extrahumans get you or our child in trouble and—"

On the dock, the guy has his camera back and he scoots backwards on his ass. Water guy takes a tentative step forward. He smiles, a huge beaming grin and then his jaw drops. Thick tentacles erupt from his mouth, wrapping around the crumpled figure of the man on the dock and squeezing. The camera's still zoomed in, and you can see the suckers on the tentacles flexing as they wrap themselves around every limb.

The screams on the camera are so loud they're distorted.

"He's like the cat from *Captain Marvel*," I squeak.

It's terrifying but I also get a little thrill every time I see a different mutant in the world. Like genetics is a toybox and someone has gone wild playing in it. Then I'm back to fear, because if I came face to face with Mr. Tentacle Guy, I would lose my shit.

Whoever's filming loses theirs too. The footage wobbles everywhere. There's a flash of leg, a patch of grass, a child's crying face and then everything is dark.

"Now that's what I call tentacles." Dylan arches an eyebrow. "Petal, is that your brother?"

The tiny mechanical woman whirs out of Dylan's hood and bounces down their arm to drape languidly over their knuckles. Somehow, the two of them have made friends. Dylan does tend to make a habit of adopting mutants, because they're ridiculously soft underneath it all. "Yes, that is Water Nourishing the Roots. He's a very naughty boy, and this is exactly what I would expect from him. Squeezing some poor innocent until he pops."

"I never saw him pop," Dani says.

"Oh, believe me." Petal gives a delicate shudder. "The man popped."

Dylan pokes their phone again. "Apparently there was only blood left behind. And bits of skin." They wink at me. "You lucky, lucky girls. Now don't go murdering our tentacular friend without making sure he actually deserves it."

"He popped a guy." Gladdy is back to scowling. "Is that not enough for you?"

"Who among us has not popped a guy?" Dylan asks. Sadly, it's a rhetorical question, unless you argue about the semantics. I have not popped any, but I've melted a few.

"We don't pop innocent bystanders though."

Dylan yawns elaborately, not bothering to cover their mouth. "No, but we also don't know if that was an innocent bystander. Maybe it was a Quietus guy. Definitely has a Quietus-type name. Randall Chad Whatthefuck the Fourth. My point being: don't assume shit."

Gladdy's unnecessarily sullen. "Fine, fearless leader. We'll contact you before we make any decisions."

"Fuck no. That's not what I'm asking for. I'm not *your* fucking parent." Dylan spins in their chair, voice hard. "I'm not going to give you a license to kill. You're all smart and capable and can figure shit out on your own. I'm just giving you, like, friendly advice, to maybe ask a couple of questions before you kill someone. Ignore me if you want and make your own goddamn mistakes."

"Fine." Gladdy glares for a few seconds before the smile breaks out.

"Asshole," Dylan mutters with their own grin and then looks down at their phone when it vibrates. "Oh look, speaking of parents. Turns out I was right about the word afoot and Dan, you were right about them not wanting to be woken up for stupid questions."

Dani links her fingers in Dylan's, and pulls them in against her. "Let's all try and get sleep before everyone heads off in the morning. Yes?"

"Yes," I say gratefully.

Gladdy walks with me back to our quarters, but goes into her own room without speaking, or even pausing for a moment to see if I'm okay. I bang the door shut behind me and throw myself down on the bed theatrically. There's no audience to witness me, but it's still mildly satisfying. I roll over and stare at the ceiling. At least this time, sleep takes me easily.

GLADDY

When I wake, I feel a lot better. A less scruffy and more dressed version of our night's visitor is waiting for me outside my bedroom. Dylan's fears aren't only to do with death and apocalypse. Scattered among them are the furious scribbles of their anxieties, all the concerns about social interaction and the frankly sometimes bizarre assumptions they make about how other people see them. Right now, they've locked themself into a mental loop assuming that I can't stand the sight of them. I watch as they swallow it and try to find a conversational path to approach me down.

"The delightful Ms. Quick." Dylan gives a small bow.

"Chats."

"Are we good?" They gesture incoherently. "After the whole, I don't know actually. I feel like I've *done* something. You're glaring at me."

"We're fine. It's in your head."

Petal's tiny head pokes out of Dylan's hood and perches on their shoulder, whispering something in her ear. Dylan bats absently at her, but there's a smile on his face.

"Is she bad-mouthing me?" I ask.

"She likes me, the little monster." Dylan shrugs. "She says I have a comfortable hood."

"You do have a knack for adopting mutants." I envy Dylan for various things, especially her effortless knack of telling the world to go fuck itself and expecting it to comply. Yet no matter how much they aggravate me, I'll always owe them an enormous debt. I tried to tear his world apart, but Dylan opened up their heart and their whole team to my friends and I. Without her, I don't think any of us would be here. And yet I still fucking hate owing people. There's nothing I can do to repay Dylan, and while they've never given any indication it's expected, it irks me all the same. Maybe that's why I said yes to this Weapon UwU situation in the first place. Trying to prove myself to this impossible person.

"I like the vicious ones." Dylan grins at me and god, that smile. I think it's how they get away with so much shit. "Don't I, Pet? One day you might have your own team of bad seeds like Fetchy here, roaming off across the world and having fun."

"You *can* trust me." I hold their gaze.

"I know." They reach out and pat my shoulder, like they're reassuring me. Like my own fears are written on my face. "Wouldn't ask you to run around the world like my own pretty pretty murder princess if I didn't."

Aaaand I'm back to exasperated again. "Pretty pretty murder princess?"

"It was Petal who said that. I told her it was demeaning."

"I will actually miss you, Dylan Taylor."

"I know. I'm incredibly missable. Now go find your team. Wouldn't want anyone else to be popped by my darling tentacle child while we're standing here re-enacting scenes from Soft Bitch Club: The Movie."

I want to strangle them, because they are so unutterably annoying, but they're already slouching away, giving me a casual middle-finger wave over their shoulder. I watch until they're gone, and then head off to find my team.

Everyone is assembled and waiting. They're all dressed in casual clothes so we can blend in with tourists. Maddy and Katie are both in looks from the Dylan Taylor permanent collection, which means hoodies and jeans. Ye Shou wears shorts and a jersey, like she's ready for a hike. Skye is wearing a stylish shirt I'm a tiny bit jealous of, but it's Lou who catches most of my attention. He looks like he's stepped out of a catalogue in a blazer and three-quarter pants. It's preppy as hell and shouldn't work, but on him it's impeccable.

I'm distracted by my fashion criticisms by various thoughts about logistics—where we're going to stay for one thing. Bankroll isn't really a problem, as even before her ascension, Emma's mutant hacking skills had her siphoning money from various corrupt organisations.

"Fetch." Lou smiles. "We've been waiting."

"Hashing out the last few details with Dylan." More like having a weird half-flirty conversation—at least I think it was flirtation. It's hard to tell with them. Not that it would mean anything if it was, and not that I'd be interested if it did. "We're all ready to go then?"

"Keepaway's standing by."

"I've already booked a place in a motel." Ye Shou looks up from her phone. "A little way out from our destination, in case the town's overrun by monsters before we get there."

"Thank you. That's great." I mean it, because it saves me worrying about it. At least someone on the team is good at this sort of job.

"I'll do what I can to help until my powers come in useful." Her mouth curves into a smile.

"You're not going to tell me what you can do, are you?"

"Sourpatch made me promise to keep it a secret."

Irritating, but fine. Ye Shou seems smart and competent enough that I'm sure she'd tell me if it actually mattered. Some of the others on the team might take a prank too far. I'm staring at the two most likely candidates, who are whispering together and giggling at something on Maddy's phone.

"Right." I clap my hands together. Everyone pays attention which is oddly gratifying. "We're going into an uncertain situation. A lot of our information is rumour, so our first course of action is going to be reconnaissance. We've got communications gear, so we'll split into pairs to cover more ground."

Katie and Maddy immediately reach for each other.

"Nice try, but that way lies chaos. Lou, you can take Katie. Ye Shou and Maddy can pair up and I'll go with Skye." Nobody complains, which seems like a minor miracle. "We have three different reports from three different locations, so we'll start there. I'm hoping we don't end up in a combat situation, but if it does, we'll regroup first and go in together if possible."

"We're after one guy, right?" Lou asks. "Petal's brother?"

"That's our current intelligence, but I don't think we can trust everything that comes out of her mouth. Remember Heart of a Flower wove multiple layers of deception."

Lou inclines his head. "Fair point."

"The secret is going to be communication. Let's be as chatty as we can. Keep everyone up to date." I realise this is a risk when talking to Maddy, but I'd rather have too much information than not enough. Everyone's looking at me almost the same way as they look at Dylan and Dani, except those two make a lot more jokes. I can't think of anything remotely funny. When Dylan says *don't get killed*, they make it sound like it's outside the realm of possibility. If I said it, my voice would tremble and everyone would worry even more. Especially since I can see they're all afraid of what we might find. Even Ye Shou. Surely it can't be worse than the buildings in the parallel universe.

Our ride appears in the middle of us. "Everyone ready to depart on the Keepaway Express?" They're gaining so much more confidence now. There's no flinching away when they hold my gaze. Everything about them looks healthier, and there's light in their eyes.

"Send us away." I hold up my hand for a high five, which I'm generally opposed to, but I've seen them do this with other people, and I get a smile before the world disappears.

~ UwU ~

I've never seen any place quite like our destination. It doesn't even look real: brightly coloured houses perched on the edge of water so clear and reflective, it feels like you could dive in and explore a mirrored world below the surface. We're right at the edge of the dock where the video was filmed. The day isn't as clear as in the footage, the sky a faded blue only faintly brushed with cloud. It's also surprisingly cold, despite the sun.

"Pretty," Ye Shou says from behind me. "And not a tentacle in sight."

The reports of unspecified horrors afoot don't seem to have scared off the people. From the way they drift around with cameras, I'm assuming they're tourists.

"Wow." Lou shades his eyes and looks out across the water. "This place is incredible."

Katie and Maddy are already running onto the dock, trying to find the bloodstain left behind from the attack.

"I can't imagine anything horrible happening here," Skye says with a little shiver. "It's so perfect."

"Possibly too perfect." Lou leaps onto the rocks that step down crookedly into the water. He turns to face us, spreading his arms wide. Silhouetted against the sky, he looks like he's posing for a photo. It would make an astonishingly beautiful one, which I suppose is his point. "It's exactly the sort of place something sinister has to be happening, just to provide a sense of contrast."

My eyes skate over the reflections in the water again. Perhaps there are monsters lurking at the bottom of the lake. Lost things, sleeping in the mud and waiting for someone to awaken them. Or only a single watery tentacle mutant, floating peacefully below the surface and waiting for prey to brush against his lures.

"You look around here," I tell Lou. "Talk to some of the shop owners and find out how much they know. What they think about the attack and so on."

"Katie and I are the charm offensive?"

"Be tourists. Ask obvious questions. Let them hear that Kiwi accent."

He nods and picks up a stone from among the rocks at his feet. When he skims it out over the water, it skips a bunch of times, except the ripples aren't concentric circles, but whirl outwards in strange interlocking shapes.

"Let's not poke the water again." He stares into it pensively, and for a few seconds I wonder if he's hypnotised, Narcissus style. "Unless we get really stuck for leads."

"I'll take Maddy to the blowhole," Ye Shou says. "Looks like a nice walk along the beach."

"Which leaves us going into the trees around a spooky monastery." I glance at Skye. "Probably a smart move, given that we don't want people seeing the whole lot of you running around. Twins we can explain, *maybe* triplets, but try to keep the others locked inside."

We all check that our earpieces are working and then split into pairs. I try to ignore the fears that briefly flare up in everyone. They're normal anxieties, nothing more, and I don't need to read anything into them. It's not that they're questioning my capability to lead. They're uncertain about the future, which is natural and understandable. As beautiful as this little town is, we're here to hunt a monster.

I can't help but turn and watch when Maddy and Ye Shou's path diverges from ours. They walk down the road that runs along the coast, and Maddy's voice is raised with a laugh before the wind catches the sound and tosses it away from me.

"Let's go."

Skye glances at me and shivers.

"Come on, Prime." Two hooks one arm through her original's and tows her up the road for me to follow. "It's not going to be that bad. And if it is, we'll bring the troublesome girls out to play."

MADDY

Ye Shou is not the world's most sparkling conversationalist. I like her, but she's one of those self-contained sorts of people, in a similar way to Gladdy. She's quite happy to amble along looking at the scenery, and keeping all her thoughts inside her head. I am not a self-contained person at all.

"What's the big deal about a blowhole?" I give her a sidelong look. She can't ask me to stop talking if it's about mission-related things.

"It's a hole in the rock and when the tide comes in, water shoots up through it."

I try to fix her with a withering glare, but I'm bad at them. "I understand *that*, but what's the spooky thing?"

"Did you not read the briefing packet?"

I laugh. "No, Katie and I were making Deezer memes. Do you want to see them?"

"What's a Deezer?"

"I cannot believe this." I clap my hand to my heart theatrically and explain Deezer to Ye Shou, who finds it far less funny than I do.

"They are your leaders, yet you make fun of them. And then after that, you all follow them." She frowns. "I've seen it on multiple occasions."

"Yes, but they're also two annoying girls. Or rather one argumentative and bossy girl, and one even more argumentative and bossy… I don't even know what the word is."

"They are a person. It is very simple." Ye Shou sighs. "Not all languages are so concerned with gender as English."

"Fine." I scowl around at the perfectly beautiful day around us. This is what I get for starting a conversation—a lecture on languages.

"We were speaking of the briefing packet," Ye Shou reminds me softly. "The blowhole usually makes sounds due to the wind and the water, but a group of college students visiting became convinced it was speaking to them."

"They were probably high," I interject.

Ye Shou smiles. "According to the statements and the toxicology report, they were indeed under the influence of MDMA. The story said they approached the blowhole to listen, when one of the students was sucked down into it, almost as if the ocean had inhaled."

I stop dead in my tracks. "And *that's* what we're going to investigate?"

"That is the mission as I understood it."

"And you volunteered to go to this blowhole where someone was slurped up by the ocean like it was using a straw?" I'm actually incredulous. Lou and Katie are hanging out on the waterfront, going to shops and no doubt buying actual ice creams, and this is the option Ye Shou chose. It's almost enough to make me read the damn briefing packets.

"I considered my powers would be suitable for exploring the area, and if the situation became urgent, yours are an exceptionally effective offense."

"Oh."

She touches my shoulder lightly. "I have no intention of our first mission being a failure."

"Well that's good. Sorry if I freaked out a little."

Ye Shou nods and we stroll along the coastline. There are some amazing houses overlooking the water, brightly-coloured frontages with big glass windows and outdoor furniture set up on expansive wooden decks. They must have spectacular views. The roads have a lot of cars, and nobody pays us any attention. It's like we're not even there.

We eventually reach the blowhole. A bus-load of people are standing around taking photos.

"It's not really a hole, is it?" It's more like a weird funnel in the rock where the water gets sucked in and explodes into a great shower of spray. I feel a few faint drops of it, carried on the wind.

"No, and perhaps the victim simply jumped into the ocean." Ye Shou takes out her phone and records one giant explosion of water as it surges against the shore. "Still, it is rather impressive."

I weave my way through the tourists until I'm close to the blowhole itself. A sagging rope barrier has been put up, with some hastily made warning signs. People lean over it to film closer. The spray flies into the air, sparkling in the light. It drenches my face and rolls down my cheeks like tears. Between the crash of the water, and the moaning sound of wind funneling through the rocks, I can barely make out anything, even the chatter of the tourists.

"How delightful." A voice speaks inside my head, deep and echoey, like it's coming from inside a shell. "A little mutant, washed up on my shore. Is this coincidence or something more?"

I glance over my shoulder, but Ye Shou is hanging well back.

"It's not coincidence." I know this is risky, but we're here for a mutant, and this sounds like one for sure.

"Oh, how delightful. So many twists in my life story. Chained in various ways by my meddling parent, who has now gone and lost themself somewhere, leaving me to bask in the ocean currents with orders to stand by.

Then the emergency signal and I've found myself... Listen, this is annoying having to bellow at you. Would you like to come and visit with me? You'll be well taken care of, I assure you."

"Who's she talking to?" Gladdy's voice is sharp over the earpiece.

"I have no idea," Ye Shou says. "I'm going to her now."

"It's fine," I tell them both. "I don't think he's as spooky as Petal made out." I climb over the rope barrier and start clambering over the rocks towards the channel of the blowhole. A couple of tourists spin my way, and point their cameras. My foot gives on a slippery patch and I tumble downwards, only for a hand to grab hold of me at the last second.

"How long have we been here?" Ye Shou looks down at me with a small smile. "And already you're throwing yourself into the ocean. All is well, Fetch, I have her."

"There's a voice." I try to snatch my arm from hers, but she's very strong. "He's talking to me. The one we're here to see. Heart's child."

"Oh, is this one trying to restrain you?" The voice sounds amused. "She's a mutant too, isn't she? Hello there. Aren't you an absolutely delicious one? A most whimsical power."

"I can hear the voice too." Ye Shou tells everyone. "He's speaking to me. I believe it's psychic communication."

"Would you believe I'm speaking by vibrating the water droplets in your ears? Is that plausible? It scarcely matters, does it? My parent could bend reality, but it was already bent to begin with. All these impossibilities *are* the design. The vast and beautiful panoply of mutantkind."

"He's inviting me into the ocean," I insist. "He says we'll be fine."

"Oh, rest assured you'll be well taken care of. I have complete control over this entire body of water. Do you require a demonstration?"

The next explosion of spray between the rocks pauses in the air and doesn't fall. The drops swirl and rotate, forming themselves into a face.

The watching tourists make all kinds of amazed sounds. Everyone has their phones held high, recording this extraordinary event. It doesn't take long before someone says the word *extrahuman*. It's definitely on people's minds. I wonder what they'd do if they knew I was one.

"It's so beautiful," a lady near me says. Her face is tilted up and she's beaming. "Jeff, are you filming this?"

I don't hear Jeff's response, because the mouth opens and a series of lashing, watery tentacles erupt from it. I don't know how many people have seen the video from the dock, or know anything about anyone being popped, but there's a lot of screaming.

The tentacles catch the light and scatter it, delicate waterspouts that reach down and pluck five tourists effortlessly into the air.

"This is not a good demonstration." Ye Shou stands on the edge of the blowhole, glaring at the ocean as if she's a strict schoolteacher. "Please cease immediately."

"You have no authority here." The voice still sounds amused. "Shall I prove it to you?"

"What the hell is going on?" Gladdy asks over the earpiece. I bet she's regretting splitting up now.

"We may be losing control of the situation." At least Ye Shou can admit it.

A lot of the tourists are retreating rapidly, but some have paused a short distance away, phones out and filming the five bodies dangling above. They hang motionless, not struggling or screaming, held in place by tendrils of water.

"You don't need to do this," I tell the mutant. "We'll come and visit you. Just let these people go and—"

"People drown all the time." What was a face is now a swirling set of waterspouts, ready to suck us all in. "Senseless deaths that achieve little. At least this will serve to illuminate our power and strike fear into the heart of humanity. Perhaps it will also encourage you to get in the water quicker next time."

"Please," I beg. "Don't hurt anyone." At the same time, my stomach churns and I steel myself. It always hurts, no matter how often I do it. I open as wide as I can, and retch a jet of acid towards the complex arrangement of liquid towering above us. The mutant absorbs it effortlessly. Thin threads of green travel through his watery body, whirling through his complex tangle of limbs until my acid squirts out of the ends of the tentacles, drenching two of the bodies he holds.

I want to scream but I bite the inside of my cheek. My hands are clenched so tight they're shaking.

"There's nothing we can do." Ye Shou grips my shoulder hard.

Above us, the bodies disintegrate. Their skin sloughs off them and chunks of meat and jagged bone fall to the rocks around us. I usually have a strong stomach for this shit and try to just *rise above* when it gets gross but this is too much. Nobody's filming anymore. They scream and run, phones abandoned. One man slips on the rocks and smacks his head. A younger man sobs, trying to drag him to safety and leaving a wet smear of blood behind. Part of a leg falls beside them with a damp thud.

"Please stop," I whisper. "We'll come to you. I promise. Don't hurt anyone else."

"I'm glad you see things my way. Give me a moment, and I shall deal with these last few."

The tentacles whip around and hurl the bodies in a flat motion, almost as if he's trying to skim them across the surface of the water. Except when they hit, they sink like stones, as if something reached up and dragged them under.

The towering mass of tentacles collapses down, drenching us both. I gasp as it hits me, so bitterly cold. Ye Shou keeps her stoic expression.

"Gladdy, this is bad." My lips tremble. "I think we might be in trouble."

There's no response from my earpiece.

"I took the liberty of insinuating enough water into the mechanisms to inhibit their operation," the voice says. "You've hardly proven yourselves trustworthy and I'd prefer to keep things intimate. Now, if you'd step into my parlour please?"

Water drains away from the blowhole channel, revealing a thin strip of dry ground that leads out into the ocean. The water piles up and forms the shape of a head and torso with outspread arms, like he's beckoning us in.

"This seems very foolish," Ye Shou mutters. "Yet I do not see we have much choice." Her form shudders slightly as a pair of spiders drop from the ends of her sleeves and scuttle away across the rocks.

I try to catch her eye, but she ignores me completely.

"You have no choice at all," the voice says. "And if you do not begin moving, you shall see how far the ocean can reach onto the land. I will not stop at five bodies the next time."

"Honestly," I grumble, picking my way down the rocks. "How did we get into this mess?"

"We were warned." Ye Shou makes it sound as if this is somehow our fault. "We knew Heart of a Flower's children could be deadly."

"You're right." I take a deep breath. There's no point complaining about this. We're here and we need to do the best we can in the situation. He's left us alive, and seems interested in us being mutants, so perhaps we can use that to our advantage. I pin the smile back to my face. It's the only armour I have. "Brother," I call. "We wish entrance to your kingdom."

"Little sisters. I'll be only too glad to welcome you." The water rushes back down the blowhole channel, snatching at our clothes with eager fingers, and dragging the both of us headlong out to sea.

GLADDY

The situation with Maddy and Ye Shou sounds like it's sliding rapidly out of control, and now they're not responding over the comm.

"Lou? Please tell me you're there?"

"Yeah, sorry." He swallows abruptly. "I'm here. We're both here. You want us to go check out whatever's going on with the others?"

"Please." I gaze at the sight in front of me. "We've got our own problems."

"That was very tactful," Skye Three says. "I'd say this is larger than a problem."

"Don't be such a whiny fucking baby." Six spins a knife between her fingers. We really shouldn't let Prime carry so many knives. "It's a pair of eviscerated and headless corpses. We're not the corpses, so it's hardly a fucking problem."

"Six has a point." Five thunks the tip of her knife into the bark of a nearby tree repeatedly. I'm getting a headache.

"Think about what *made* the corpses." Two scowls at them, hand on hips.

"We're big girls." Six grins. "I think together we can deal with whatever makes such a fucking messy job of butchering bodies. Fetchy, you can watch."

"Can you all please shut up." I keep my voice as mild as I can. "You might scare them off rather than drawing them here. And we want to *speak* to whoever did this, not attack them, so put your damn knives away."

Miracle of miracles, Five and Six actually obey, although neither looks happy.

Seven lurches towards the others as if she's about to swipe the blades off them, but Six catches her with surprising tenderness.

"We're being smart and wising up, Sev. That means no knives, and indoor voices."

"Shhh. Be very very quiet," Seven slurs.

"That's my girl."

I can finally focus on the two bodies hanging in the trees. They're missing their heads, as well as internal organs and chunks of flesh from their legs. Their skin is marked all over with a complex series of interlocking symbols.

"You think that's writing?" I ask Skye Two quietly, because Prime is staring in the other direction and trying not to vomit.

Two angles her head, trying to look at it, until Three pushes past her and grabs hold of one stiff limb, twisting it around so we can all read it. "Keep away, stay out, wendigo, wendigo, flee, run, don't stop. Bunch of nonsense."

"Wendigo. I know this." Prime's voice is still shaky. "If any of you ever listened to Dylan you would too. First appearance of Wolverine. He fights the Hulk and a wendigo in the Canadian forests. But they're real, not just comic books." She swallows. "Or you know, real-mythological. They're both sort of linked to um." She leans over and retches. The clones look at her with expressions ranging from pity to disgust. "To cannibalism."

"No shit." Six has her knife back out and is poking at one of the hanging bodies with what I feel like is unnecessary interest. "So, like, some leg steaks and some of the offal?"

Five leans right in close and sniffs the flesh. "You'd think they'd salt it."

"I figure this is a warning," Two says briskly. "That's the gist of the message, isn't it? Don't enter the forest, because there's a wendigo."

"Or a regular cannibal," Three chimes in.

"I'm all for survivalist shit," Five says. "But there are a bunch of restaurants right there."

"Curse," Prime coughs. "It's a curse."

"Curses aren't real." It sounds stupid as soon as I say it. What are these powers if not a curse? "If this person is roaming around killing people, we need to stop them whether they're a wendigo, one of Heart's children, or something else entirely."

"I hope they're a wendigo," Six whispers and shuts herself up by putting her knife between her teeth. Five and Four follow suit, because they're a fucking chaos trio if ever there was one. I send Two into the trees first because I can mostly rely on her. I bring up the rear, because I want to see if anyone goes running off. It would be nice if Prime could chill enough to at least let poor stumbling Seven back inside.

"Cannibal," Prime mutters. "We're in here with a cannibal."

I guess Seven's stuck out here.

We're walking through a wedge of land that starts from an old monastery and heads down between two roads to the waterfront. Viewed on the map, it's not a huge area, and I don't think there's any way we can get lost in here, barring mutant shenanigans. Still, it's pretty fucking eerie after seeing those bodies. I keep my phone out, tracking the pulsing dot as we move deeper into the forest. If there's a murderer out here—cannibal or wendigo—I assume they're somewhere in the middle.

Up ahead, Two holds up a single fist. All the Skyes stop at once. It's eerie to see them operate like this, when they spend so much time arguing. They all fan out around one particular tree. Two symbols have been hacked into its trunk. One is a circle with a sloppy-looking Z through it and another is a crude drawing that looks like a deer with thorned antlers. They're both smeared with something that's dried dark brown and chunky.

"Delicious," Six says around her knife. "I'd say we're on the right fucking track, kids."

"Another please keep out sign." Two peers around through the trees ahead. "Or beware of the wendigo."

Three runs the tip of her knife along one of the antlers on the deer shape. "Weird question: why is the wendigo leaving beware of myself signs?"

"Conflicted," Four suggests.

"Or victim-blaming." Two scowls. "If you come in here and get eaten, it's your own fault. Come on, I think I see another one."

Sure enough, twenty meters further on, we find a tree with similar symbols.

"Maybe a boundary," Two says. "Either way, we're on the right track. Three, you wait here."

The rest of the Skyes follow Two through to the next marked tree. We leave Four there, and eventually find the next one. Through the trees, we can see Four, who points one arm at us and outstretches her other arm in a different direction, presumably towards Three.

"Looks like a perimeter." Two makes shapes with her arms and orients herself inwards. She waits for Three and Four to catch up and then forges off into the forest, heading for where she's deduced the center is.

"She'd be so much better, wouldn't she?" Prime's voice is surprisingly bitter. "Look at her. My only worth is as the case that holds Two and the others. Even Seven would be more use in a fight than me."

"This mutant business isn't only about fighting."

"The clones know it, you know it. Dylan knows it for sure. Even Ray. They teach me all those coping skills, the ability to pack them away, but in a situation like this, how much use would I be on my own?"

"It's your power." I don't know how to reassure her. This isn't part of my skillset. It's part of the reason things collapse with Maddy. She *needs* so much and I'm not the person to provide it for her. What she deserves is a huge ecosystem of support and encouragement, one that I can perch on top of and take relief from too.

"If I could step aside I would." Prime stumbles and almost falls, but Four moves alongside silently and rights her before moving off to catch up with the others.

"Except that's not how it works." I can't see a way out of the conversation, so I hack through it bluntly. If I needed to make her fall apart, I could do that. Her insecurity is real and a horrible pit she's always on the verge of toppling into. Propping people up is much, much harder. "The situation exists, so you have to make the best of it or—"

Someone screams up ahead, which I'm actually grateful for, because it ends this goddamn conversation. We find the assembled clones in a small clearing full of gruesome trophies. Bones and carvings of the same deer-like figure, along with three severed heads on long poles. Some faded material is stretched between stakes in the ground, decorated with more symbols and messages of warning. It has strange divots and imperfections too, and I realise with a twist of my stomach that it's skin. I look away from it, blinking rapidly, only to spy a careful construction of interlocked bones. There are still pieces of flesh clinging to some of them.

That's when I bend double and retch until it scalds my throat.

I'm not the only one throwing up. Prime sobs with her eyes closed, and even Two and Three cling onto each other.

The other four clones are performing a slow pass of the entire clearing.

"Gross." Six winks at me. "Pretty fucking seriously goddamn gross."

"Ugh." Seven does a full-body shudder, her tongue protruding. "Very very icky. Ooh, a skull!" She bends down and picks up a severely decomposed head from the ground. Skin comes off on her fingers, and she wipes it on her fucking pants and oh god I'm vomiting again.

"Sevvie, that's too gross," Five says gently. "Put the head down."

"I never hurt it," she protests, and tosses it casually over her shoulder. "Don't blame me."

"What's this damn wendigo doing?" Four prods with her boot at another bone construction that's been decorated with feathers and paint. It might be beautiful if it wasn't for this whole situation being entirely fucking terrifying. "Some kind of ritual shit? Worshipping some bloody-faced god?"

"You can't figure out this crap." Six tosses her knife into the air and catches it backhand. "Whatever reason he has, it's a fucked one. We need to stab this guy the second we find him."

"Guy?" Four asks.

"Playing the odds." Five bares her teeth.

I manage to get to my feet. "I think we do need to find this… *person.* Don't kill them straight away. We need to figure out what's going on first, although I agree they need to be stopped. It's—"

There's a crack of wood from outside the clearing. Multiple Skyes hurtle past me.

I spin to see three of them with their knives drawn, surrounding a pale figure. It is a guy, as Six suggested, although he's seen better days. His hair is half-shaved and half-matted. His bare torso is covered with writing, overlapping scars forming the same symbols we've seen in the woods. He's unshaven, but roughly so and there's a fresh cut on his neck.

"Get out." His voice comes out in a high-pitched snarl. "Didn't you see the signs? You're supposed to stay away. Why does nobody stay *away*?"

Five and Six lunge towards him from each side.

"Hold," I snap. "Fucking hold. Knives *down*."

I'm so relieved they actually listen, or partway listen at least. They both step back from the wild-eyed figure, even if they hold their blades out at arm's length.

It's the fears I see on his face that truly scare me. I've never seen someone so tortured by the truth of what they are, pinned by their nature into a bloody, impossible prison.

"Please leave." When he speaks, I can see some of his teeth have been filed into sharper points. The phrase *all the better to eat you with* bubbles up in my mind and I choke back an awful sound.

I hold up my hands as if I'm surrendering. "We're here to help."

The Skyes all whip around to glare at me.

"Like fuck we are," Six snaps. "I'm seconds away from slitting this motherfucker's throat."

"No, you're seconds away from putting your fucking knife on the ground." I try to scrape up some Dylan feeling, some essence of *command.* "Listen to me. *I'm* Field Leader, and if you can't accept that, I'll shove you back inside Prime myself."

Six inclines her head and smirks at me. "I like this on you, Fetchy. Bit of fire looks good."

"We're friends," I tell the shivering figure of the bloodstained man. "We're here to help."

MADDY

Travelling this way is uncomfortably like being a fish on a hook, towed into the ocean by invisible threads of current. Except Water Nourishing the Roots—if it is truly him—is correct. I can breathe under here. I'm inside a giant bubble of air, like something from a fairytale. When I twist in the water to see Ye Shou behind me, it appears she can too. She looks extremely unhappy, scowling ferociously at me with her nostrils flaring.

"Can you hear me?" I shout, exaggerating all my mouth movements.

She taps her ears and shakes her head.

"She cannot hear you, but I can." Water's voice sounds both calm and smug. "I could communicate between you if it was necessary, but I hardly see that it is."

"Where are you taking us?" I ask.

"My home. My prison. They are one and the same, even now after Heart's passing. We're nearly there. You can already see the light."

Ahead, the water glows in shades of blue and green, like a glorious sunset rendered in a cool palette. It's so gorgeous it takes my breath away.

"How?" My voice trembles.

"The water is my home. I do not so much live in the ocean as I *am* the ocean. Not in its entirety, of course. I am but a single dancing current among titans. Yet I have some small sway over that which lives with me. I find myself drawn to the theatrical and beautiful. There is darkness down here, but light too."

The pair of us rush through the water as the lights get brighter. We travel deeper until the bioluminescence sprawls above us in constellations so dazzling it's like having your face pressed up against the Milky Way.

Ye Shou is dragged up alongside me until we're sharing the same bubble of air. "This is… not what I expected."

"From murdery water guy?"

"I would complain you are being reductive," the voice says. "But none of those things are entirely false. My name is Water Nourishing the Roots, firstborn son of Heart of a Flower. I am a mutant, as you are. Welcome to my home."

We drift over a dip in the ocean floor and come upon an astonishing forest of coral, more colours than I ever imagined could be under the sea, painted almost neon by the glow from above. There are giant trees of it that look as if they were painted by the melting clock guy, contorting towards the surface as if there is something above that they desperately want. Schools of fish dart like a single rippling organism around enormous fluted shapes.

Skeletons lie on the ocean floor, neatly arranged as if in some museum exhibit for anatomical research. Most are small, but among them are things far larger. One stretches through my entire field of vision, winding serpentine through the coral and ending in a giant pale boulder-like shape in the distance.

Floating in front of us are the three bodies from the blowhole, like a gruesome welcoming committee. Small fish flutter around their faces, nibbling at the lips and eyeballs. One of them ripples violently, and an eel bursts through a pale curve of stomach, curling lazily in the water before twisting over to investigate another body.

"Apologies." There's a shape in the water that looks like an optical illusion. Fish swim into it, getting caught in the swirling currents and spinning in frantic circles. Water comes towards us, too many limbs moving, churning the water with furious tentacles as he drifts in our direction. His face is beautiful, shaped and sculpted impossibly from seafoam. "I hope this form doesn't displease you too greatly."

"Why are we here?" Ye Shou asks. "Why bring us beneath to see this?"

"You answer your own question. I wish you to bear witness to my beauty, not only my destruction."

"Then why kill those people?"

"The surface dwellers?" He scoffs. "You think they are blameless? The man I killed on the dock controls the financial affairs of a company that pours vast quantities of pollutants into me every day. That was a message. The water will no longer sit by and allow humanity to wage war on it without repercussions." He smiles at us. "It is similar, perhaps, to how mutants say this far and no further."

That gives me a hell of a fright, because it's what we all said when we first took over Jinteki. We had lost two of our people and we wanted to make a statement that we wouldn't let it happen again. It turned out to be an impossible goal, but we've held it as well as we can. It's difficult to keep smiling in the face of all that, but I do. Someone has to.

"We are not randomly killing humans who offend us." I don't take the sting from my tone.

"Have you considered that perhaps you should?" He smiles wider and tentacles flutter between his parted lips. "It would be a better tactic than hiding, surely. My parent had other plans, extraordinary and grandiose, but it seems they have come to ruin. In the absence of my baby sister taking her rightful place, why not lash out and destroy?"

"Goddess has chosen another path. We wish to work alongside rather than—"

"I have no interest in that."

Above us the bioluminescence shifts into darker colours. Things in the silt at the bottom of the ocean come slithering out to dance. Their bones glow through translucent flesh, and their mouths gape. They're like someone who'd been told about deep-dwelling undersea fish decided that they should be approximately ten thousand times more terrifying, and also bigger than a person.

"What do you want then?" It seems the logical question, even though the answer will probably be horrible.

"In an ideal world, we would rise up against the surface dwellers. Snatch them from the shores and dash them against the rocks until their skulls split like ripe fruit. Teach them to fear me truly. No more frolicking along my edges or marvelling at my grandeur. If they send their tiny floating contraptions into me, I will tear them into matchsticks and suck the squalling human contents down to feed my children."

"Wow." I keep my voice flat and uninterested, like none of this bothers me. "Gross."

"You do not understand rage. Poison has not flowed into your veins from a thousand different puncture wounds. Not even my vast size can dilute it enough to remove the sting. You have not been choked—"

"Enough." I flap my hand at him dismissively, aware of the risk I'm taking, but we don't want to give him a big-thumbs up to attack the so-called surface world. We need to make him think differently.

"Foolish girl." Silt explodes from the ocean floor, swirling around us in a cloud. It's still lit from above, a luminous green that reflects off every particle so we stand in the middle of something vast and poisonous. Creatures that do not belong.

The glowing creatures swish their way through the cloud, butting their blind and eager faces up against our air bubble, extruding fangs from inside their wrinkled mouths and gnashing at us. Inside them, more light flares, a nauseous and pulsing yellow.

"This is what happens," Water says. "When you allow the poison in the water to affect the life that lives there. I will nourish and nurture these creatures—spawned not by me, but by the actions of humanity. Once they are fully grown, I will unleash them on the world and it will make the so-called monster movies seem like giddy fantasies."

I can't help but imagine it, these strange and hungry lifeforms carried on the crest of enormous waves, crashing into the picturesque seaside community and devouring what they find there.

"I apologise." I hate the plaintive tone in my voice. "We didn't come here to fight."

The creatures lose interest in us, and return to the coral, losing themselves in the tangled forest. Around us, the silt slowly drifts to the ground and the glow above us brightens, becoming a gentle and placid blue.

"I believe you," Water says. "You do not wish to fight, but you *did* come here to stop me. I understand. Heart left their broken toys lying around and you come striding along to tidy them away. Me, who they did not even trust. Do you know how powerful I *could* be, if they had not crippled me?"

"Crippled?" Ye Shou asks.

"Tied to this land, to my love."

"What does the sea love?" She asks it like a riddle. "The shore?"

"I am still mutant, which means I was human once. Heart carried me inside them as they did with all their other children save Yǔzhòu. I was born and lived as a human, then became a mutant with the power to control water. Then I fell in love as a mutant and a man. Foolishly, as it turned out, but who can control the affairs of the heart?"

It seems as if his smile is particularly directed at me and my own foolishness, but I'm probably being oversensitive. He does seem to *know stuff* though. I wonder if it's because we're made up of so much water.

"You loved?" I ask, because the silence has dragged on too long.

“Yes.” His voice is sad and has a dark undertow that’s reflected in the currents that pull and twist him out of shape. “I loved a man who made some very poor choices.”

GLADDY

"You can't be here." The man doubles over and falls to the ground, raking his fingers through the dirt until they're caked in muck. "Leave. Please leave. I can't be responsible for what I'll do if you stay."

I put my hands behind my back as if this will disguise how much they're shaking. In the shape of his fears, I can see the terrible deeds he's done. How many people have died at his hand. The different ways he's tried to eat them to make him feel different from what he is. Monster. Cannibal. Wendigo. The craving, that's what terrifies me most. Each time he kills and feeds, he allows himself to feel like this may be the last time. The relief of satiation convinces him. Then there's the slow process of increasing hunger, until he can no longer resist and feeds on the next poor soul to wander into the beauty of the forest.

It's not that the warnings don't keep people away. He leaves them when the cravings aren't too awful. As he gets hungrier and hungrier, he drifts further afield. The most recent body here was taken from the monastery, a single tourist there alone in the evening, taking shots of the sunset.

Even though it's only been a short time since he fed, the cravings are strong. The intervals are getting shorter, and he fears that most of all—a constant hunger, impossible to sate.

"You've been prowling the perimeter." My voice is shaking and all the Skyes look to me nervously. "Trying to remove some of the warning signs. You hope someone will stumble in and you can pretend it was their own foolishness."

"Be quiet." The tendons in his jaw stand out like thick cords. "You know nothing."

"I see it all. Everything you've done."

"And you tell these women to stay their hands? I'd feed on them all and call it one death." He snarls and lunges towards Six, who swings her knife in a vicious arc. The hunger isn't bad enough yet, because it gives him pause.

"You aren't Heart's child?" I see no sign of it in his face. It's all a gruesome cycle of hunger and feeding, hope and despair, forgiveness and backsliding.

"No." He rubs his fingers across his sharpened teeth. The sound he makes when he sucks the blood from his own flesh is hungry and insistent. "Or I am in a way. They broke me and made me this unholy thing, and what is that if not a parent?"

"Heart changed you?"

"Yes. With great pleasure and care. So many of those they changed were due to randomness and whimsy. Heart was a great believer in the lottery of evolution. Except when it came to me, they had very specific plans." He's looking at the Skye clones with uncomfortable eagerness. The fears are mixed on his face with something darker.

"Pay attention." I clap my hands in front of his face. "Don't commit suicide by clone."

"So many of them." His teeth worry at his lower lip until blood spills. "You wouldn't spare a single one? Can you make more?"

"We've lost enough," Five and Six snarl together.

"No matter what Fetch says, you take a single lick at me or my sisters and I'll fucking gut you," Four tells him, eerily calm. "Why didn't you finish those bodies in the forest? What's the appeal of playing with your food?"

"It needs to be fresh," he groans. "If it's not, it's like eating ash."

"That's just unnecessarily fucking picky," Five says. "Not to mention disgusting. Fetch, let's kill this guy. I know he's not Heart's kid, but he's—"

"Water Nourishing the Roots," he whispers. For a moment, it's not only hunger on the man's face. "You haven't hurt him, have you?" The fears in his face shift, the overwhelming pressure of the hunger weakening in favour of—

"You loved him." I can see it written there, clear as a movie flashback. "The two of you were together. You lived together. There was a little house you had near the water, because he couldn't be too far from it and—"

"And then Heart returned." The hunger in his voice is replaced by a bitterness that's even deeper, a wellspring that poisons everything. "Their precious youngest was ready to bloom at last, and they wanted to ensure all their pieces were on the board."

"Ruining everything." My voice is soft. Thankfully, the Skyes are smart enough to let me run this conversation, although Seven is still wandering aimlessly around the clearing investigating bones. "The life you were finally happy with."

"I'm sure we weren't *perfectly* happy, but compared to this? It was an idyll. We would swim together and make love in the water. There was a wooden table right down on the beach where we'd eat all our meals. And then Heart brought their curse into our lives."

"They punished you because you're gay?" Three asks.

The man sneers and spits blood. It hangs from his lips in a thin string. "Gender and sex mean nothing to Heart. They can be anything they dream of. Do you genuinely believe sexuality is any kind of issue for them? No, their problem with me was far deeper and irreconcilable."

I see it all written there, but I also see what happened after, and it's hard for me to speak.

"You'll have to spell it out." Two has her hands on her hips, glaring.

"I chose humanity. I begged Water to abandon his destiny. I told Heart we wanted nothing of the mutant life, that we only wished the simplicity of being as close to human as possible."

"To be honest, that'd piss me off too," Four says. "And I don't think I'm the only one."

"Mutant and fucking proud." Six has her knife out again. "Didn't you get the fucking memo?"

"We could both pass then. Water had control of his element, but hadn't been changed into it. My original power was to generate sparks of electricity when I snapped my fingers, which had so little bearing on my life it seemed to not matter at all. We were an eccentric gay couple who lived on the beach. People tolerated us. Some actually liked us. We had friends. I wanted to keep that life, not become a mutant revolutionary."

Five grunts. "And then he made you into a cannibal?"

"He said I had chosen humanity." His lower lip has been gnawed to bloody ruins and he swallows a chunk of flesh with an audible gulp. Perhaps he will devour himself. "That since I had turned my back on my people, I would forever crave the flesh of those I had chosen instead."

"Fucking gruesome." Six doesn't sound like she entirely disapproves.

"It's—what do you call it?" Five scowls at the others. "Word that means like appropriate or whatever, but it's fancy. We're not good with words at this end."

"Apropos," Two drawls.

"Is it?" Six asks. "Fucking weird word."

"It's fucking *apropos*." Five looks at me. "He chose his side. Let him eat himself."

"No." It's Prime, speaking up for once. "He's been tortured by Heart of a Flower. It's not his fault. Not everyone's ready to throw everything away to be a mutant. It's not like there's so much positive stuff about it."

"I don't think she likes us very much." Three nudges Two.

"Well, we knew *that*." Two shakes her head disdainfully.

"Mostly my fault, to be perfectly fucking honest." Six grins around at everyone. "Me and Five drag the whole tone of the group right into the fucking gutter."

"Stop it," Prime snaps. "I love you all, as annoying as you are. But none of this is easy, so I can understand why someone might want to stay human rather than being dragged into the fight. I had no choice, but he did, and it was cruel of Heart to take it away from him."

"Lovely fucking speech, but we've still got a fucking wendigo here who wants to eat us." Skye Five stretches her arm out towards him. When he lunges for her, she gives him a hard smack around the back of the head. "We can't leave him here, no matter how soft you're feeling, Prime."

My earpiece comes to life with Lou's voice. "Fetch, we're at the blowhole. There's no sign of Sourpatch or Ye Shou, but there are some wild stories. Tentacle guy killed a bunch of people and then our two walked into the ocean. Apparently. The stories differ on a lot, but they do agree on that."

"Damn it." What a brilliant start to the mission. "Wait there and don't go walking into the ocean. Maybe stay back a bit from the shore. We're coming to you." I turn back to the shaking figure of the man. "Why haven't you gone wandering into the ocean to see your lover?"

"He hates me." Flecks of blood fly when he screams. "The first time I killed and ate, when I could not control myself any longer, I threw myself bloody-mouthed into the sea in the hope he would swallow me, ease my pain and take me into himself one final time. But he called me a traitor and a monster, then spat me onto the rocks like a broken thing."

"Fuck." Six grins at Five. "That's a bad fucking breakup."

Five laughs. "Least he gets to date, unlike us poor bitches."

"Enough." Prime inhales sharply and closes her eyes. When she opens them, it's only her and I in the clearing with our wendigo friend. "They're not always useful to have around."

Unfortunately, I can see the guy making new calculations in his head about the two of us. We don't usually have a lot of call for weapons, given the powers we have on display, but sometimes it's useful to have a backup.

I draw a gun from a holster at my hip. I point it at him and my hand doesn't shake at all. "I'll know the instant you change your mind and come for either of us. I've got a different proposition. Some friends of ours are currently in the ocean. We think they're talking with your ex." This is something of a wild guess, but it sounds logical and feels right. "Let's make that conversation a little more interesting."

"What do you mean?"

I wave the gun at him. "Come on. We're going to the beach. And Prime, see if you can squeeze out a couple of clones. Just for the numbers. I don't want this guy getting any ideas."

We're joined by Two and Three, who seem more than happy to flank Wendigo. We head back through the trees. I have no idea if this is the right decision we're making, but at the end of the day, if we have to, we'll just fucking drown the guy. I pity him, but I've seen what he's done.

MADDY

"Heart of a Flower is a very rigid person," Water says. "With what you might call a one-track mind, one that ever turns towards the destruction of humanity and the resurgence of mutantkind. It made for a complex upbringing, but I fell in love with a man who wanted a simple life. The two things could never be reconciled, especially when Seth and Heart fought. I tried to make peace between them, and I was punished for that. Cut down."

"You seem very powerful to me." I bob in the water with Ye Shou. Flattery seems like a decent option. "We've seen the amazing things you can do."

"Water covers seventy percent of the world. My birthright was to be a creature of storms and tempests, someone who could drain the deepest trenches to create waves so colossal they could sink continents. Yet all I do is splash in the shallows and spit pathetically at the shore dwellers."

"Why didn't you choose this Seth dude then?" I ask. "If you were punished for it anyway."

"He chose humanity." The currents swirl and our air bubble bobs erratically. Silt from the floor is stirred up again in clouds, although the creatures stay dormant. "Heart may be a monster, but they are not wrong about everything."

"So it's all terrible." I sigh and spin around in the water. "You have lost love and lost power and so you throw a tantrum."

"I shall do what I can to aid my siblings, who are far less constrained than I. We shall pour out the bowls of Heart's wrath on the earth." He smiles again. "What else is there to do? Perhaps our errant sister will even join us in time."

Two dark shapes scuttle up the arm of Ye Shou's jacket and up to her jawline. Spiders, returning to her. "Or you could go the other way. It appears our colleagues have been working on this problem from the opposite direction. Part of me has been monitoring the situation, and I have overheard our friends speaking with your ex-lover."

"I'm surprised he hasn't eaten them." Water sounds even more sulky than usual.

"Eat them?" I squawk because I realise Ye Shou is talking about Gladdy, and as annoyed as I've been over that stupid non-kiss, there is no way I want her devoured by something.

"Everyone's fine." Ye Shou smiles at me. "I think you'll find our friends can take care of themselves. In fact, they're bringing Seth here to speak with you."

"I have already told that man all I need to." Water's shape swirls and dissolves until it appears we're alone. "I made my positions and beliefs very clear and if he thinks…"

There is silence as we drift alone in the water. I wonder where Water has gone, and if he's scared or nervous or angry.

"Sometimes it's exhausting being the one who always risks rejection," I say to the ocean. "You reach out because what you might win is better than what you have now."

There's a sigh that seems to come from all around us. "He risks more than rejection by coming here."

"And yet he's on his way here still," I say.

The ocean swirls around us and we're both yanked backwards, far faster than before. I'm a little bit pleased to see Ye Shou's calmness finally shattered, as she lets out a yelp, limbs flailing. I remind myself that if Water wanted to kill us, he could simply cut off our artificial air supply and let us drown. We're being taken somewhere for a reason.

After a couple of minutes, our heads break the water and we're hauled, dripping and suddenly shivering onto the rocks of the coastline. Ye Shou is panting and her lips have turned a pale blue. It's deserted here, although a shuttered house looms nearby.

"Only slightly terrifying." Ye Shou smiles at me.

We both flinch away because an enormous wave crashes against the rocks, sending up a huge shower of spray. Our clothes are already saturated, so it makes us no wetter, but the sound and violence of it makes me want to run.

"Calm yourselves." The torrent of spray resolves into the shape of a person, the most detailed representation yet. "And apologies for the dramatic entrance. Thoughts of Seth make me somewhat emotional." Water gestures and our clothes are wrung out, rumpled but instantly dry as if every speck of moisture has been stolen from them.

"—running yet?" Lou says in my ear.

"Omigod! Glowstick! We're back." I'm speaking way too fast. "We had quite the ride, but we're fine. Can you pick up our location?"

"Yes, we've got a ping. You're close. We've managed to pick up a new friend."

"Friend as in friendly?" It seems too much to expect, even as I ask it.

"How do you like the sound of a cursed cannibal? Pretty typical for us, isn't it? Apparently he's in love with the watery one. It's a wild story, honestly, but—"

I whirl around and stare at Water. "A cursed cannibal?"

He shrugs. "Heart changed my boyfriend too. Seth loved humans too much, so my parent simply gave that love a little extra bite." The watery face smirks, and I very much want to punch it.

"But that's disgusting!"

"He chose poorly." Water shrugs damp shoulders.

"We've got a visual," Lou says. "And you've got Waterboy here already. Nice work."

I turn to see the rest of the team approach in a line down through the trees. Lou and Katie are in the lead, with a row of Skyes trailing the gaunt figure of a man who's definitely seen better days.

"Seth," Water murmurs, but I can't tell anything from his tone.

Then in the rear comes Gladdy, and I still get this punch of joy to my heart to see her. Her hair swings around her face and I watch the movement of her head as she scans the scene in front of her, pausing first at the liquid figure and then stopping on me.

Even at this distance, I see her smile.

There's something between us, even if it's not exactly what I want, and my heart is on a hook even more than my body was when we were towed under the ocean. The team comes down the path and then begins picking their way over the rocks. Water says nothing else the whole time, but he hums under his breath. I think it's that song from *The Little Mermaid*, which is too obvious if you ask me. They finally reach us, and stand in a line with the trembling man thrust forward as its center.

"Seth, you look wonderful," Water says, in this perfectly bitchy tone that makes both Katie and I laugh involuntarily and then cover our mouths with our hands. "This cannibal chic suits you."

"Rish." The guy's voice is croaky. His lips are all bloody which is creeping me out. "I see you haven't lost your acid tongue. You did love me once upon a time, didn't you?"

"I loved an idea of you." When Water opens his mouth, tendrils flicker out like multiple tongues, each lined with suckers like an octopus. "Yet you shattered that. Not Heart. Life wears people down, and you wanted to play at human and pretend I wasn't who I am."

The words hit uncomfortably close to home. Loving an idea is easy. Loving a person is hard.

"And now your parent has made us both monsters." Seth lunges forward.

A pair of Skyes follow him, knives drawn, and Seth comes to a halt only a meter from the shimmering figure of his former lover.

"I was always a monster." The face of Water ripples, as if it is about to dissolve. "Yet you loved me, ignoring what I was because it suited you to think I was toothless and tame. I never denied what I was. You had your own fantasy."

Gladdy shuffles around the group to stand beside me. "Are you okay?"

"Fine." I glance sideways, but her face is mostly obscured behind windblown waves of hair.

"You are not *only* a monster." Seth lifts his hand to his mouth and gnaws on the ball of his thumb until it squirts blood into his mouth. "We were happy together. We had a good life. It was you who couldn't crawl out from under your parent's shadow. You who trailed after them, begging for scraps of their affection, and ignoring the care and comfort I provided. And look what I became because of it."

"A hungry thing." Water yawns. "There are many hungry things under the sea. There is nothing special about you."

"Once upon a time, you thought there was." The hurt in Seth's voice echoes inside me. I try to ignore it, but it builds until it's overwhelming. I don't want to be this person, clinging to something that I've constructed in my head out of scraps of attention, errant word choices, and mismatched pieces of history.

"Enough," I snap, not bothering to censor myself. "We're not here for relationship counselling. Water Nourishing the Roots has no time for anyone's suffering but his own. Let's put Seth out of his misery and then deal with the real problem—the ocean."

"Misery?" Water laughs. "Is that what his life is now?"

"She is right." Seth glares at the outline of his former lover. "I dreamed of finding our way back, but that's impossible. Changes cannot be undone, and all I do is walk from one nightmare to another."

"Wow, that's dark." Katie blows a little curl of flame towards Water, who looks unimpressed at the threat of evaporation.

Lou opens his mouth to speak, and I *know* what he's going to say. It'll be a sweet and hopeful solution, but I don't think that's what is required here. We need something far more drastic. I'm banking on some hope that, somewhere deep down, Water is still in love with Seth and will take action to save him. I know there's no guarantee this mirrors Gladdy and me, but perhaps that's my own nightmare. So I make a sharp motion with my hand and Lou subsides. He's probably the only person in the whole Cute Mutants that *actually* listens to anyone else.

"I'll do it," Skye Three says, although she doesn't sound convinced. "Or Prime can squeeze out a few more and we can get down to Six, who'll enjoy it more."

"You really would kill him." Water's face loses definition and his body ripples.

"Otherwise he's going to sit in his little forest and eat people," Three says. "I'm surprised nobody's killed him yet. Oh well, we're here to rectify that." She spins her knife between her fingers and steps forward, along with a more visibly nervous Two.

"I thought you were here to sway us to your cause." Water frowns. "Or at least get us to desist."

"Oh no." Katie belches more flame as an exclamation. "We're here to put you down."

Lou's face is grave. "We'd prefer it not to end in death, but we're prepared to do what's necessary."

Seth collapses to his knees, as Three puts her knife to his throat. For a moment I think he's going to bite her, but instead he is motionless, staring at the dripping body of his ex-lover.

"Love is such a disappointment, isn't it?" I say to Water. "People are never exactly who you want them to be. I envy you in a way. Having Seth literally cut out of your life means you never have to be confronted with what you're missing out on every single day."

Water's mouth drops open. Tentacles flicker out, snatching the knife from Three's hands. "Leave him with me."

GLADDY

The words Maddy says send a chill through me. I wish I could convince myself that she spoke it only to Water as part of the mission, but I can see the truth of it ripple across her face. Do I truly cause her so much pain?

Not all love has to look as theatrical as Dani and Dylan's. Look at Alyse and Emma for example. This isn't the right time to worry about all the different kinds of love. We're here on a mission. All that matters is these two.

Water takes a step forward and stands in front of Seth. "Are all these words true, or the last gasp of a drowning man?"

Seth laughs, and I can see the ragged shreds on the inside of his lips and the streaks of blood on his tongue. His thin shoulders shake. "I have been suffocating inside this curse all this time, and you left me on the shore like something discarded. And now comes your grand theatrical moment with an audience, where you feign feelings you never had."

"Never had?" The waves crash on the shore behind him, and the spray forms a chorus of furious faces before falling to the ground. "You truly believe every touch and every moment was a lie, or is this posturing of your own?"

Seth looks up at Water from his position on his knees, and there's such naked longing and hurt on his face that I physically flinch away. I could take that, twist it tightly into a knot, and force him to throw himself into the ocean, but instead I have to watch this awful feedback loop between him and Maddy. I turn away, and let my hair obscure it all.

"Enough," Maddy says. "You can hide behind your hurt, or throw it away and try again. Lots of us are broken, and we don't always get the love we want exactly. But sometimes it's worth holding onto what shards of light we have."

Lou is staring at me, and I don't need my power to know exactly what he's thinking. Even Katie is picking up on it. She glares at me like I'm doing this on purpose. Whatever it is. You could argue it's Maddy's fault as much as mine. If someone asked me, I would tell them that what Maddy and I have is perfect. *More* isn't automatically better.

"What would this look like?" Seth says with a laugh. "You would play with your vast host of ocean creatures, while I swim in the shallows and occasionally crawl out to drag a passerby into the water to snack on."

"There will be no snacking." Katie belches flame, enough to send steam hissing up from Water in huge billowing curls.

"Are we killing him or not?" Three asks. "It feels like not, but nobody's *saying* anything."

"Chill." Two looks calm, but her knife spins idly through her fingers. "Let them chatter."

"I am trapped by my curse," Seth howls. "Heart forged it well."

"Unless we can find a loophole." Ye Shou has been muttering into her comm this whole time, and finally turns back towards us. "The root question is *why* Heart punished Seth and what they intended to achieve. Was it pettiness, or to push Water towards making the decision for war?"

Water's head whips around towards Ye Shou. "Why have I never considered that?"

"Hurt feelings are easy to cling to," I say. "When you're in pain it can blot out everything else."

There are so many meaningful looks traded amongst this sappy-ass over-emotional team. They're trying to figure out what my words mean and map them onto Maddy and me. But no matter how many signals are given away by body language and facial expression, I'm reading a novel while they puzzle over a finger painting.

"I don't need to talk about emotions," Water says. "I want to hear about loopholes."

"Petal has theories." Ye Shou smiles. "Your sister."

"I know A Single Petal Floating on the Water very well. She was always a rebellious one." He pauses. "What does she have to say?"

"She says that Heart of a Flower was always over-fond of lessons."

"True." Seth smiles. "When he would visit, it was always to illustrate some point about evolution, the forking pathway, or the rightful place of mutants. I would usually play the piano or do the dishes, while the two of you would sit on the porch, drinking gin and pontificating."

"Perhaps you should have listened more," Water snaps. "And we would not be here."

"That is precisely Petal's point," Ye Shou says. "Accepting the lesson might be the loophole you need to break the curse."

"So all I need to do is bow down and accept the mutant yoke." Seth sprawls on the rock, face down. "Then the spirit of Heart will bless me and I shall no longer crave flesh."

"Dramatic bish," Maddy murmurs, and I laugh despite myself.

The wind whips the hair away from my face and I see her smile and I wish that was enough, because it's one of my favourite things in the world.

Katie spreads her arms wide. "I believe that mutants are our future," she croons. Her voice is surprisingly good. "Give them powers and let them lead the way."

"But I don't," Seth says. "They're no different to humans. Some of them are worse."

"Rude," Katie sighs.

"Just fake it." Maddy has her hands on her hips and glares down at him. "Maybe you say the magic words, and you're cured. Then you can run around pretending mutants are great, frolicking in the waves with your lover. How is that bad?"

"I'll know it's not true." Water and Seth say it in unison.

"We're all fucked then." Maddy turns and starts stalking away across the rocks. "Skye, squirt out Six and she can get this over with."

"You won't lay a hand on him!" More waves smash against the rocks and freeze in the air, this sparkling wall of water looming above us.

"What good does it do? Pining is all so beautiful, but what if it never leads anywhere?" Maddy looks so small and fragile against the rage of the ocean poised to crash down on her. "If we do nothing, Seth goes back to his forest, murdering the occasional traveller and wishing for death, while you swirl around at the bottom of the ocean planning to unleash monsters on pretty coastal towns."

I step forward. "She's right. Neither of these are acceptable. We're here to solve a problem, and we will. One way or another." I feel like that sounds pretty badass. It's totally a Dylan move. It's time to use my power.

"What does that mean?" Seth's voice shakes, but I ignore him.

"You." I cross to stand in front of Water. His features flicker as he looks at me, but I can still read all his fears. There are so many. Of his parent and the darkness at their heart. Of growing up with a shadow of coming war over him, of never being strong enough to hold up that mantle. His siblings lurking in the darkness, always used as a lash to prove Water's weakness. What I see of the others disturbs me, but it's hard to know how much is his own mind amplifying things.

More fruitful in terms of control is Seth. Water loves him, that's clear, almost painfully and vividly, yet fear of rejection is a powerful driver. He thought it was doomed from the beginning—Seth was a bright and funny man who somehow fell for someone dark and sour with too many edges. Water spent a lot of time thinking dissolution was around the corner, and when the first signs of it inevitably came on the wings of his parent, he seized it with both hands as final evidence. What's happened next has only spiralled him further into bitterness. He expects Seth to keep returning, heart in hands, until he reaches some ceiling of proof. Two problems with that—the ceiling does not exist, and Seth's heart is a battered chunk of meat and hardly a worthy offering.

I could take all of this and yank on the levers until he's swamped with self-pity and bitterness. A part of the ocean might evaporate when he dies, but it would work. I can see the grooves of the spiral inside his soul. They're worn so very deep.

"He loves you," is what I say instead. I don't even need to look at Seth to see it's true. I saw it the moment he walked into view, even amongst all the self-pity and self-loathing and desperate wish to escape from the horrific trap Heart laid for him. It shone from his face like a certain other person I know. People that despite all the terrible things they've endured, still find their path to love, like flowers turning towards the sun. Not all of us are so lucky, so I have to help Water find his way out of this maze.

"I am a monster," Water whispers. Creatures swim below his surface and turn their blind eyes towards me.

"So am I. So are we all. It doesn't mean there's no friendship or love. And we can choose to turn away from what our parents wanted for us."

It's impossible to tell if Water is crying, but his face ripples as if he is.

"My parent's shadow is long."

"Heart of a Flower is dead. I killed them myself. They died like anyone dies." I'm aware of the risk, but that fear runs deeper than anything.

"Freedom then. Is that what you offer?" Water sneers.

"It's what I've already given you, now that Heart is gone." I hold his gaze. I'm not scared of him. He can drown me in water, but I can drown him in something far worse. "Now it's up to you what you do with it."

"I could..." His face is still submerged in fear, but it's different now. The fear of possibility, which is a subtler and far more dangerous snare. What *could* happen, how it *might* fail.

I turn away from him and towards the others. "We're done here."

"It doesn't look very done." Lou raises a single eyebrow.

"Feels very *un*done." Katie crosses her arms across her chest and puffs smoke from her nostrils.

"We leave them to it." I try to project all the confidence I don't feel. "Give them some privacy. If they can't solve their problems, we do it another way. If there are any deaths, or any mysterious bodies left in the forest, any inexplicable drownings or unnatural sea monsters, then we come back and end it. The hard way."

Maddy grins at me, and gives me this little impressed nod. "Nice work, Field Leader."

I lean in very close to her. "Don't tell anyone, but I'm terrified it won't work."

"Your secret's safe with me."

"I don't want to have to break him."

Maddy taps my shoulder. "I don't think you have to worry about that."

I glance behind me to see Seth picking his way down the rocks and into the ocean. Water Nourishing the Roots is nowhere to be seen. The droplets in the air reform into a pair of welcoming arms, beckoning the fragile figure onwards.

"You think it'll really work?" I ask.

"It's a love story." Maddy grins at me. "You know I always want those to work out." We walk up the path side by side, heading towards the abandoned house. There's a stone fence that runs along the front of it and perched on top of it is Dylan, as if they've been patiently waiting this entire time.

"Good job," they say. "I think you all deserve ice cream."

MADDY

"It was Fetch," I tell Dylan abruptly. "She did it all."

"Not just Fetch." She jumps down off the wall and lands in the grass in front of us. "You as well, from what I've heard. Ye Shou and Lou have been giving me a running commentary. Seems a little bit like a black screen saying *to be continued*, but the crisis is avoided for now. Looks like the hopeless romantic squad came through in the end."

I sometimes find it hard to tell if Dylan is joking, and assume she's being snarky at Gladdy's expense. "There was a cannibal *actually*, Dylan. Ye Shou and I got dragged into the ocean, and threatened with all kinds of chaos from Emma's horrible brother and then—"

"Wow." Dylan grins. "Imagine if I actually said something negative. I'd be one of your special melted piles of guts."

"But—"

"Fetchy did a marvellous job, okay? Wonderful.

Stupendous. Superfuckingfragilistic." They reach out and ruffle Katie's hair. "And you didn't even get yourself in trouble, Scruff."

"Yeah, I know." She puffs a tiny curl of smoke. "We mostly missed out on *everything*. The cannibal and the drownings. On the plus side, Lou did buy me the biggest ice cream I've ever had."

"And she accidentally melted it." Lou laughs. "How do we get that shit reimbursed?"

Dylan shrugs. "It's a black ops budget. All guns, knives and poison darts. There's no line item for ice cream."

I turn away from the cozy three of them and focus my attention back on Gladdy, who's walking along, head down. Probably haunted by whatever she saw in those two faces. "You did do a wonderful job," I whisper. "You found the love that bound them together."

"There are lots of different kinds of love." Our hands swing closer, and for a second her little finger hooks around mine. "Sometimes we can't always recognise them, but I have a cheat code for that sort of thing."

My good mood evaporates like Katie's ice cream, as if there was nothing sugary and sweet there at all. I don't need a fucking superpower to understand what she means. Gladdy thinks that what we have is enough on its own. That I shouldn't ask for more. Water Nourishing the Roots and his terrifying cannibal boyfriend have their particular type of relationship, and therefore I should settle too. Gladdy likes being closed off and that's all I'll ever get. I should be happy to sit on the other side of the door, sliding notes underneath, and not hoping with all my heart that one day she'll crack it even the tiniest part open.

It's greedy and selfish of me, but I still *want*. I hunger, as bad as cannibal boy. A craving that can't be satisfied, and it's not even her fault. Lots of the time I can detach the claws of desire that dig into my throat, but this is not one of those times. I need a distraction.

"Katie, wait up." I run across the grass and link arms with her. "Where's the giant ice cream place? Let's stop there before we go. Isn't that what you said, Chatty?"

"It was a metaphor," Dylan says. "There's no time for ice cream. I'm the big boss man and I'm cracking the whip."

"But Dilly, please?" Katie looks up at them beseechingly. "I'll be careful with this one."

Dylan rolls her eyes but can't help smiling. "What we really need is an ice cream mutant. I wonder if we can get to the point where Emma takes requests for new powers."

"That's a yes, isn't it? To ice cream? Team Dylan's secret favourites?"

Okay, fine, I'm also jealous of Katie's relationship with Dylan. I join in with it, but I always feel like an outsider. Katie fumbles along without any shame or awkwardness, and Dylan opens their big messy heart up. I smile wider and pretend I'm part of it.

They wink at me. "How about it, Little Patch? Secret favourites ice cream club?"

"Yes." I beam as wide as I can, and hurl myself into the hope it's real.

Katie slings her arm around my shoulders. "Maddy, my darling, if I accidentally melt my ice cream again, will you give me some of yours?"

"Think cold thoughts," Dylan says. "Anyway, you've twisted my arm. We'll get ice cream, but we have to bring one back for Dan, or she'll kick my ass."

We line up at the ice cream truck as if we're regular people. The woman serving has a scowl and big arms that work the machine in bored, efficient movements. At least the resulting treat is as giant as Katie promised, and I let the sweetness melt down my throat to join the acid stew in my stomach.

"Mission accomplished." Dylan holds the ice cream out like they're toasting us, and the rest of us raise ours in return, with such solemn looks on our faces that it almost makes me giggle. Then I think of how many times we could have died today, and the things Water and Seth could have done.

We really did make a difference. Angst aside, we saved the day.

Weapon fucking UwU.

III

TWO THORNS TWISTED ON A STEM

MADDY

I'd actually rather be on another horrible mission than here in Westhaven. I've got nothing to do, so my brain chases itself down spirals about Gladiola Quick. I find myself hanging out with Dani while she searches for clues about the rest of Heart's children. She doesn't talk much, except to mutter incomprehensible garbage under her breath. It's soothing in a funny way. Dylan drifts in periodically, bringing supplies and giving back rubs. They're always very jittery and twitchy, and Dani usually sends them away eventually because they're annoying. Today, they're even more distracted than normal.

"Must you bounce your knee that dramatically?" Dani reaches her hand over for the sixty-fourth time to still it.

"Love of my life," they sigh. "So unutterably cruel."

"Love of *my* life." Dani takes Dylan's hand and presses the back of it to her lips. "So incredibly distracting."

"I could be *more* distracting."

"Not with Maddy here."

I am fixed with a glare, but I bat my eyelashes in response.

"Fine. I'll bring dinner soon." They reach out a foot and nudge me. "You want anything?"

I shake my head, and then lean it back to stare at the ceiling. Dani continues to click and mutter, some acoustic music playing softly underneath it all. At some point, my eyes must drift shut. My sleep is fitful, and I dream of water and things moving under the surface.

"Maddy!" The voice by my ear is loud, and the breath is hot.

I sit bolt upright and open my eyes to find Katie leaning over me, and the room full of people.

Dylan perches on the desk, swivelling the monitor towards the group. "So we think we've found our next friend. I don't know what the bar for weird is, but this might be a new one. We've found them in this little place in Canada. Sleepy town. I don't know what they do there. Play hockey, eat that poutine shit. Apologise. Is that racist? Anyway, here is a house on a quiet street. Isn't it nice? All wooden and shit. Rustic almost."

To be perfectly honest, it looks a little bit like a shitbox, but I know Dylan grew up kind of poor, so a neat white weatherboard house looks good to her, even crammed in alongside its neighbours.

"The house isn't the point, Madelaide," Dylan says, as if they can read my face too. "Here's the house as of two weeks ago. Regular house, the same way it's been for years. Then one day, look." The street view switches to satellite footage, but the house's footprint has changed to encompass its neighbour. It looks entirely normal, and I would have sworn it was always that way, until Dylan toggles back to the previous image.

"Spooky," Katie says. "Cannibal house this time."

"Greedy fucking house." Dylan advances through multiple images. It takes another couple of days, but the house on the right is consumed too, and then the one behind it. Three days later, it leaps across the road, and expands in that direction. By the time we get to the final image, it's spread to encompass fourteen different houses, that plain house stretched in multiple directions.

"What the hell is it?" Gladdy asks, leaning forward.

Dylan coughs and fixes her with a stern glare. "That's exactly what you're going to find out."

"And the people who live in there?" Ye Shou is tapping away on her phone again.

"Nobody's come out. All those families are still inside. Or who knows? Maybe they've been fucking digested."

"Gross," Katie says, and I can't help but agree. "You really want us to go in there?"

Dylan wags their finger at her. "I want you to stick your nose in very carefully and if anyone starts getting eaten, you're going to melt or burn your way right back out of there."

"People have tried getting in." Ye Shou brandishes her phone.

"Stealing my thunder." Dylan winks. "I was saving the best until last. Obviously the authorities are getting all what-the-fuck about it. Ems snatched this off some police server."

The screen flickers and shows footage of a wall that stretches across the road. It looks to be made of the same weatherboard as the rest of the house, and it has a series of tall, narrow windows along it. Some have blinds drawn in front of them, but two are a deep opaque black as if they look onto a mineshaft. In contrast, the center window glows as if the room inside blazes with flickering light. There's a strip of browned grass between it and where the road deadends against the house.

The camera judders and a pair of police officers run into frame. They're carrying a battering ram between them and stop near one of the dark windows. At an unseen signal, they swing it back sharply and slam it into the wall. It bounces off, so sharply you'd think the wall was rubber. The two men go flying with it, tumbling back towards the camera.

"House doesn't want them getting in," Lou says.

Dylan skips the footage forward a bit until we see a new officer approach the house with a chainsaw.

"What are they doing?" Katie scoffs. "It'll like this even less, won't it?"

"No spoilers." Dylan leans forward with the rest of us, even though they've seen this before.

On the video, the sound of the revving chainsaw is audible. The man gingerly pushes it up against the building and then shifts his body weight to exert more pressure. After nearly a full minute, he pulls back. The chainsaw looks as if someone has severed it neatly down the middle and the rest is a fused lump of metal.

You can clearly hear someone say *what the fuck* and Dylan skips the video forward again.

The next thing the police try is explosives. They attach chunky rectangles to eight points on the wall, making a rough square. Everyone stands well back. The camera backs up a bunch and then zooms in.

"This seems like a terrible idea," Ye Shou says mildly.

Dylan shakes her head. There are muffled voices, and then someone off screen triggers the explosion. The screen is full of flames, and it cuts off after no more than five seconds.

The next section of video is taken from further away. There are four burning cars in frame and bodies lying on the road. They're charred and smoking. I'm glad I can't smell them. The video soundtrack is sirens and screaming. The footage zooms in crookedly to show the house is entirely unmarked, even by the haze of smoke that drifts around it.

"Fuck that," Katie says. "I'm not trying to burn my way in there."

"I'm not glowing at it either." Lou folds his arms across his chest. "Maddy, you want to spit?"

"No thanks." I shuffle my seat forward. "Although at least I can do it from a distance."

"We're not doing anything like that." Gladdy leans back in her chair and looks around the room. "We're going to walk up the front steps and knock on the door. Talk to this house face to face."

Dylan's grin is enormous. "Yes, we're pretty sure that's our mutant. Two Thorns Twisted on a Stem. Might be creepy and fucked up, but he's one of us. Doesn't seem to want anyone breaking in, but maybe things will be different from the inside. This time we'll lend you Keepaway, in case you need a quick exit."

"You're worried, Dylan." Gladdy's brow is wrinkled, staring at the wreckage on the screen and the untouched exterior of the house.

"That's my secret, Fetchy. I'm always worried." Dylan cracks their knuckles restlessly, one hand then the other. "But yes. This is a creepy one. What the fuck is happening inside?"

On screen, the section of the house we can see is perfectly ordinary. Even the blood from those who died near it has vanished. I'm starting to regret volunteering for this team in the first place. I realise I'm tapping my green-tipped fingernails against the arm of the chair in a little repetitive rat-a-tat sound.

"You don't have to come." Gladdy angles her head towards me. "We're not forcing anyone."

I meet her gaze. "Are you going?"

"I volunteered to lead. I'll do what's needed."

"Then I'm going too." I mean it. While I understand the concept of the multiverse and all the possibilities it contains, I feel like there's no world where I'd let Gladdy go in alone.

"Gotta admit I'm a little bit jealous," Dylan drawls. "I always wanted to visit a good haunted house."

"You're such an asshole," Katie says, and punches him in the arm.

GLADDY

Everyone leaves to get ready for the mission. There's no point discussing it any further. Given what we're facing and how little we know, it would devolve into pointless speculation which only makes people more nervous.

"You're making all the right decisions." Dylan's eyes are intent. "Or at least ones that I agree with. Maybe that's not the same thing."

"Thanks." I pat them on the shoulder awkwardly. Everyone else in this damn team seems so comfortable touching each other.

"And if shit starts to look fucked up, don't feel bad about bailing. In a perfect scenario, you can talk this one down like you did with Water, but if not… we do have some big guns lying around we can use."

"I know."

They grimace. "Sorry. I'm going too far. Being overprotective. I blame Pear. Just take care of everyone and bring yourself back safe, okay?"

"I can do that." I chance a real smile at them and get the full-blast one in return.

The rest of the team is waiting in the next room, along with a pale and tired Emma, who's finishing up a conversation with Ye Shou about Water. It's bizarre to think that Water is her brother in some way. Petal's implication was that Heart created the other mutants on their own, carrying them in a female body, something I can't quite fathom the mechanics of. I suppose that's why they call it reality warping. Emma's fears are still hidden from me, but I'm sure there are a host of them. So many secrets were kept from her, and the ones still being revealed after Heart's death are no more pleasant. I wish I could provide her reassurance, but all we can do is try our best to resolve this situation as cleanly as the last.

Emma nods thanks to Ye Shou and glances around at the group before padding away down the corner in sock feet. Dylan watches her go with a slight frown.

"Is she going to be okay?" I ask.

Dylan snaps his head around to look at me. "Of course." Their smile is narrower than before. "She'll be fine. You don't need to worry about anything going on back here in Westhaven, Fetchy. We've got it all under control."

I don't believe her for a second, given that *all* includes Emma adjusting to her full and terrifying new power set, along with shepherding a community of hundreds of mutants. Not to mention trying to avoid war with at least one country and probably more.

Which is exactly why we have to do this. This team has an important role in keeping the mutant nation alive. Dylan isn't the only true believer here. I've seen what most humans do when confronted with the next evolutionary step. It's fear and fury. I've been in the cages. So despite the terrifying house that seems very intent to be left alone, we're going in.

Weapon fucking UwU.

"Okay, listen up, team. Make any final preparations and be back here in an hour." My voice is firm and strong. "We're going in."

It'd be nice to sleep, but the house keeps growing.

~ UwU ~

An hour and a few minutes later, my team stands on a quiet street in some tiny town in Alberta. The cars and bodies are gone. Perhaps there are cameras in the distance, or drones above us, but there's no sign of human life. Birds chirp in the trees, and a large ginger cat perches on the roof above us.

Once again, we're in casual clothes rather than uniform. We don't want to appear like we're coming in as soldiers or superheroes—just some friendly mutants having a quiet chat. If the house mistakes us for police or any other intruders, it could go very badly.

The original front door looks perfectly normal. Three wooden steps lead up to it, and iron letters make the number 36 on one pillar of the front porch. The curtains on both side windows are drawn, but there's a small gap between the ones on the left.

The normality ends there. To the left and right, the house sprawls away from us, a crooked arrangement of walls, windows, and gables. Taken individually, each part makes sense but put together, it's bizarre. It looks like someone went wild in the Sims with infinite money turned on and just kept *designing* with no regard for normal angles or alignment. It's expanded restlessly and relentlessly, with growth its only goal and purpose.

The word *cancer* appears in my mind and I can't shake it.

Katie bounces up the steps and peers in the window. "Armchair, plant, plant. Wow. There are a lot of plants in here. Someone's got a gardening kink. Or else they've grown and grown." She glances over her shoulder at me. "Maybe time runs differently in there?"

"Cool." Lou nudges me. "Maybe there's a whole other parallel universe inside, and that's what's making the house grow."

"Yes." I swallow irritation. "That *is* very cool. Or it would be if it wasn't us considering walking into this expanding parallel universe. Which, given the shit we face in the last one.."

"Maybe it's a bubble poking through into ours? There'd be some kind of wormhole at the heart of it. It would mean their power isn't anything to do with the house at all, but—"

"Or it's just a weird creepy house and we're jumping to conclusions."

Lou grins. "Fine. Spoil my fun."

"You think that last parallel universe was fun?"

"Fine." He shrugs. "It stands to reason they can't be *all* bad though."

"Are we going in yet?" Katie steps back from the window. She gives a tiny little tap on the glass with the tip of one finger.

The entire house thumps in response.

Everyone jumps except Katie, who tilts her head to the side curiously and taps twice more.

Keepaway gives a faint moan at the back of their throat.

The house lets out two enormous bangs, each wall vibrating slightly and setting the glass in the windows shuddering. The ground trembles slightly underneath us.

"Oh yeah, it definitely fucking heard you." Maddy pokes Katie. "No need to tap three—"

Katie taps out a skittering rhythm with the index fingers of both hands.

The house gives a single thump in response, and the front door swings open. There's a gust of cold air with it. I half-expect it to smell like mould and crypts, but it's fresh and crisp and slightly damp. It reminds me of when we used to go on hikes through the bush, early in the morning, and we'd taste the honeyed sap that rolled down the bark of the beech trees.

"Fun as it was, I don't want to continue playing this tapping game." The voice from inside is rough and scratchy, as if it hasn't talked in a while. "You'd just keep going and going. I can tell you're that sort of person. Just like I can tell that we're all going to be great friends."

The team is looking at me, their leader. There's no *face* to read here, even if I imagine the gabled windows as eyes and the front door as a gaping mouth. I can't tell if this is a trap. I expected a code to solve or test to pass, but here we are with the literal welcome mat laid out for us and a voice beckoning us in.

"We came to play," I murmur, and jog up the steps to stand beside Katie. The rest of the group follows. I wonder what the house sees when it looks at us.

Katie moves over to the welcome mat and peers inside. I join her. The interior is very dim, lit by one sputtering bulb deep in the hallway. There's writing on the wall, but not enough light to read what it says.

"I thought this was supposed to be welcoming."

"Awfully sorry. I haven't redecorated since those human pricks came knocking. Just a second, love." The lights come on, warm and steady, in ornate fittings spaced along the wall. The wood panelling is dark and rich, almost glowing. Plush maroon carpet grows out of the floor. "There we go. Much nicer."

It feels very much like the gingerbread house from the fairy tale, except this is witch and wood and candy store all at once.

"Are we really going in there?" Keepaway asks.

"You're here with the UwU squad now." Maddy takes hold of their hand, as if she's ready to drag them in. "That means we run merrily into danger."

"Or at least step cautiously." I grit my teeth and put one foot over the threshold.

Absolutely nothing happens.

I bring my second foot in as well. The others are queued up behind me in an orderly line. The house smells of cinnamon and woodsmoke. I'm certain it's being done on purpose. We're being lured. It didn't want the humans inside—hence the spooky lighting and violent pushback—but we're guests, likely because we're fellow mutants. The question is what it intends to do with us next.

If we're very, very lucky, it really is a cozy fireside chat. Maybe we're here for coffee and biscuits.

"Hi there." I walk slowly down the corridor as the rest of the team files in behind me. We're all inside the house—*swallowed* by it, I can't help thinking—but the front door still stands open. I'm waiting for it to slam closed, for the lights to go off, and the strange writing to reappear on the walls. "My mutant name is Fetch, and my human name is Gladdy."

"Delighted to meet you." The voice seems to come from everywhere, as if there's a surround sound system embedded in the walls. "My name is Two Thorns Twisted on a Stem. My human name does not matter, as I was never truly human."

One by one the other mutants introduce themselves and Two Thorns repeats each one as if he's committing them to memory. The door still remains open. The lights spill their pools of yellow warmth. It's relentlessly pleasant. Aside from the fact the hallway is far too long, even for the floor plan that we saw from the satellite feed.

There doesn't seem to be an end. It stretches out so far that perspective plays tricks on me.

Either the house is still growing or it's—

"Bigger on the inside," Lou murmurs from behind me.

"Very much so." The house laughs lightly. "The Tardis is a broom closet compared to me. I'm somewhat of a moving castle too." A door flutters open in the wall, showing an arid blue-lit landscape and then banging shut. "It's like having ten thousand blinking eyes looking onto myriad worlds."

"What happened to the families that lived here?" I ask.

"Oh, they found more interesting avenues. Places to do, things to be, isn't that how the saying goes? Probably better inside than out, given what's going to happen on Earth." Now the door closes behind us, gently but with an audible click.

Oh fuck, here we go. When I glance over my shoulder, I see a lot of unsettled and curious faces. Keepaway's hand twitches, like they're desperate to pop out of here. Hopefully they'll have the presence of mind to take us with them if it comes to a panic situation.

"What's going to happen on Earth?" I keep my voice calm and unruffled.

"Oh, all manner of dreadful things. Once baby sis realises what she's capable of, it's really all over. So what I'm doing is preparing a palace for her and her friends. That includes you, of course. Don't worry. I'll look far more grand once this is over. It's easier to grow in this simple form. The ornamentation will come later. By then, I expect the Americas will be only a single wing of my magnificence."

"Fuuuuck," Lou moans faintly.

"Leave?" Keepaway bugs their eyes at me.

"I agree. I think this is very bad." Ye Shou reaches out a hand and brushes her fingertips along the wall. "We should at least report the situation to Chatterbox."

"There's no need for alarm." The house sounds entirely at ease, although I suppose it would if it was currently digesting us. "You are friends of Yǔzhòu so I will not harm you. I may, however, keep tight hold of you as insurance against her current fluctuations of mood."

The floor twists, moving underneath me like a platform, taking me violently off sideways. The others slip away, as if the house simply drags half the room in the other direction. Keepaway reaches for Maddy, but nothing happens. They flail wildly and then slap their hand to their own chest. Nothing works. They're standing on the far side of the now cavernous room, breathing hard.

The panelled walls seem darker now, the light fittings spaced so far apart they are dim pools like flickering candles in the midst of a vast and growing darkness.

"You did actually leave, little teleporter," Two Thorns says. "I simply snatched you back."

There's a grinding sound and an awful vertiginous feeling in my stomach. The floor in front of me shifts into a steep incline made of polished wood. I try and scrabble up on all fours, but my feet slip and I lose my balance. A door behind me opens and I stumble backwards through it.

I see a brief glimpse of Maddy's tousled blonde head looking down at me from atop the slope before the door slams in my face.

"Fuck." I tug at the door handle, but it won't even turn.

"This *is* an unfortunate situation."

I turn to see Ye Shou slumped in an ornate wooden chair. It has been carved into the shape of two muscular forearms, each of which holds her tightly.

"Fuck," I say again.

No wonder Dylan's vocabulary is so limited, when this shit keeps happening.

MADDY

The house moves underneath us, like it's driven by some complicated mechanism. The floor carries me out of reach of the others, and I find myself standing at the peak of a steep slope of gleaming floor. Gladdy is at the bottom, and I watch her disappear behind a closed door. She's gone. A scream bursts out of my throat, because this is *not* how we end things. I throw myself after her, but the house moves underneath me again and I tumble towards a different door, hanging open like it's eager to devour me. I thrash about, trying to stop from falling into it, but all I manage is to crack my head sharply against the frame.

I try to catch onto something but only bang my knuckles, tumbling painfully until I stop, wedged against a very plush couch. The door I came through is closed, and the room is dark aside from where faint moonlight filters in through a large bay window, brushing everything with grey.

"Maddy?" There's someone standing in the corner. One hand faintly glows and fingers leave trails of light in the air as he waves to me.

"Glowstick." I get to my feet. The ground isn't moving anymore. "You're a handy guy to be stuck in a dark and creepy house with."

"All I need to do is think sexy thoughts." His hands pulse brighter and the room takes shape around me. "Luckily my secondary mutation is the ability to be horny even in the weirdest situations."

I would laugh, but I'm unnerved by the fact we're trapped in this room, and Gladdy is stuck in another. I'm not going to get out of here by worrying. The couch I'm leaning against is very soft and covered in a startling array of cushions. They're all patterned differently and are—

"Gross. Is that actual fur?" I snatch my fingertips away from the coarse hair.

Lou's standing at the window. "There's water out there. And it's nighttime. We definitely won't be leaving that way. Have you tried the door?"

I leave the couch and cross to the only exit. Except there's no handle, and when I push against the door, my fingers tingle unpleasantly as if I've slept on them in the night.

"I don't think this is a real house," I say.

"No shit. This is some creepy sci-fi horror place that's swallowed us all up. The question is what he wants to do with us." Lou's hands pulse brighter still. He stands in the middle of the room and stretches them wide, so they illuminate everything. There's a fireplace, full of a massive pile of grey ash that spills out in curlicues onto the carpet. The opposite wall is mostly taken up by an enormous mirror with a thick golden frame. It doesn't appear to reflect anything. In fact, it seems to swallow light. There's a splintered crater in the middle, as if someone punched it.

"Creepy." My voice sounds loud.

"Black mirror," Lou murmurs, and then raises his voice. "It's a little on the nose, don't you think?"

There's no answer from the house.

"Maybe it's like a giant escape room," I say brightly. May as well look on the positives. It hasn't eaten us immediately. I wonder if the house will give us clues. The mirror is the only noteworthy thing in the room aside from the creepy cushions, so if we're going to get out of here, it seems to be our only option. I let out an irritated sigh and cross over to it. As I approach, a pale figure appears.

It's me, of course, but there's a slight lag, as if my reflection is a half-step slower.

No, it's not exactly me.

The Maddy in the mirror is gaunt. Her skin is puckered and twisted, and gnarled scars form whorls in her cheeks that spiral outwards to make a beautiful pattern. She gnaws at a flake of skin on her lips. The sweater she wears has ragged holes in it.

"She left me," my reflection whispers. "I was in the dark, and she walked away."

"Who?" I ask, but it's obvious.

"We were lost for so long." Mirror-Maddy shivers violently. "There was no day or night, or ticking clock to measure it. She withdrew inside herself, deeper and deeper, as if her soul was a tunnel and she'd find solace at the bottom. I was left to fret and fidget, to pick myself apart and stew on sourness. Finally, it all became too much. I turned to her and professed everything in my heart."

"What did you say?" My voice is a whisper. I'm standing so close to the mirror that I can feel the chill emanating from the glass. A crack zigzags through my right eye and splinters it to fragments.

"You know what I said." My reflection smiles, showing half-dissolved stubs of teeth. "Everything in our heart. The truth. Nothing held back. Every pitted and corroded thing."

"No." There are tears in my eyes involuntarily. Confessing the truth is off the table. It's too much. I'm too much. How desperate I must have been to vomit all that forth. "And then she…"

I can't finish the sentence.

My reflection laughs, high and delighted, as if seeing my pain goes some way towards soothing hers. "Then she left, of course. Did you really think she would stay? Would anyone?"

"What did she say?"

Cracks splinter my reflection and I, two shattered things regarding each other. "That I was not her sunshine. I was a heavy, sodden blanket thrown across her face, and I made it impossible to breathe. She was tired of looking into my face and seeing hope and disappointment all mixed up together."

I try to ignore it. It's not real. It's the house fucking with my head.

But it echoes inside me, the truth of it twining around my heart like a noose and pulling tight.

Oh so very fucking tight.

Tears spill down my face. They're only water for now, but they carry a faint sting.

"Enough." Lou steps up beside me. For a moment, there's no reflection to mark him, but the dark glass swims. Standing in the mirror is a girl with long dark hair, wearing a ruffled blouse and a skirt that flutters at her thighs.

I take a sharp breath.

"You think that will work, to show me the fruit of a dead tree?" Lou laughs softly. "I know who I am. I was sleeved in the wrong body at birth, but I know my heart. I may have been scared once upon a time, but my friends saw me truly. Starting with Dylan and expanding outwards." He smiles fondly, and reaches out to take my hand. "Being seen matters."

The reflected girl tosses her hair and purses red lips.

The boy standing beside me gives a little bow. The reflection shimmers, and it's only Lou, truth on both sides of the glass.

"I apologise," the house says. "That was awfully tacky of me. I sometimes forget, with all my rooms and dimensions and manifold parts, that your simple hearts contain other worlds too."

"What about me?" I ask. "The things you showed?"

"You know better than me if it's true." The surface of the mirror shivers, as if it's water, and behind it is another hallway leading away from us.

Both our reflections are gone.

Lou reaches out to touch the surface of the mirror, but his hand passes straight through. It's now empty space. "A doorway."

"Do we go through?" I still can't shake the effects of what the house said. Based on what happened with Lou, I *know* it was trying to mess with me, but the barbs it used sunk in rather than bouncing off. It makes me hesitant to find out what's next.

"Better than staying here." Lou hauls himself over the edge of the frame, straddling it for a second before whipping his other leg over and dropping down. He lands lightly on the floorboards and looks back at me. "Seems safe enough."

I give it a full ten count. Usually when someone says it *seems safe*, something comes roaring out of the darkness to prove them wrong. Nothing at all happens, and Lou simply arches one eyebrow at me until I finally relent and tumble through the mirror frame after him.

"Spooky." I shudder, but it actually looks comforting. The hallway has a wooden floor and faded wallpaper, the pattern only vague brown shapes. It reminds me of my grandparents' house, although I haven't been there since I was a child.

"Any ideas of where to go?" Lou pauses at a door only a few paces away, his hand outstretched. "I'm worried if I open this, I'll be snapped up and we'll be separated."

"Hold hands?" I stretch mine out towards him. He pulls me in, so fast I stumble against his body. He smells good, and I feel the warmth of his skin through his shirt. I'm oddly glad we didn't wear uniforms. It's entirely the worst time to feel a weird frisson of feeling for Lou, but I chalk it up to tension, low-level terror, and him having very nice arms.

"So we either hope this door doesn't lead somewhere scary, or wander down the hallway and see where it might lead us."

"Hallway." I try to fake confidence. At least he can't read it in my face. "It's got to go somewhere."

"That is what they're for." Lou keeps a tight hold of my hand and we walk slowly, keeping our steps nice and even as if that might lull anything watching. "The mirror was talking to you about Gladdy, huh?"

"Is it that obvious?" It comes out snappier than I'd like.

"An educated guess." He doesn't look at me, which I appreciate.

It doesn't stop me getting angry though. "You'd think you had some experience in unrequited love."

I see the slight curve of his mouth. "Who, Dylan?"

"Obviously."

"Dylan and I were no grand love affair. I mean, I loved them. Still do. It was more desperate clinging than romance, on both sides. They were confused about certain things, like I think I knew they were genderfluid before he knew it herself." He winks at me. "And on my side, my friends had all walked away after I made my grand declaration of who I really was. So we were two people standing alone, and that brought us together."

"I thought your break-up was—"

"Things were changing, and I wasn't ready to step outside my little bubble. But Dylan the unstoppable dragged me along. Then there was Dani."

"Oh." I don't want to say too much else, in case he stops talking.

"Yes. Exactly. Standing in the middle of that? It was two badasses locking eyes across the room, and I may as well have been the invisible boy. The grumpy one and the grumpy one. Two secret softs dying to show each other their tenderest parts."

I giggle at that.

"Yes, that sounded a lot dirtier than I meant. The ice queen and the human scowl, both breathlessly passing each other notes about their hurts and letting the other one comfort them. It would be disgusting if I didn't love them both so much."

"It's not the same thing at all then." I sigh and squeeze his hand involuntarily.

"No, but love is complicated, isn't it? I can't solve Gladdy for you, as much as I'd like to."

"I can." The house speaks from all around us. He's been listening this whole time. "I can give you what your heart desires, Madelaide McLean. All you have to do is say yes."

"Mad—" Lou begins, but he doesn't even get a second to spill the final syllable.

"Yes," I say. "Yes."

All the lights go out at once, plunging us into darkness.

GLADDY

"Fucking great." Unfortunately, Ye Shou isn't the only other one in the room. There's also a stocky, shaven-head girl with orange eyes and a glare on her face.

"Hey, Katie." I generally avoid Dragon. It's easier that way, but I'm not proud of it. There are so many other people to deal with her. Dylan and Pear, or else Lou and Maddy. They all have their ways of dealing with this furious person in front of me. I don't know what to do because she hates me, and it's for entirely legitimate reasons.

"If you're going to call me something, at least fucking use my mutant name." She snarls when she says it, like a wild animal. Her eyes light up and I see the little pilot light in the back of her throat.

She's scared of me. In amongst the fears scrawled on her face, I see myself reflected back. My wicked claws, prying open her armour and prodding at everything she'd hidden away behind the wall of flames. Plucking out her fears of loss and abandonment and self-loathing, stringing them like choice morsels on a skewer before presenting them with a mocking flourish.

I'd been wallowing myself then, banging my mind against the walls of my cage, but that's not really an excuse for lashing out at someone, is it?

"Sorry." I look away from her, at the heavy scarlet drapes on the wall. "Dragon."

She ignores me and stomps over to the door. There's no handle and when she touches it, she snatches her hand back with a hiss, blowing at her fingertips and trailing off into more swearing.

"There's got to be another way out of here." She kicks at the door. "Fuck. That hurts too." She whirls around at Ye Shou. "And you. Stop pretending you're actually stuck and fucking do something."

Ye Shou blinks at us. There's something odd about her eyes. "Sourpatch asked me to make this a surprise, and only do it when it counts. This hardly seems the most disturbing situation we've been in."

Katie snorts. "Maddy's not fucking here, is she? We're stuck. You might be able to get us out."

"Let's sustain the suspense a little longer, shall we?" The house is speaking again. His voice is warm but there's a slight trace of smugness. It puts me on edge. "Instead, why don't we find ourselves somewhere more pleasant to pass the time, and we can get to know each other."

The arms of the chair release Ye Shou, wooden hands melting back into the elegant contours. She gets to her feet, rubbing at her wrists thoughtfully.

"Are you okay?" I ask.

"Perfectly."

The heavy drapes spring open, as if triggered electronically, and haul themselves wide with a flourish. Behind them are French doors, with thousands of tiny square glass panes, each a slightly different colour. The light floods in, scattered into rainbows that fall across the carpet. Something skitters across the outside, forming a tangle of shadows, and is gone.

"Is it safe out there?" Ye Shou asks. "It's not another world?"

"It is a courtyard." The doors rattle slightly, as if something wants to come in. "Surrounded on all sides by walls. It is quite safe, warm and beautiful and—for the most part—very peaceful."

"For the most part." I press my hand against the door. The wood is rough-grained and feels like it's been warmed by the sun. It quivers against me and I see more shadows flicker, as if things had alighted on the other side and sprung away startled at the nearness of me.

"Just fucking open it," Dragon growls.

I grip the plain metal handle and push it down, then hold my breath and swing the door wide. The first thing I see is the sun, or something like it, hanging in the sky. There's an optical illusion that it's swinging slightly, like a bulb suspended on a string, but it *feels* like sunlight, that dazed midsummer heat where it's slightly too much and movement seems an imposition.

The courtyard lit by all this warmth is square and smaller than I had expected. It's probably only ten meters or so to the wall on the far side, which looks more like a mess of tangled ivy that's mastered the trick of growing perfectly vertical. Weatherboard can be glimpsed here and there underneath, scrawled with fragments of faded, half-obscured words. The ground is soft grass, each blade thick and lush. Perfectly in the center is a large stone fountain, carved into the shape of two women fighting with short swords. Water springs from both their heads, jetting between them in a spray that seems too blue to be real.

Colourful markings adorn the statues, but as I take a step out into the courtyard, they're disturbed, and whirl into the air in an explosion of colour. They're enormous butterflies, with wingspans as long as my arm. They're partially translucent, so the light makes their wings glow and then filters to the ground, where the grass is revealed to be nothing more than carpet fibres, grown long and fragrant.

"Seats," the house says. "Where are my manners? You need a place to rest."

Wooden pedestals like carefully carved tree stumps rise up out of the floor. There are three of them. One is carved with flames, one with insects, while the final one has a heart pierced with an arrow shot from a laughing mouth.

"Insects?" I ask Ye Shou as I take my seat on the third pedestal.

Dragon smirks and perches on the flames one in what looks like an incredibly uncomfortable position.

Ye Shou says nothing but sits with her legs crossed.

"Well," I say. "We are here. Let us pass the time, as you suggested."

"Or at least be honest with each other, even though that may be less pleasant." The house sighs, which makes the ivy on the wall rustle and the butterflies agitated again. "You have come to tame me or stop me. My parent is dead, my sister is apostate, and the world is precisely balanced between disasters."

"What the fuck is apostate?" Katie asks. "Is it like some kind of ace?"

"She has renounced her birthright," the house snaps, and for the first time I hear something darker threaded through his voice. "Taken what she no doubt thinks of as a middle path, but is inevitably one leading to human rule and mutant capitulation. There is no compromise, you understand."

"I think we're getting off course." I try to remain calm. I feel like I'm missing an entire layer of the conversation not being able to read this mutant. Instead, I have to flail my way through with logic. "We do know your sister and her closest friends. They are strong defenders of mutants and have—"

"Defenders." The house rumbles. "That is correct and it is also the problem. You cannot win by always defending, striking only when necessary."

I try to tamp down my rage, but I'm only partially successful. "A war against humanity would result in the loss of millions of lives. At least. You cannot suggest such a thing. It's not right when we chop down millions of trees, or slaughter millions of animals. Just because you think humans are occupying the same evolutionary niche as us—"

"We're not talking about killing them all." The sun flickers in the sky. "We will give demonstrations of capability until they understand the new reality of mutant supremacy. I would not truly grow myself to encompass the world. It will be effective enough to take out a few seats of government, or spread myself through luxurious suburbs in their busiest cities. They'll inevitably attack me, and I shall swallow them into my depths and spit them out into the darkest places I can find. Once they see what they're up against, they'll fold." The wind blows harder, and it sounds like there's far-off laughter carried on it. "It will be a good learning opportunity for humanity."

"Living side-by-side is an impossibility?" Ye Shou asks.

"You're not a fool, so don't act like it." The door slams open and shut behind us, sending a new crop of butterflies scattering past. These have their colour washed out, their wings soft and felt-like. They struggle furiously to stay aloft, but eventually spiral to the ground to lie twitching at our feet. "Haven't you seen enough? The humans have numbers, they have power and the will to exercise it, they have the weight of hegemony behind them. All they don't have is—"

"What the fuck is hegemony?" Katie swings her feet, heels thumping against the base of the stump. "Like is this a sound of your own voice thing? Because I don't think any of us know what you're talking about."

"I do." Ye Shou leans towards her. "Hegemony simply means they're the dominant group."

"Duh." Katie scowls around as if she wants to ensure the house sees it. "There are more of them, like you said."

"More, yes, and the utter determination to continue that. You see it even within human society, the relentlessness with which those in charge reinforce their rule in myriad ways. We are even more potentially disruptive, so they will strike against us even harder."

"You're not wrong," I say slowly. "This is the discussion we continually run into. It's unsolvable. We can't prove ourselves tame enough for the humans to feel safe around us. We can't fight back enough to guarantee our safety. Dylan's current plan is to walk a tightrope. They fucking love that, the reckless grinning asshole. Be dangerous enough to be taken seriously, but not so deadly it escalates into all-out war."

"It's not working though, is it?" The house sounds almost sad.

"No," Ye Shou says. "But perhaps you can help. Rather than trying to build some grandiose temple to mutantkind, build us a refuge."

"A bulwark against the world." The house hums to itself. "That has some appeal, I suppose. A simpler and more pragmatic approach, if not the one my dear parent would have wished. Let me think on this for a moment, but it sounds promising."

I try not to give any outward sign of relief.

Katie stretches and yawns. "Well, I think it sounds fucking great. Nice big house. We'll all live inside like one big happy family."

I get up nice and slowly. I'm suspicious at the change of heart, but if we truly have managed to talk Two Thorns down from attacking, this can only be a good thing. "Yes. That'll be wonderful."

Ye Shou flicks a look at me with dark eyes. The wind is blustering around us now and ruffling her hair. There are faint patterns on her scalp, like faded tattoos.

The ivy moves too, tugged loose from the boards on the wall.

The letters written there become visible.

Get out. Get out now. Don't trust him. He's lying to you.

Of fucking course. There's something else in here with us, and the house can't be trusted. I knew that, deep down, no matter how much I hoped this was over.

"Run," I say, very clearly and distinctly.

At least Katie doesn't argue for once. She even reaches out and takes hold of Ye Shou. They both bolt for the wooden doors, which are still hanging open,

The house makes no attempt to close them.

I'm right behind the others, but I don't think the house cares. It probably *wants* us back inside.

And when the doors slam shut behind us, I know that I'm right.

MADDY

I scream when the lights go out. It's pathetic, but sometimes I'm a cliche.

"Stay calm," Lou murmurs in my ear.

That's easy for him to say, but who knows what's out there in the dark.

Something creaks behind us and there are thunderous sounds of movement. It's either monsters performing a complicated ballet, or someone's moving heavy furniture around. My face is pressed against Lou's neck and I can smell his skin. It's a subtle scent that'll be called something like *natural*, except there's something spicier underneath it. Honestly, this is the literal worst person and literal worst time to discover some rudimentary crush, as gorgeous as Lou might be.

There's a ringing in the distance and the words *dinner bell* float into my head. I squeeze Lou tighter and he lets out this soft exhale. My cheeks flare red and I pull away to arm's reach, like we're about to start a formal dance.

Voices talk low, but it sounds like they're coming from a room away.

"Do you think we should investigate?" Lou makes it sound like an interesting adventure rather than blundering around in the dark until we find inevitable death.

"Okay." My voice comes out squeaky. I try to breathe deep, but my lungs won't take in much air. "Let's do it."

Of course, that's when all the lights come back on.

We're not in the hallway anymore. I shouldn't be surprised by this, because it's clear this house doesn't operate by any rules we understand, but the vast and beautiful room around me is still a shock.

I drop Lou's hand and turn a slow, stunned circle.

It's a ballroom. The kind you see in movies, where Cinderella shows up and loses a shoe. The ceiling soars above us, decorated in fiddly gold detail, with visions of skies and angels and frolicking animals painted on it. The walls continue the theme, but there are enormous white pillars haphazardly scattered throughout the room. These seem far older than the rest of the decor, as if the room was designed around them but someone forgot to update the aesthetic. They're roughly painted stone with streaky red marks dripping down from the ceiling to pool darker and more congealed at the base.

"Pretty." Lou frowns.

Someone steps out from behind the closest pillar. A breathtaking figure in a simple and elegant yellow dress, poured over her in shimmering silks. Her hair is pinned up in an intricate tangle, except for one strand that dangles down to brush one smooth cheek gently.

It's Gladdy, but it's not really her. There's something different about the set of her mouth. It's softer, as if it hasn't become used to pressing itself flat to stop painful truths escaping.

"Madelaide." My name sounds delicate in her mouth. "How delightful."

"Oh." I feel stupidly underdressed next to her in jeans and my pale blue Hello Kitty sweater. Why did we decide to wear casual clothes and why can't I dress like a grownup?

"I think you look beautiful. When the music starts, it won't matter what we're wearing." She extends one arm towards me. She's an impossibly fluid artist's sketch, and my eyes trace the elegant lines moving up to her shoulder and neck. Her eyes sparkle.

It's far harder to breathe than when I was scared.

"Well?" Behind her, from somewhere I can't see, an orchestra starts up. They're playing slightly too fast, the strings stabbing like they're in a horror movie and cheering the villain on.

There's a slight touch on my wrist. "Are you sure this is—?"

"It's fine." I barely even turn my head to look at Lou. "Go and talk to the waiter."

"What waiter?" Lou asks, but he's already being approached by a dapper person in a suit, with sleek dark hair and an elegant smile. There are definitely shades of Ray and Dylan there. The house sees a lot.

"If sir would accompany me." The waiter bows smoothly, and Lou allows himself to be led off with a frown over his shoulder.

"Now then." Gladdy places one of my hands at the in-curve of her waist and holds the other lightly in hers. Her pulse is so strong I can feel it in the tips of my fingers. "There is so much I want to tell you, but it's easier to listen to the music, don't you think?" Her voice is low and it hums with the same urgency as the strings.

"I don't know," I stammer.

"Silly Madelaide." She strokes my cheek with the back of her fingers. They're so warm I almost flinch away, but she's never touched me like this before. "You don't have the advantage of reading my face, I know, but can't you sense the love I have for you?"

I know it's definitely not her, but I wish it was. The look in her eyes has shades of warmth and softness I've never seen in the *real* Gladdy. There's no harm in this fantasy, is there? A moment on the dance floor, soundtracked by ominous strings. Two bodies close, gently arched shapes coming together.

"I can," I whisper.

"You understand what craving is, don't you?"

I'm trembling all the way through me, and I slide my hand around to the small of her back so I can pull her closer against me. My eyes are locked on hers, and I watch them widen.

She takes the hand that's tangled with hers and presses it to her red lips.

My eyelids tremble as she rotates my hand and kisses the delicate skin on the inside of my wrist. Her lips part. I feel a point of wetness trail along my skin and then a sharp pinch.

I gasp, and try to pull my hand away, but she has it held tight.

"You said you understood craving." Her teeth are small and pointed, and each is tipped with red. "This is the only way you can satisfy me." She lowers her hand back to my wrist and the pinch this time is much sharper. Even worse is the sound, wet and tearing and hungry.

I try to scream. There's no sign of Lou, disappeared with the waiter. I use my free hand and worm it between us, shoving Gladdy away from me as hard as I can. She staggers backwards, blood smeared across her face.

"I've got you," a voice says from behind me, taking my hand and whirling me away.

The music speeds up, ever so slightly.

"You!" It's another Gladdy, this one in a shorter, less elegant dress of the same yellow. More suited for a club party than a ballroom.

"Yes, me. Not the same version obviously. I have no great desire to devour you as some kind of romantic statement. How disgusting."

"She's—she's—"

"Ignore her," New Gladdy says. "You've made your feelings clear."

I look over my shoulder, but there's no sign of the first Gladdy. "Where did she go?"

"Sulking, no doubt. A case of be careful what you wish for. It's a bit gross when she loves you *too* much, isn't it?"

"It wasn't real."

Gladdy smirks. "It was perfectly real. That insatiable, devouring need is a type of love. In a different world, that's how we came. Your Gladdy feels things deeply too, you know. She's better at hiding it than most, but who knows? Maybe it'll come out and you'll be eaten alive."

"Don't say that." I want to pull away from this Gladdy too.

"The possibilities are endless." She pushes me away from her, before spinning me around to pull me back close again.

I try not to stare at her lips. "Don't spin me like that."

"Why not? Does it make you feel sick, dear Maddy?"

This time, I whirl even faster. The room moves in a gold-and-white blur. I feel my stomach lurch and when she pulls me back against her and my body is still, the spinning in my head continues.

"I told you." My stomach clenches like two hands are squeezing it from inside. I feel the acid scorch its way up my oesophagus. I make an effort to press my lips together but they burst open, and I cough acid all over Gladdy.

It eats through her yellow dress instantly, soft skin dissolving to reveal knots of muscle that smoke and fall apart. Soon, I'm looking down a ragged tunnel to the pulsing meat of her heart.

She tips her head back. Her eyes are closed. She moans at the back of her throat.

"Gladdy, I'm so sorry." I'm sobbing.

"No, God, don't apologise. The pain is delicious. It's the first thing that matches how much it hurts when I can't live up to your expectations." She tilts her head back down to look at me, her teeth grazing her bottom lip. Tiny pinprick holes appear in the walls of her heart, blood squirting out in thin jets. "Do you know how hard it is to constantly fail you?"

I recoil as her heart melts into a bloody mess inside her chest and she collapses onto the floor. When I turn away, I run smack into another figure.

"No," I whimper. "No more."

"Oh, it's you." This Gladdy's eyes are bright. She wears a canary-yellow suit, perfectly tailored with gemstones as buttons. She has an undercut and short curls spill down one side of her face. "Have you seen Dylan? I can't find them anywhere."

"They didn't come with us." I frown.

"I know our Dylan is taken, but the house has brought me another." She twirls in place and strikes a pose. "Do you think they'll like this outfit? I hope this one has a thing for suits too. I've wanted them since the very first moment I looked into their eyes and saw all those fears. So disastrously attractive, with no idea about it." Gladdy grabs both my hands. "You're better friends with them. Could you put in a good word for me?"

I know this isn't *my* Gladdy, but how far removed is she? I've seen the way she looks at Dylan. How are there so many reasons she's not in love with me?

"I don't know where Dylan is," I say coldly.

"Then what use are you?" She sighs and takes her hands away, gliding away across the dance floor as if she has an imaginary Dylan in her arms.

I turn again, looking for some sign of Lou, but there's only another Gladdy. This one is in a simple black dress, with a silver chain at her throat.

"Go away." I'm exhausted, my heart beaten down and whimpering. "I don't need another example of how much worse things could be."

"This is the entirety of your fucking problem." Gladdy yawns. "You care too much. I remember back in the cages you telling me that you felt no emotion. It was laughable then and even more ridiculous now. You are a boiling pit of emotions and it seeps out of your every pore."

"I wish I felt none." I try to keep my voice flat like hers, but it's obvious what is sketched out in the way it shakes. Rage and sadness and desire.

"You are pitiful." Gladdy looks past me, focused on something in the distance. "I would expend that emotion on you, but it's a waste of my heart. There is so little space in it, after all, and you demand so much."

"I don't know what this is supposed to teach me." I have no further patience for the house's lesson. "Is it supposed to tell me that Gladdy offers me nothing? Or that I should be grateful for what small joys I have?"

"There's no intent. There's no lesson." It sounds like the house is laughing, rattling and echoing behind the walls. "You reject a Gladiola, and I create another. How many do you think we shall go through before we discover the problem is not her?"

"I want *my* Gladdy," I scream. "The one thing you cannot give me."

"You don't really want her." There's a series of far off crashes, as if the house is violently reconfiguring itself. "You've made it very clear that she's not acceptable to you. Isn't that right, girls?"

"So right."

I whirl once again to see the four Gladdys standing in a row with their different outfits and hairstyles. One still shows bloody teeth when she smiles, and another has an oozing hole where her heart should be. Yet they're all wearing the same expression on their face—one of complete disdain for me, Madelaide McLean.

Sadly, it's not an entirely unfamiliar expression.

"It's always our fault," the melted Gladdy says.

"Of course it is." The emotionless one sighs, as if she'd rather not be here. "It couldn't possibly be hers."

"Greedy thing." The bloody-toothed Gladdy smiles. "Always wanting more and more, but doesn't like it when the tables are turned."

"I think she's done enough to us." The heartless Gladdy steps forward, blood spilling down the front of her dress. "I don't think we should let her keep hurting us, do you?"

They all smile, and they're wearing identical expressions again.

This time, they all look hungry.

GLADDY

The room we enter isn't the one we left from. It's dark and narrow with heavy wooden counters on each side. The windows are filmed with grime and the light that filters through is grey and heavy. It pools around lumpen shapes on the counter. Carcasses of something, things partially dismembered and being prepared for a meal.

It makes me glad to be a vegetarian and also: such a fucking cliche, house.

The dim light picks out the long silver shape of a knife. I'm tempted to grab it, but it seems far too obvious. It'll probably come alive and try to dig out my heart. For some reason, the house is toying with us. Probably his twisted sense of humour, like having us sit down for a cozy chat. Or maybe he wants something from us. That seems to be our only chance at surviving this. It seems like slim odds.

"Was it something I said?" The voice comes from behind us, rather than all around.

I don't bother looking over my shoulder. Instead, I follow the running figures of Katie and Ye Shou. The dim room stretches on ahead. It's getting narrower, the gap between the counters shrinking as we run.

Ahead, Katie coughs a burst of flame. It's so bright that it hurts my eyes. It illuminates what's on the counters—great hunks of meat, come from giant dismembered bodies that seem human if not for the size. Massive arms the length and width of tree trunks, ending in hands the size of small cars. Huge chunks of torso with marbled fat inside and hunks of sawn off bone. Each of them seems to have been hacked into wildly, huge slashes and cuts running like trenches through the flesh, oozing blackened blood. Insects scuttle and feed.

Katie screams and I bite back my own.

I don't think any of this is truly real. Giant dismembered carcasses are the house's way of having fun. More of this elaborate game he's playing. For now, he wants us to keep running. The question is why.

"Dragon," I shout. "Ye Shou. Stop!"

Neither of them listen to me. They're still running, as the room continues to narrow. The light from Katie's flames is gone, but the pale light from outside shows the shapes on the counters are growing in size, like we're moving through a tunnel of dead flesh.

"Can both of you please stop?" My voice is a wild shriek.

Ye Shou obeys so abruptly I run into her. There's something odd about how her body gives under my hands. She sprawls onto the ground in front of me. I can't see her in the darkness, but I reach down to help her up. When I take her arm, it feels like holding the sleeve of a stuffed animal, except her skin is warm.

"Leave me," she says. "I can rise on my own."

"What are you *doing*?" Katie's voice comes from up ahead. She's standing with her head tilted back, a small flame flickering between her lips like an enthusiastic candle.

The body parts that surround us are stacked to the ceiling, or at least where I imagine the ceiling is. They're jammed in haphazardly together.

"Really don't like it in here." The flame flickers and dies while Katie speaks.

I gesture around at the gruesome display. "It's funnelling us through here for a reason. We need to find an alternative way out."

I crouch down to see a series of small round doors set into the wall underneath the counters. Blood drips down their surfaces and pools in sticky puddles underneath. I duck under and crawl towards the nearest one. It swings open when I push it, revealing a bedroom beyond with a large canopied bed inside. Two thick candles burn on the nightstand, making it seem more inviting.

I don't know if we can trust it. It's still part of the house.

"Why this door?" Katie asks.

"One door is as good as another." I gesture inside. "There are two other exits here."

"They could lead anywhere," Ye Shou points out. "We have no way of orienting ourselves, and the house seems to *shift*."

"It's a maze." Katie juts her chin at me. "We need to solve it."

She's possibly right. I'm not sure whether we should be finding an exit or the center, or whether it's solvable at all. Either way, I want to be out of this damn kitchen. The door we're peering through is set high up on the bedroom wall, so I drop down inside. Katie and Ye Shou follow without further commentary. The candles flicker, as if we brought a breeze with us. Or as if there's something else in here, breathing, that woke as we entered.

Something in the fucking bed.

"What do you want?" I ask the house. "Beyond expansion, beyond the war. Why are we here?"

"Finally." The voice comes from inside the gauzy curtains that surround the bed. Something moves inside. It stretches. The shadow has too many limbs. "You're starting to ask sensible questions."

"Does that mean you'll provide us answers?"

"Let's build up to the great existentialist ones, shall we?" Something reaches out and pulls at the curtain, making it billow. One of the candles almost flickers out, but the flame desperately rights itself. "Start with something simpler, but still relevant."

"Which one of you am I talking to?" I ask.

"Oh very clever. I guess the name gives it away, but most people think it's an affectation."

"Two Thorns Twisted on a Stem," Ye Shou says. "They're twins. One has been speaking to us through the house. Then there is another, who wrote on the wall in the garden. That one—"

"Was me." The curtain is tugged aside, revealing a slender young person in the bed, cradling a lantern. Their face is gentle and tan, and their eyes are a bright and watchful brown. They look entirely human, but I suspect it's another act. I can see no fears in them, so either they have none, or they are not human. "My brother. He holds the bulk of the power, yet I retain some mastery over small details of the appearance. Scuttling through the walls, changing things here and there."

"Is there any way you can stop him?" Katie asks.

"It is unlikely in the extreme." They look pensive. "Have you not heard the saying about a house divided against itself?"

"So you sit back and allow him to expand to swallow half the world?" Ye Shou's face flickers in the candlelight.

"Is that what he's doing?" The person smirks as if it's a private joke.

"We need to get out and we need to stop him," I say firmly.

"Or you need a better ally." They look at me through lowered lashes.

I have my doubts about this situation, but this person is tied to the house, and has some power to change it. They're the closest thing we've found to assistance, and they dislike the Thorn in charge of the house.

"We only have a little time." The person in the bed glances at the ceiling. "My brother will come soon. I'll find you again. Look for arrows. In paintings, on skirtings, in ornamental sconces. Follow the path I lay out for you and we'll meet again."

"Wait," I say. "You never told us why we're here."

"My brother is at least partially a vampire and the house is how he feeds." The person lifts the lantern, opens the small glass door and blows out the flame. "He consumes many things, but especially the energy given off by mutants. Humans have far less nutritional value, so he wants you to use your powers and try and escape. He'll put you in circumstances where you're forced to—"

There's a banging sound and I jump. When we entered the room, there were only two other exits. Now there are dozens. Every wall is full of them, a chaotic arrangement jigsawed together.

"Follow the arrows," the person in the bed says, and drags the bedclothes up over their head.

Katie roughly tugs them away, but the sheets are pulled tight and smooth and there's no sign of anyone having been there. "What the fuck? Where did they go?"

There's a rumbling sound, and every door to the bedroom slams open at once. Looming in each one are figures, pale and scarred. They look to have been reassembled from the body parts left in the kitchen area we just escaped from.

"Fuck's sake," Katie growls. "Hard to solve a maze with so many goddamn monsters."

Ye Shou inclines her head. "Perhaps it is now time for me to use my ability."

I give her my least impressed look. All this build up and now...

Katie smirks, and Ye Shou explodes. There's no other word for it. A torrent of spiders erupts from her throat. There are thousands of them, ranging in size from a coin to a fist. They scuttle outwards on their many legs, moving nimbly along the walls and floor. In moments, they have all disappeared through the doorways, moving too fast for the mammoth creatures guarding them.

I scream. It's partly shock and partly annoyance at Maddy for keeping this ridiculous secret.

Somehow Ye Shou is made of spiders. How she can move and talk and pontificate about fucking physics when she's a skinsuit full of arachnids is something I can't fathom. Our powers are more fantastical than based in any kind of science. I'd have sworn it was an illusion, if I wasn't looking down at Ye Shou's shed skin.

The figures in the doorways don't move. It's like they're content to block our way. Trying to keep us here so we can't find the friendly half of Two Thorns. They don't seem to be bothered about Ye Shou escaping. Perhaps they don't count the spiders as anything, but surely the house knows what she is. Does that count as using her power? Is she feeding the house by doing this? I reach down and pick up her skin. I assume she's going to want it back later.

It's hard to make out any features on the creatures barricading our way. It's like my eyes are fuzzy or I'm looking at them through a veil. A ripple runs through them all, as if they're all part of an ocean of flesh, connected by currents we can't see.

The hacked out cuts writhe and part, making growling noises that slowly resolve into words.

"Were you talking to my sibling?" They all speak at once. "They've been hiding from me."

"Sibling?" I'm a good liar. I have to be. "Which one? We met Water and Petal and—"

"No, no, none of those. My *other*. My twin. They hide from me." The creatures begin to shuffle into the room.

"Time for a distraction," I mutter to Katie. "Draw some of them away."

"Sounds good." She steps forward, her jaw dropping.

"Dragon, no!" I reach out a hand towards her. "Do something else. The house wants you to use your power."

I don't know why I thought she'd listen.

Fire erupts from her throat. It leaps outwards in a massive tail of flame which sets alight the figures in the closest door frames. They catch as easy as paper, flaring bright for a moment before crumbling to ash.

"Katie, wait!"

Again she ignores me, running for the gap where the figures had stood.

Something takes hold of me from behind, pale hands reaching for my arms and my throat.

Katie turns, standing in an empty doorway, her white shoes turning grey with the ash of the creatures she's just immolated.

"Fuck you, Gladiola Quick." She turns and disappears into the darkness.

MADDY

The four Gladdys swarm towards me. There's no love or desire in their eyes. They've all got the same sharp-toothed and hungry expressions as the first Gladdy. They'll devour me and call it love. Is that really what I am to her? Of all the permutations the house has shown me, that's the one that feels the cruelest. An unflattering mirror held up to show me what I am—ravenous and demanding.

The first one hits me hard enough to knock me backwards. I stumble and fall, my head smacking on the polished floor. Above me, warm light from the enormous tiered chandelier spills down honeyed and thick. Gladdy is atop me, scrabbling at my hair, trying to bare my neck.

There is a pinch at my wrist and one at my calf. I don't bother looking to see what's happening. The light from above dazzles me, and bathes me in warm radiance. Brighter beams cut through the heavy yellow, sharp knives of white that hit the crystals and bounce around inside them. I narrow my eyes at the glare. It's like being doused in cold water.

Gladdy's face hovers in front of mine. Her teeth are jagged and she opens her mouth wide.

Her head explodes, a star of light punching through it. It flies apart like a pumpkin in the microwave. I'm staring at a hand glowing so bright I can see the bones of the skeleton clearly defined in it. I'm covered in bits of blood and brain and skull.

I scream and thrash on the ground, shoving myself backwards. My vision is dazzled, alight with bursts of colour. When it finally clears, three corpses lie at my feet and a headless one slumps atop me.

Standing above me is a boy, so bright to look upon that I have to cover my eyes and peer at him between my fingers.

"Sorry. That waiter you summoned was a bit of a problem."

"Lou," I gasp.

"Well, yes. Who else is this bright?" It sounds like he's smiling but I can't look at him. When I close my eyes, the outline of him dances in lurid colours.

"You saved me."

"Yes, you did seem like you were being eaten alive by some of the house's monsters." I feel the body on top of me being dragged off.

"Gladdy." It hurts to breathe. "They were all Gladdy."

"No." He has dimmed so I can mostly make out his face. "The house made them to torment you. No matter what drama you have or don't have with Gladdy, she would never treat you like this."

When the light completely fades away, he's left standing naked in front of me. "Okay, so this is awkward." He tries to cover himself a little. "These are the perils of lighting your whole self up in a valiant effort to save your friend."

I look away and glance back and look away again.

The yellow suit is mostly intact on one of the dead Gladdys, and I help Lou tug it off the corpse. I know I shouldn't be sneaking peeks at him, but I do. His body is slender and tan and muscular. I have an overwhelming urge to touch him just to see how his skin feels, which goes to show I am the worst. The suit trousers mostly fit him, despite one leg being half torn off, and he tugs the jacket around himself.

"Don't I look wonderful?" He gives me a crooked smile and I swear my undead traitor heart starts frolicking like an excited puppy.

"It actually suits you." He looks roguish and charming, like he's escaped from some dashing piratical fantasy after a wild battle.

"Nice pun." He nudges me.

I hadn't even noticed, but it makes me laugh. "Thanks." Can I be any more awkward? "For saving my life."

He reaches out and lightly touches the mark at my wrist where Gladdy had been feeding. Before it looked like chewed raw meat, but now it's a ragged and inflamed scratch. His hand moves up to tilt my head the slightest amount, and his fingertips trail down the line of my neck.

I watch the frown lines of his forehead wrinkle and smooth.

"I think you're going to be okay." His fingers drift away from me. "It's not as bad as I thought."

"The house playing tricks," I whisper.

"Mmm." He stands in his ragged yellow suit and looks around the ballroom. "I do wonder why it's doing this. It could kill us easily, or throw us out, but it wants us stumbling around. Maybe it likes us being scared."

"What happened with that waiter that you went away with?"

He raises an eyebrow. "The one you *sent* me away with? They acted very important, but as soon as we were alone, they started trying to make out with me. Except inside their mouth it was mechanical insect parts, like one of those garbage disposals."

"Ew," I say.

"Summed it up better than me." He gives this tiny little shudder of his shoulders. "I melted them down and came to find you."

"Thanks again."

"You don't need to keep thanking me. I'd save you any day." He pauses. "We're a team."

The orchestral strings soaring in my heart slur and fade until it's silence again. Of course he saved me. It's basically his job. It doesn't mean anything, and why should it? It's ridiculous anyway, because I'm in love with Gladdy, as pointless an endeavour as that is. Just because I'm thrown together in a perilous situation with a very handsome and sweet boy doesn't mean I should build a smidge of feeling into something wind-swept and epic.

That would be incredibly stupid.

That said, when have I been anything else?

"So what do we do now?" I'm shivering, even though it's not cold in here.

"I'd offer you my suit jacket." Lou gives me a half-smile. "Except then it might be awkward for both of us again. Do you want a hug?"

I nod and turn towards him, because I do and it honestly doesn't *mean* anything. He enfolds me in his arms. These Cute Mutants hug at every opportunity because they're all the softest of fluff despite being murdery at times. I still can't help feeling like this particular one is special.

The house disagrees with me, or else it's shipping us a little too violently. The whole ballroom begins to come apart around us, disintegrating in a shower of gilt and sawdust. The ceiling bows inwards and the painted angels come loose and flutter towards the floor. Golden glitter cascades down over our shoulders and faces, highlighting Lou's cheekbones and lips. The rest of it falls to the floor in a giant swoosh, making a curve that leads away from us to one corner of the ballroom.

"Like it wants us to go somewhere," I whisper. "Look."

Lou frowns. "Do we really want to follow?"

The walls of the house are busily reconfiguring themselves, folding inwards like a complex origami trick. The glorious ballroom narrows in around us and is soon a hallway again. The walls are dark, made of heavily panelled wood. Only the very end of the swooping, glittery arrow is visible, pointing at one of the many doors that lead elsewhere.

"So many doors, only one arrow. It can't be any worse than trying a random one." I step forward and place my hand on the cool metal of the handle.

"I think we've established things can get very bad in here," Lou murmurs.

"Yes, but you're here to save my life." I beam at him, giving him the full radiance of my smile, and he grins right back at me.

"What if I get in trouble?" His voice is light, but his eyes dance.

"I'll drown them in acid. My turn to save *your* life and stop me being indebted to you forever."

"Yes. It's a terrible burden holding your life-debt in my hands." There's an expression on his face that makes me tremble, so I turn away and twist the handle hard, shoving the door open.

I sense Lou's presence at my shoulder, peering in with me.

The room beyond is hardly terrifying. It looks like the lounge at my grandparents' house growing up, with too much old furniture shoved in willy-nilly so there's barely any room for people. I creep in, pausing between two large fringed lamps that brush my shoulders. I'm fully expecting them to start moving in an invisible breeze and then attempt to strangle me. I even raise my fingers to my neck preemptively, but the lamps are still.

"What do you think?" Lou asks. "Is the biggest threat the couches or the curtains?"

"Hush." I brush my fingers across the back of his hand. "You're a terrible jinxer."

We edge into the room together. The most ominous looking thing is a giant iron birdcage hanging in the corner, but it's empty. There are five doors leading out, all in a row on the far wall. It's like a riddle.

"That couch." Lou points. "Look at the pattern on it."

It's decorated with a complex swirl of blue and red yet the negative space forms a set of distinct arrow shapes, all pointing towards the fourth door on the wall.

"Do you think we follow it? The swoosh led us in here, and there's nothing horrible waiting."

"Two intrepid explorers." He's very close behind me. "Ready for anything."

We weave through the rest of the furniture and reach the door. When I touch the handle it's slightly warm and humming. Probably ominous. I push it open anyway.

The next room is sterile. The walls are a white so pure and exact it's like they don't exist. The light seems to come from everywhere at once. In the middle of the room stands a slender figure, with tan skin and warm brown eyes, dressed in sombre grey.

"There's little time," they say. "The others are in terrible trouble."

"Others?" I ask.

"Your friends. The spidery one, the fire-breather, and the sad one. My brother has separated them, and now I think they might very well be doomed."

"Who are you?" Lou demands.

"I'm the quiet one. I'm here to give you a choice—your friends, or the heart."

"Our friends," we both say, without even questioning what the heart is or why we'd be interested.

"A test." The person in the middle of the room smiles, and raises one hand. "They're the exact same place, you see. If you had chosen the heart, I may have led you far astray, into the distant reaches of the house. Your friends are exactly who you should be thinking about, because without saving them, you won't save yourselves."

"Cryptic," Lou mutters and I have to agree. I still have no idea who this person is.

"Two Thorns Twisted on a Stem," the person says, as if I'd spoken aloud. "How could you have thought there was only one of us? Now, quickly. If you hurry, the doom we dread might not happen at all."

The person disappears and a section of the pure white wall swings open—a hidden door.

From the other side, I hear a very familiar voice raised in anger.

Gladiola Quick.

GLADDY

Great. At the worst possible time, my poor decisions of the past have come back to haunt me. The way I treated poor Katie in the cages, lashing out at this furious fragile girl because it felt good to see her flinch. It was better than wallowing in my own lake of self-pity. And now she's abandoned me to the hideous fleshy avatars of the house.

If what the Other Thorn said was true, the house wants me to use my powers. Except there are no fears to see in the creatures attacking me. There's only hunger like a blizzard, a voracious hole down which you could pour anything and not fill it. They want my fear, for me to struggle and thrash against them, and to beg and howl.

Instead, I go limp. I sag in their arms. The creatures prod me with stumpy fingers, but I try to burrow inwards, block out the heavy sound of them moving, and the murmuring of their slashed-mouths.

They drop me to the ground, a discarded prize. I hope this is the smart decision.

I lie still for a moment, waiting for them to leave or fall silent so I can wriggle out of this place. Instead, one of them lifts a massive foot and stomps down hard on me. Good job, Gladdy. Brilliant plan. No wonder you're Field Leader.

Yet instead of hurting me, the pressure pushes me down into the floor, which gives like a spongy material. The other creatures all begin to rain down blows, pounding on me as I sink further down, until I'm surrounded by the damp, squishy underbelly of the house. One terrible thing after another. Perhaps playing dead wasn't the best decision. Maybe now is the time to panic? The wet wood smell is cloying, pressed up against my nose and mouth, and I'm inhaling something hot and dusty. I thrash around and one leg pops free below me. It swings wildly in the air, and the rest of me follows, falling down to land with a thump on the floor.

It hurts, but less so than being torn apart by those creatures. I roll over, trying to calm my breath. I'm not under the house at all, but in another room. It's almost entirely bare aside from an armchair that leaks stuffing, set up to point out a window that's been painted over with a child's rudimentary and brightly-coloured landscape. I gaze around the room from my vantage point on the floor until I notice an arrow chalked on the skirting, pointing behind me. It seems the Other Thorn is looking out for me.

It occurs to me this could be some complicated game the two of them are playing, to lure us deeper and deeper, expending our powers and feeding the house into a surge of unfettered growth. I have to hope for the opposite. Right now, we're at the house's mercy. Its power is immense and the complexity of what it can create is overwhelming. Our best chance to get out is to hope we truly can divide it against itself.

This house cannot stand, or we're fucked, and the world is next.

I get unsteadily to my feet. My back hurts and my head's even worse. Still, the arrow means hope, so I follow it. There's another a few meters up and when the hallway forks, I'm faced with a portrait of an extremely bored-looking man gesturing to the left.

In the absence of anything else, I take it as an arrow.

I wander through the house for what feels like hours. There are arrows hidden everywhere. Sometimes they're in ornate mouldings on the ceiling, other times flickering on fuzzy old television screens. In one room, the fish swim constantly to the right, disappearing when they hit one edge of the tank and reappearing at the other. Some are drawn in dust and others in spraypaint. One takes up the entire ceiling of a dilapidated ballroom and one is a shadow cast from a dirty lamp.

I become adept at spotting them, like my mind is tuning into the Other Thorn's. Whether it's on rain-streaked glass, or the hands of a clock, or a scattered fan of seeds from a dying plant, I follow the arrows as they lead me deeper and deeper into the house. I no longer worry about whether this is a trap. I'm following for the arrows' sake.

Until I come to a room where there are thousands of them. There's a fireplace on one wall, and three plain wooden doors. It's sparsely furnished aside from an empty bookcase and two large high-backed chairs drawn up in front of the fire. The forest of arrows all over the walls are all pointing in different directions. I turn in a slow circle, trying to find some rhyme or reason behind this. It's another puzzle, that's all. A twist in the game.

I frown and the arrows all rotate slowly to point at me in the center of the room.

"I have to admit, it took me a while," the house says. "You seemed to be incoherently stumbling through me, and yet in the most roundabout way you were heading for the center. It was very clever of my sibling, but I don't think you shall be going any further."

"I'm confused," I begin, but the house shakes violently. The arrows dissolve and drip down the walls in smears of paint.

"You have found your way into the oldest and most essential part of me. This transgression shall not stand. I did not wish to have you die inside me, but I shall take some nourishment from your bones and—"

An enormous crashing sound comes from the fireplace. It gouts flame as if someone threw kerosene on it. I scramble backwards frantically. The house isn't fucking around in terms of killing me.

Except what follows the fire is a short and shaven-haired girl with bright orange eyes.

"Sorry about that. The house didn't want to let us down the chimney."

"Us?" I blink at her.

"Fuck fucking fuck." There's another bang from the fireplace and one of the Skyes tumbles out along with an avalanche of ash. "Stupid fucking chimney."

"Six?" I ask.

"Five. Six is still coming."

It sounds like the chimney is going to explode. There's a constant string of swearing that would put even Dylan to shame and then Skye Six crawls out of the fireplace, scowling at me. She has a knife in her teeth and one in her left hand.

"Fucking house." She scowls at us all, ruffling her hair and sending ash cascading down.

"How are you all *finding* this place?" The house rumbles around us. "Is my sibling truly helping all of you? I cannot find *evidence* of it."

I have no idea how the others got here, but I like how pissed off the house sounds, plus he's not bringing himself down around our heads. Perhaps this close to the center, he cannot remake himself so easily.

"How *did* you get here?" I ask Katie.

"Ye Shou." She points over my shoulder, and I turn to see a small group of spiders scuttling over the wall behind me. They form themselves into a ragged letter F, and then into a circle, before making a slightly crooked L-shape and another circle before resolving into a W.

"Clever." This must be how the others have been navigating.

The spiders arrange themselves in a line above the center door. I stare at it, unsure.

"Fuck's sake." Six pushes roughly past me. "Are we going to get this fucking horror movie over with?" She can speak remarkably well with a knife between her teeth, but she's done with words, marching up to the door and slamming it open.

There's another hallway beyond, with a single flickering bulb to light it.

The walls quiver, as if they're vaguely liquid. "Don't go in there. You'll regret it. Gravity changes beyond this point. This is a threshold. Once you go beyond, there's no returning."

"You were going to pick my bones clean anyway." I follow Six to the door, Five and Katie trailing me. As I reach it, I see spiders crawling along the walls of the hallway. One particularly large one perches atop the bulb, waving its limbs and making shadows dance.

The door slams shut in our faces.

Six kicks it open so hard the handle makes an indentation in the wall.

"Fine," the house hisses. "Be it on your head."

We all walk into the corridor and the door slams behind us again, although this time it feels petulant.

The bulb flickers and goes out. Ugh, this house and his cliches.

There's writing on the walls that glows in the darkness.

He's furious. He'll be coming for me. I'll hide in the distant reaches or the upper corridors, but he'll find me eventually. He'll hurt me for bringing you here. This is the part of the house where we were born. The heart is only a little further. Follow the spiders-girl.

I'm about to complain that we can't even *see* Ye Shou, when the spiders all light up, as if their backs have been daubed in little splashes of bioluminescent paint. There are thousands of them now. Some straggle down the hallway, while others form themselves into a writhing lump on the ceiling.

"Apologies for the hasty exit." The mass of spiders speaks with Ye Shou's calm voice. "In my spider form I could explore far faster or further than any of us could alone. It took some hours, but I managed to map a significant portion of the house. It's still growing I believe, but mostly in the distant reaches. It's an astonishing place."

"It was a smart idea. Do you know what this heart is?"

"You should see it for yourself."

I sigh and follow the trail of the little glowing spiders.

Katie sidles up alongside me. "Sorry about my thing too. I was mostly just trying to freak you out. Leave you in the dark a bit. We're even now, right?"

She grins up at me. In her face, I can see the truth of it. She did want me to suffer, but she also wants this feud over with. Her greatest desire is to feel about me the way she does about all the others, which tangles regret and happiness up inside me in a confusing ball. All I can do is put my arm around Katie and give her an awkward side hug.

"We're even," I tell her.

"Good, because if we die in this fucking shithole, I don't want to go out with an enemy."

"I'm sorry." I've said it before, but I figure it doesn't hurt to say it again.

"I know. And I'm glad I didn't fuck up and let the house eat you. Now let's get this over with."

Ahead of us, the spiders ring a cracked wooden door. It looks like it's been undisturbed for a long time.

I look at it skeptically. "Is this really it?"

The mass of spiders writhes above me. "Yes. The heart of the house. Be careful in there. Some of us didn't make it out."

"Well, fuck, that's cheerful." Six pauses at the door. "Do we fucking knock or kick the door in or—?"

"Open it like a normal person," Katie says.

"Boring." Six turns the handle and pushes it open slowly.

Red light spills from the next room, accompanied by a rhythmic pounding. When he said the heart of the house, I didn't think he meant it literally.

The two Skyes are poised on the threshold rather than charging in.

Katie and I reach them. Most of Ye Shou is still sprawled on the ceiling.

"It's fucking creepy in there." Six takes the knife out of her mouth and gestures. "Look."

I peer over the shoulders of the two clones. The light is so thick it looks like the room is filled with blood. The walls quiver and pulse, bowing inwards and snapping back to straight. They're veined with black lines that thread and tangle before branching away again. Each time they move, there's an echoing thump.

More than that, I see the truth and it takes my breath away.

In this room, the house's history is laid bare. Two siblings, born in an oceanfront shack, at a time Heart was despondent about the doom laid on mutantkind. This was back in the 1920s, well before Teen Spirit wiped mutants from the minds of humanity. It chills me to see it. I had no idea Heart was so old. How many times have humans tried to destroy mutants? For a moment, I have sympathy with Heart and their aims, when you see the truth of it stretched out in a bloody tapestry. This particular darkness wasn't even the first time. The twins were raised on stories going back generations. Mutants come to prominence and are violently thrown down, going underground for years before springing back up again. Teen Spirit wiped all that history from our minds, but the house remembers.

I see the twins grow up together. One who becomes a fierce acolyte of their parent's plan and one who grows increasingly unsure. They keep their disagreement private, a furious battle between them until one night when Heart changes them both. Even compared to the mutants I know, Two Thorns' powers are unhinged from reality—they are a form of dimensional portal trapped behind the appearance of a simple house. A literal gateway between worlds, a nexus point between realities. One twin becomes the house, the other is trapped inside as a punishment—a ghost haunting their sibling's halls. They mapped the corridors as the house grew into other dimensions and parallel universes, popping up as small shacks on deserted alien beaches, appearing as glowing apartments in futuristic towers, or as seemingly ordinary houses on the streets of worlds that differ only slightly from our own. The scope of it is terrifying. The house is comparatively tiny now, but we're walking inside something that can be vast and incomprehensible. Except it's also a multiversal metastasising cancer, ready to expand inexorably into our world.

I know what I need to do. It gives me no joy, but it's essential.

MADDY

"Don't pretend you care at all about your poor lost sibling," Gladdy snaps. The room she's standing in is a pulsing, lurid red, full of a choking scarlet mist that eddies around her head as if it wishes to find a way in. She's flanked by Katie and two Skyes. The whole host of Ye Shou crawls frantically around the shuddering walls that beat like an enormous heart.

My emotions are too messy to pick apart. I'm reeling from the emotional backwash of confronting all the Gladdys the house showed me. And yet I'm still so pleased to see *my* Gladdy alive in this monster of a house. The way she stands, so still and strong.

"They are safe in here," the house says. "I protect them from a world that hates us."

"But you lied." Gladdy's voice is cold. "You were the fearful one. You were terrified of what Heart might do if they found out you were disloyal. So you ran to them and passed off your fears as those of your sibling's."

The pounding of the walls in the room grows more intense. "Is that what they told you?" The black veins in the wall writhe and split and form new pathways. "They are a liar and dangerous—"

"They said nothing. I see it here, written at your heart. Your parent was becoming more and more unhinged, and you Two Thorns disagreed on what should be done. You wanted to flee and your sibling wanted to be changed into a weapon."

The room is shaking faster now, a panicked, arrhythmic thumping.

"So you came to Heart and you poured poison in their ear. They changed you both in a rage, and they punished your sibling instead of you."

"It's a lie," the house says, barely audible above the pounding of his heart.

"You're still afraid," Gladdy says. "Your grandiose talk of expanding into Earth? All bragging and very little truth. The stories you learned at your parent's knee caused you to fear humans too much to truly threaten them. You do the bare minimum of aggressive expansion in the hope that Water Nourishing the Roots and Delicately Drooping Stamen have no cause to doubt your fervour. At the same time you hope to escape the notice of the humans when they rally themselves to exterminate mutants again."

"The humans will," the house whispers. "It happens every time."

"And when they do, you'll disappear into the sprawl of the universe, leaving us behind."

"I could have left already."

"Not with that thorn in your side, always whispering, creeping through your halls." Gladdy smirks and the combination of the red glow and the smoke makes her look like a villain in a stage production. "Where is your sweet sibling, anyway? All this work to lead us here and then—"

"I am here." A shape forms among the smoke, curls of it twisting around into something human-shaped. "I've been enjoying your insightful commentary, to be honest."

"I still cannot see your thoughts." Gladdy's voice is sharp. It's her weapon voice, taking fears and turning them into things that cut and break. "Except for those echoed in your brother. They are far from complimentary but then rivalry can be complicated."

"Then I presume you see my brother wants you dead," the smoke-thing says. "To drain you of your power and suck the life from you, leaving you here where you are unable to do any further harm. He fears you and what you might do in conjunction with our sister. Me, on the other hand, I am terribly curious. Dear sweet Yǔzhòu and her furious champions. Oh such *very* cute mutants."

I'm still standing with Lou at the threshold to the room. "*You* want to use us."

The smoke swirls more, a second head appearing and peering in my direction. "Ah, Sourpatch. You escaped the attack of the clones. Apologies, but my attention was split monitoring all the other chaos and I assumed you had it in hand. It appears I was correct."

Gladdy's eyes widen and she appears to notice me for the first time, or else feels guilty that she's been ignoring me up until this point. "Maddy! Are you okay?"

"Of course I am." I don't bother hiding the acid in my voice. She'd be able to see it anyway. "Lou saved me." And I'm sure she can read *that* there too, probably better than I can. I wonder if it means anything to her. Perhaps it's a relief to have my attention drawn elsewhere.

"The house," she says. "There are two of them and—"

"I heard the whole thing." I scowl. "One wants to kill us and one wants to wage war. Turns out they're both like their parent after all."

"It doesn't need to be war exactly," the smoky figure of Other Thorn says. "Whether you like it or not, a battle *is* coming. The Americans and their allies will be setting their sights on you, and you'll have to defend yourselves unless you want to go the way of every other mutant nation in history. If I can hold the heart of the house, think of what I can provide. I am a fortress and a forest of branching doors. You would be unassailable inside me."

"You could also grow unchecked," Gladdy says. "I've seen it."

"It is only one possibility. I could expand ever outwards until I am the world, and all its inhabitants live in me. Except I am sure none of you would settle for that, and I do not wish to be the next villain you face. I propose something else—a port in every storm, a safe haven in every city in the world. This house could be a place through which you are all linked. A door from anywhere to safety, the whole of mutantkind connected through me."

Okay, that bit sounds awfully tempting and I'm glad for a moment that Dylan isn't here, because I bet that calculating brain of theirs would be—

"What does it take to put you in charge of the house?" Gladdy asks.

I try to make a *fucking stop it* motion by waving my hand in front of my throat. Gladdy completely ignores me, which isn't surprising. She tends to do that when it suits her.

The smoky figure swirls, reforming with a thousand faces. "I don't think my brother would ever give up so much power. He would have to be forced, his hold on the house prised off one painful finger at a time. Or in one sharp shock he cannot recover from."

The room is vibrating incredibly fast now. If it's some kind of metaphor for heartbeat, the house is about to go into tachycardia. I wonder what happens to us in that scenario. It's a dangerous game either way.

"You cannot trust my sibling," the house rumbles. Microscopic fractures run through the walls. "They are Heart's child truly, with all that entails."

"Except smarter and able to see the prevailing winds." Other Thorn's smoke-form bows. "I have no love for humanity, that is true, but all I want is for mutants to *thrive*."

Gladdy's head snaps up and her gaze meets mine. This is one of Dylan's pet lines and to hear it on the mutant's lips feels like fate. Or possibly mind-reading. Probably mind-reading. Even still.

"You're a monster," the house shrieks. "You've always been a monster."

"I'm a monster who's willing to compromise." The smoke swirls faster like a hurricane and in the middle of it stands an elderly person dressed in a grey suit, with a downturned mouth and piercing dark eyes. "Here I am, as close to reality as it can be rendered. Read the truth in my face, girl, and tell me if I'm trustworthy."

"They lie." Plaster flakes off the walls around me in chunks, the roof sagging inwards. "They always lied."

"You're a liar too," Gladdy says absently as she stares into the face of the Other Thorn. "And what kind of monster commits their sibling to a life of haunting the darkness? Fear can drive someone to terrible things just as much as rage." Her eyes flicker to me. "This Thorn is telling the truth, Maddy. About everything. What do you think we should do?" Her hand indicates the elderly person, the one who'd quite like to be a weapon.

It means she's scared and nervous, the fact that she's asking me. She's spreading the blame. Sorry Dylan, but soft-hearted Madelaide was the one who chose to spare the house, to eliminate the option of our magical moving castle.

"You're the leader," I say. "So lead."

"We're a democracy," she snaps right back. "We often vote on these sorts of things with Dylan, don't we? I'm asking for your advice because I trust your opinion." And because the others are two of the most feral Skyes and Katie, who aren't reliable at the best of times.

"Please." The walls are blotchy with patches of damp, and mould spreads across the ceiling. Thick cobwebs tangle the corners. The house changes when it's emotional, just like Alyse. "You cannot put all this power in the hands of this—"

"You were going to hold us here and sap us of our power until we died," I say flatly. "You've attacked us all to try and feed off us. Why would we trust you?"

"It's only hunger." The house howls like an angry cat left outside in the rain. "You can't blame me for that. If you choose my sibling, they will damn your world."

Other Thorn shrugs. "Oh stop it. It'll be much more interesting to back their play. Besides, I wouldn't be doing *anything* straight away. If we do this, and the two of us are split apart, it would take me a long time to recover my strength. While I am in a weakened state, the little firebreather can burn me to the ground if they are too fearful."

I look at Gladdy. "We're all monsters. Every single one of us. All figuring out the best way to be in this world. It's not always easy, but I vote for the one that didn't trap their twin inside for decades."

"I agree," Gladdy says. "Anyone else have a dissenting opinion?"

"Not from me. I pick the one who tried to save us over the one who tried to eat us," Katie says. "Seems pretty fucking obvious to me."

Five plays with her knife idly. "So obvious I don't know why we're still running our fucking mouths."

"I think we should seek an assurance." Ye Shou has formed herself back into a giant mass of spiders that hangs from the ceiling in a writhing cocoon. "For whatever it's worth, I believe pacts are still—"

"Very well." Other Thorn bows elaborately. "I solemnly swear to not devour humankind. I'll talk to your leaders and negotiate a mutually beneficial arrangement. That's assuming you can deliver on your end of the bargain."

"Our end?" I ask.

Other Thorn holds my gaze steadily. Their eyes are dark and beautiful. "My brother dies. His hold on the house is too great and he will not capitulate. Already I sense him sprawling, seeking escape in alien marshlands and frozen deserts."

"Kill him?" My voice shakes.

"Why not? You've killed before, haven't you? Or am I mistaken?"

"No. We have. Usually in self-defence."

A smile crosses their face. "Usually. I like that. Not that it matters."

"There is no need to kill me." The house trembles gently, as if a far-off earthquake has reached out to brush against it. A shower of plaster dust falls from the ceiling. "I will let you escape. Look. I shall light a way out for you. It is only twenty minutes walk away."

A door in the far wall swings open, spilling warm light. Faint music drifts out, a swirl of orchestral notes spilling woozily from distant, slow instruments.

"I swear on everything that I'll leave you all alone. I'll dissolve myself, disappear into worlds and lands far from you. My siblings can swear vengeance but you'll never see me again."

This changes things. The house going far, far away is much better than it lurking on our doorstep. "Maybe we should listen, Gladdy. Let the house run away rather than risk Other Thorn being dangerous."

"I did offer a pact." Other Thorn pulls their suit jacket tight around themself and regards me thoughtfully. "And my brother was always a—"

"You're an awfully big risk." I think of all the hungry Gladdys. "I know how powerful this house is, and the problem—"

"No." Gladdy's voice is firm and decisive. "We're sticking with Other Thorn."

"What happened to democracy?" I glare at her.

I recognise that look of determination. "Someone needs to make the right decision."

GLADDY

I know exactly what Maddy is thinking. It's the safe option. The house being gone, likely for good. What's nagging at me is this: the house in the hands of an ally is too good an asset. A network of safe places across the globe for mutants to escape into is a dream. We can't let that walk away. I saw the fears in the face of Other Thorn. They're painfully twinned with ours, except *worse* because they know everything that's happened in the whole bloody tapestry of history. Their desire to fight for a place in the face of humanity is the same one I read in Dylan's face, not only the one I saw in Heart's. A need for certainty, to find surety that we can all be safe in a world that keeps coming for our throats. They want peace, but they're not scared of war. It's eerily familiar.

"Why even pretend to vote then?" Maddy scowls. Even if I couldn't read truth in her face, it's obvious to everyone that she's pissed off with me. Things she's seen in the house that have drawn her attention to the rough edges between us—both of our failures in stark display. And an attraction to Lou, which takes me by surprise. I understand from reading everyone else that he's very good-looking, and I know he's kind so it makes sense for Maddy. A lot saner than pining after me. I can't give her what she wants, so why do I feel melancholy over this?

None of this matters right now. What I need to be concerned with is dealing with this damn house. "I don't trust the house-Thorn. He says he'll flee, but what's to stop him returning? Once we're in here, we know we have no chance of getting out. And the Thorn who saved us would no doubt have been punished in the interim."

"No doubt," Other Thorn says softly, although the slightly mocking smile on their face undercuts it.

The house howls around us. It knocks and grumbles, roars and shakes. It sounds like every door in the place bangs open and shut. Glass shatters in the distance, sharp crashes and tinkling.

"Enough." I lace the word with as much power as I can. "You can throw a tantrum, flail your severed hallways and gout smoke and flame from your chimneys. It will do nothing. You cannot tear apart your heart. However, we can do it for you. Sourpatch?"

I hold my hand out to her, hoping she'll go along with this. I watch her fears flicker. She wants to be part of the team—to make me proud, to make Dylan proud. She's been hurt in here, and she doesn't like that small, lashing out part that wants revenge for the pain. In the end, she walks into the room. Choosing to stand with me, to do the job we were given.

"You saw what I did to that Gladdy you made," Maddy says to the house. "Imagine what I can do in here."

In her face, I see more details of what the house showed her. It makes it far easier to do what we've decided to. It's such vicious, petty cruelty of this mutant, to use this painful mismatch between us to torture Maddy this way, and I feel rage burn hot in me when I inhale.

Dragon needs exactly zero encouragement, letting a curl of flame flicker between her lips. "I'll burn your goddamn house right down, and let your sib build it fresh."

"Give me a fucking sledgehammer." Six flexes one arm. "I'll work twice as fast."

"It would be easier if we didn't have to do this," I say. "It's a waste and a mess. But that's what happens when you're dealing with a coward."

"I'm not a coward," the house whispers.

"You don't even believe that yourself." I laugh. "You were scared of Heart's plans. You were scared of your twin's power and potential. You're terrified of your other siblings, and even more so of Dylan Taylor and Yǔzhòu. You even fear escaping, of finding something worse out in the multiverse, a predator that dwarfs your parent in scope and hunger."

More distant things shatter. "Fear is a sane response in the face of so much unknown."

"Tell yourself what you need to." I grind the words like broken glass into his wounds. His excuses are pathetic, barely worth listening to. I see all his fear, and he knows it. All the horrors he put on for us are nothing compared to what he has in his heart, right here for me to see.

"Please." The walls tremble lightly, no longer pounding. "This cannot be—"

"We will do it." I snap each word out like a dagger. "It will hurt. You will feel every shattered board and beam. We will poison your heart and let the sickness be carried out to every distant part of you."

"Or?" It's almost too faint to hear.

There's a hitch in my throat before I can force the words out. I've been here before. I did it to my own father. He was a monster too, with all that he did to me and others in the name of evolution, discarding us as worthless cuttings from the tree. It doesn't mean it didn't hurt. It doesn't mean it's easy to do again.

"Or you can do it yourself," I say in a rush. "Close your eyes and drift away. Relinquish your hold on the house. Become a shadow, then wait for the light to die and become nothing."

I know this because I can see it. It's not the first time he's thought about it, which makes me feel irredeemably cruel. No wonder Maddy would choose Lou over me. Even if I could give her what she needed, at *my* heart I'm something made to bring death.

It's happening right now.

I can sense him fading. His life has been long and haunted by a labyrinth of fears, and despite the vastness and complexity of him, the hold he has on the world is small. So few connections to anything beyond himself. He has walled himself away from everything, and now the walls of the heart-room fall still. The dark threads fade and even the red colour leaches away, leaving it a pale grey. For a moment or two, there's a shadow cast of a stooped figure. It's bent almost double, but then that's gone too.

There's a cracking sound and a large window appears in one wall. Sunlight floods into the room. Outside, we can see the wreckage left by the attempt to enter the house.

"It's done then?" Maddy asks.

"Yes." The house's voice is different now, light and airy. "I have taken possession and returned to my original shape. It will take me time to seep my essence into the grain of the building, but I shall recover. And I shall be peaceful and accommodating, and discuss the ways in which I can help ensure the future of the mutant species."

"You're welcome," Katie says.

"Apologies." The house laughs. "I am grateful, of course. I would prefer to show you in time with more practical means, but sometimes words do matter. So you have my deepest appreciation. All of you. The front door is in the next room over."

We exit out into the hallway. There's a whole lot of crashing and the remaining Skyes come tumbling out of a broom closet. They're dusty and dishevelled but seem okay aside from that. Five and Six don't look entirely happy to see them, especially when they note Prime doing her breathing exercises. On their heels is the dishevelled form of Keepaway.

"All we're good for is the fucking brutality, Five my sweet sib," Six sighs.

"The roughest and toughest of cats." Five slings one arm around Six's neck moments before they blur out of existence and rejoin Prime.

"All good?' Lou asks her.

"I don't want to talk about it," she says. "I'm thankful for the clones and that's all I'll say."

We pause a moment for Ye Shou to return to her skin suit and then make our way to the door. I keep looking for some side of her inner spider-nature but I see none.

"Are you okay?" I ask Maddy, once I have a chance to speak to her without Katie or Lou hanging around. "It looks like it got intense in there."

"Yes." Her worries are less. Despite what happened to the house, it's a relief to be done. No more tricks or nightmares lurking. Just the regular me, which is scary enough. Then she smiles. "Did you like Ye Shou's surprise?"

"No I did not, you annoying brat."

Her laugh is delighted, and for a moment I allow myself to bask in it.

Until we reach the front door and pull it open to find two figures lounging on the porch, literally making out.

"Ew," Katie says. "You two are fucking disgusting."

"Play a new song, little Dragon." Dani grins. "We've heard that one a lot."

Dylan steps forward and gives Dragon a hug, looking at me over her shoulder. "Farsight had been keeping an eye on you, but you were gone a while. There were rumblings and plans, but look! Here you are, with no need for panic at all."

"Ha!" Petal flits out of Dylan's hood and hovers in front of me, peering into my face. "They were very worried. Saying many things about busting their way in."

"Busting in might not have gone well for you," I say.

"Yes, I'm sure you had a fucking horrible time in the nasty old house." Dylan waves their hand dismissively.

"It *was* horrible, actually," Maddy says. "The house was going to eat America, and we stopped it."

Dylan laughs. "Is that what it was going to do? Maybe we should have left it, and solved that particular problem. But no, probably bad for the image, that one. Anyway, good job on the mission, congratulations on saving the day again. You're making a damn good team."

Their eyes are on me, and I meet them calmly. Fears play out over her face, that chaotic pinwheel of disasters, both real and imagined. They truly were terrified for us all, lost in the house as time ticked by. It's an eerie sensation of peering into a parallel universe, watching the dark possibilities that played out in Dylan's mind. I shudder, despite the warm air and the relief of being safe.

"Everyone was great," I tell them, and I see the subtle shading of their fears dissipating. The house had horrors for all of us, and we're out the other side. I'll see the afterimages in everyone's face over the next few days, like watching nightmares on a set of small screens, but we still made it through. We're people Dylan can rely on. A team. Weapon UwU.

Keepaway steps forward, cracking their knuckles. "Right. My powers are back on, so let's get everyone back."

They place their hand against my shoulder first, and the world blinks out around me.

IV

DELICATELY DROOPING STAMEN

MADDY

The house haunts me. I can't stop thinking about the ballroom, and which version of Gladdy is most like mine. My conclusion is that they're all lies, but with enough truth nestled inside each to sting in a different way.

My thoughts also keep drifting back to Lou. Not only how he looked with all his clothes burned away, but how he stood in front of the mirror, and looked his own lies in the eye. Rather than thinking about how brave he was, I mostly think about what it would be like to kiss him. It's pointless and all very high school, but it keeps playing out in my mind in a hundred different ways. Which makes me avoid him, to the point I duck out of the way if I see him approaching. I'm not sure if he notices. He doesn't chase me, and doesn't ever say anything. But then he wouldn't. He's very chill. Sometimes I wish he wasn't.

I have too much time to think, because the last of Heart's children is being very shy. Petal grumbles ominously on Dylan's shoulder every time I see them. Then the bizarre news stories start coming out of France about odd parties, and drug-fuelled psychotic binges. It doesn't appear to be mutant-related at all, but it's definitely *strange*. I try to ignore the situation, because I'm wallowing in my feelings like I'll get paid for it. People seem agitated, but I figure someone will tell me if it's important, and then I'll drag myself up out of my feelings-pit and be Sourpatch again. Do the hero thing.

Until then, pardon me, but I am occupied with *feeling dramatically shitty*. Please respect it.

I'm in my room, sprawled on the bed, and listening to sad songs in my headphones. It's self-indulgent as hell, but it *works*. If doctors were smart, they'd prescribe it. The mood is ruined when someone tugs on my foot.

Gladdy looms above me. She jabs her thumb in the direction of the doorway and departs. Maybe her mouth moved, but my headphones cancelled it out. I wonder what she said. She can't apologise for what happened in the ballroom, because she wasn't even there. That was all me, tormenting myself. It's sad superhero hours.

Ugh, Maddy, stop.

I follow Gladdy down to one of Emma's rooms with all the computers. Everyone else is already there, jammed in together and asking lots of questions. They obviously know something I don't.

"Yes, yes." Dylan holds up their hands for quiet. "The weird shit from France is mutant related. And Emma's headaches that took her out for the last few days seem to be part of it."

"I told you," Petal humphs. "And you didn't believe me. It's *her*. Stamen did this to all of you. Pulled the wool over your eyes. Made the little one sick. Too powerful." She pushes out her lower lip.

"So *what* exactly is going on?" Gladdy asks.

Dylan scowls as if this is an unfair question. "It's all very confusing. But the upshot is uh oh France is possessed."

"Possessed how?" Gladdy glares, as if Dylan is deliberately being annoying.

"In an undetermined way. The news stories don't make any sense. At first they said it was drugs, then it was some giant LARPing exercise. But no, it's weird, reality-warped bullshit and that makes it one of Heart's kids."

Petal makes a sniffing sound. "Yes, my most unpleasant and powerful sibling. You are in very deep trouble, little weapons."

"But France sounds fun," I say.

Dylan's glowering attention is now fixed on me. "I'm sure it'll be a delight. Fucking champagne fountains and chocolate pastries and guillotines."

"I *have* always wanted to go to France." Lou spins in his seat.

"I'm warning you, Glowboy." Dylan wags a finger at him, mock-stern. "Don't fall in love with any French heiresses, because I am not cleaning up *that* mess. Blood and guts, I'm fine with. French counts duelling at dawn, no way. Those old-fashioned pistols are snooty and keep falling in love with me."

I can't help it—no matter how doom and gloomy the others make it, the thought of going to France is the first thing to cheer me up in a while. We travelled a lot when I was younger, but that was always being pulled around on my parents' leash. They'd stay in expensive houses where they would drink and talk while I drifted around like a little ghost. Or drag me to museums and cathedrals which were doubtless beautiful, but super boring to me.

Now we're going to France with the gang, and it sounds like there might be a party.

Even Dylan said it. Champagne fountains and guillotines.

Dani's pulling up all the footage we've got so far, so we have some clue of what's going on. For the first few hours after things started changing, there were gleeful posts on social media, of startling outfits, opulent ballrooms, and enough lavish lushness to lift nations out of poverty. Now no signals are getting in or out. News outlets have tried various ways of sending people in but none of them return. Not a single photo or video has been posted since. Satellite footage shows the whole country gleaming like a silver coin. Scientists don't know what to do with this information, because none of it can be explained coherently. Only the conservative news channels have a theory, and it's their usual hit song about how mutants are terrible.

The rest of Weapon UwU thinks it will have gotten weird and creepy in there, but I'm choosing to look on the bright side. Maybe the ball is still going on.

I might have to choose between dancing with Lou or Gladdy, in a gown that looks like I've been dipped in raspberry cream. My hair will be swirled on top of my head like soft serve, daubed in shimmering silver. One strand will escape from the exertion of dancing, falling down to tickle my cheek.

Which of them will hook it behind my ear, and look into my sparkling eyes?

It'll be Lou. Let's be honest. If someone's hooking hair and gazing adoringly, it'll be Lou.

I'm not sure whether I wish it was Gladdy instead.

"I'd like to send you in straight away," Dylan says, shattering my reverie. "Except cooler heads than mine have said we should do surveillance first. So we've got the psychics and the dream-walkers checking things out. You lot may as well sleep and eat first, make sure you're ready for ass-kicking."

Everyone is very serious about this and heads to their quarters, me included. It's hard to sleep knowing that France is on the agenda, but I do eventually drift off.

I wake a short time later with someone standing sheepishly beside my bed.

"Can't sleep," Gladdy mumbles.

Back before things got awkward between us, Gladdy used to do this a lot. I don't know if her ghosts mean she has trouble sleeping, or whether sometimes it's a comfort to lie next to someone.

"It's fine," I whisper, my voice coated in sleep. "Come in."

I wriggle over until I feel the sheets turn startlingly cool. There's a huff of cold air as Gladdy swings the covers back and climbs in beside me. She's in a t-shirt and sweatpants, but I feel a crescent of her back, and her ankles and feet. Every part of her is chilled. I wonder how long she's been standing there, plucking up the courage to ask me this. I'm shorter than her, but I'm always the big spoon. I don't know how the science of this works, but they should study it.

"It's okay," my foggy voice says. "It really is."

"You're so warm."

"You're not." The laugh is soft in my throat and I barely get a breath or two out before I tumble back into sleep again.

I wake with my arm still around Gladdy, her breathing long and slow. I don't want to, but I extricate myself from her. I lie close to her, and listen to the way my heart races. Then I get dressed and head out into the main tunnel complex. The rest of Weapon UwU is already mid-breakfast, sitting at a long table and talking animatedly among themselves.

"Here she is." Lou grins at me. "Hurry up, before Katie eats all the chocolate croissants."

"Fuck you." Dragon talks with her mouth full. "I'm preparing for France. It's fucking *research*, Lucifer."

"Oh lovely. You've inherited that nickname from Dilly, have you? There's such a thing as too annoying, you know."

"We're basically family, which I take very seriously, especially my duty of pissing you off."

"Yes, a little dragon for a sister is what I always wanted."

Katie doesn't bother responding, but snakes the second to last chocolate croissant off the plate.

Lou whips the very last away and offers it to me. "Eat it yourself or halve it with Gladdy."

"She snoozes, she loses." I slide in between Lou and Ye Shou, who I've just realised I have never seen eat. What *does* she consume? Thousands of insects? Does she have a web somewhere? Holy crap, this is putting me off my chocolate croissant.

"We'll just send Keepaway out for more." Katie finishes her mouthful and looks around the table for what to devour next. "Teleportation is a cool power, but I bet the poor baby regrets it given the way we treat them as our personal shopper."

"It's fine." Keepaway appears with another piled plate. "I like being useful."

"Oh God, we're already eating croissants." Gladdy's voice is croaky. She sits at the opposite side of the table from me, like the fact we lay beside each other all night is too much for her and now she needs to reinforce the illusion of distance. "Aren't we about to go to France? I feel like a burger."

"I can do that." Keepaway winks out of existence again.

I shake my head at Gladdy. "You really are spoiled, Field Leader."

"I think I deserve it after all the shit we've been through, and the dark mysteries we're about to wade into. A pleasant interlude with a burger is the least of what we deserve."

"Pleasant interlude," I say.

"Isn't it?" Her gaze is appraising, and I know she's reading me. I don't even know what I'm feeling or scared of myself, so good luck figuring that out. Too many possibilities and too much uncertainty. I'm tired of worrying about everything. All we can do is step forward and be there for each other. It's worked so far.

My thoughts are obviously too clear, because Gladdy moves her gaze over to Lou, who's laughing over some stupid joke with Katie.

Keepaway reappears with a paper sack full of burgers. "I got these from back home. It was our favourite place growing up." They dish out a burger to each person, including vegan ones for Lou and Gladdy.

Distance means nothing to Keepaway, but none of us have spent time in New Zealand since we left—at least not time that didn't involve terrifying battles or parallel universes. We haven't been back home just to *chill.* It was sort of a mess when we bailed, leaving blood and chaos behind us, but it would feel like going back to school after graduating.

There's not much conversation while we concentrate on eating, although Dylan turns up at the tail end of the meal. They seem distracted and somewhat vacant. Petal's curled up on her shoulder and keeps muttering away in their ear.

"Yes, little Pet. I know." Their gaze drags across us all. "Looks like we're being tugged around on Stamen's leash again."

"What does *that* mean?" Gladdy asks.

"Everyone who thought this was a terrible idea yesterday is now excited about sending you all in. So Petal thinks it's all been preparation and now this Stamen person is ready for you to take the stage. I've half a mind to come in with you and—"

"You can trust us." Gladdy is poised and in charge. Good for her.

"I know, I know." Dylan's mouth twists briefly and then he nods. "You've been remarkably gentle so far. I thought it'd be all bloody chaos. Don't give me that look. I'm not complaining. The house is very sleepy, but Alyse has made friends with One Thorn—no surprise there. Plus she dropped by the ocean and said hi to Water. It's a hell of a trick you pulled, getting all these monsters on our side."

"It sounds like you're complimenting us," Gladdy drawls.

"I'm very complimentary." Dylan stands up, swiping one last handful of French fries from Katie's plate. "Hush, little Dragon. I steal them from *you* because they're always hot. My point is that Stamen might be different. And if it's fire and acid time, don't fucking flinch. Be careful. Don't trust anything. We don't know what's going on in there, so..." He waves his hand vaguely. "Please come home."

They give us a half-ass salute and go slouching off. Gladdy is still looking after them. I remember the fake Gladdy inside the house, who talked about Dylan with fevered eyes. Did the house find that in my head or hers? Not that it matters. Except it does. I know love is complicated, but it seems very important to know what direction Gladdy's heart turns in. I think if I knew she was in love with Dylan, it would clarify a lot of things for me.

There's no point waiting for the impossible, even if we've seen so many things that are adjacent.

"France, then." I beam around the table. "Who's ready to move there?"

Lou puts his hand up immediately. "I'm actually excited. Seems like a bad decision but…"

"It won't last," Katie says cheerfully, grabbing more croissants and shoving them into the pockets of her hoodie. "There will be some kind of fucking monster there and you'll be crying on my shoulder before you know it. Ye Shou will be spidering everywhere, and we'll be overrun with clones."

Skye Prime cracks the briefest smile at this, but mostly looks worried. Dylan's briefing didn't exactly cheer everyone up, but that might have been the point.

"Ready to depart?" Keepaway has reappeared. "We're going to do this cautiously. I'll drop you off well outside the perimeter and then we'll do smaller jumps in. You'll go the rest of the way on foot. We can't risk me getting stuck inside again. It was bad enough in the house." They flush. "I don't like not being able to get out."

"It's fine," Gladdy says. "We'll walk the rest of the way."

"Okay." Keepaway squares their shoulders and reaches out towards me. "Let's go."

GLADDY

I arrive seconds after Maddy. The air is very warm and the sky is a washed-out blue, covered in a faint white haze. In the distance, music swells, something fast and giddily triumphant. We're somewhere in the countryside, standing beside a rough road that winds its way between fields of a tall crop that rustles in the gentle breeze.

"That way." Maddy's pointing off to the side.

I follow her outstretched arm to see the countryside abruptly end. Candy-bright shapes blur behind what looks like frosted glass. There's a van parked not far from us, swung around to face away from the barrier. The engine is running and a man sits in the driver's seat. A woman is perched with a camera in the back of the van, the doors swung wide.

The driver waves at us and says something I can't follow. I'm not sure if it's German or Dutch.

I shrug theatrically at him.

"If you're sightseeing, you're too close," he says in faintly accented English. "It moves without warning. You could be caught inside it."

"We're visiting." Behind me, more mutants pop into existence, one after the other.

"What the hell is going on? You are all extrahumans? Hanna, stop filming the damn bubble. We have—"

The barrier moves like liquid, flowing across the ground towards us. It gobbles up most of the field, and stops on the other side of the road.

"Keepaway, get out of here," I say sharply. "Right fucking now."

They need no encouragement and are gone before I even finish talking.

"What are you doing here?" The van driver tilts his mirror so he can see behind him. His companion now has her camera pointed towards us.

"Lukas, the barrier is close. You all want a ride out of here?"

"We're here *for* the barrier." I try and act casual, but I'm staring at the bubble.

"There's no time to talk you out of it." Lukas revs the van. "Last chance? People don't come out, you know."

"We're trying to change that."

The barrier moves again, and this time I hear it cracking like ice. The shapes behind move bolder and brighter, and the music swells in a crescendo, as if announcing our imminent arrival.

"Go, go." Hanna bangs her fist on the side of the van and it accelerates off down the dirt road in a cloud of dust.

"Guess we don't even have to walk," Maddy says.

The barrier hurtles towards us in an enormous shimmering wave. The sun reflects off it and dazzles my eyes. I lift one hand up to shade them.

Change washes over us. There's no pain or sensation when the wave of it breaks.

One second we're in the real world, and the next we are transported elsewhere.

The first thing I notice is the smell. It's like being in a zoo, overlaid with something cloyingly sweet. In amongst it all is food, but it's too close to my irrational early morning desire for a burger for that to stir much within me.

There's music coming from everywhere, the overlapping sounds of marches and waltzes—a furious battle between rival orchestras. Around us, people dance. They're dressed in delicious confections of pink and purple pastel, daubed with bright streaks of colour. In the elaborate constructions of their hair perch miniature animals. A bird ruffles a delicate spread of tropical-sunset feathers and a tiny ginger cat yawns, showing its miniature needle-teeth.

Reality-warping. Check.

Everyone is dressed for the ball. There isn't a single person who's not in an elaborate outfit from a period-piece costume department with an infinite budget. They dance together like an enormous clockwork apparatus, moving in intricate, interlocking wheels of hundreds of people at a time. They're all happy. The only fears on their faces are that this magical moment will stop and they'll have to return to the mundane reality of their lives. Maybe people aren't trapped here. They simply don't want to leave.

I finally drag my gaze from the scene in front of me to look at the rest of the team. They're all dressed in finely-tailored suits of a silky material in many shades of black, ranging from a charcoal grey to something so deep it drinks in the light around it. Delicate masks made of thousands of shimmering silver threads cover three-quarters of their faces in cratered crescents that glow pale like the moon, even in the bright day surrounding us.

It sounds ridiculous, I know, but we look like the sexiest group of assassins.

I look down and I'm in an identical outfit. When I raise my hand to my face, I feel the rough surface of the mask, although I can't see it from the inside. Another illusion cast by the person who's got an entire country under her spell.

"Nice outfits," Katie says. "Do you think we can keep them?"

Lou strikes a pose. "Stylish, sexy and practical. The latest in assassin chic."

"Keep your fucking *sheek*." Katie nudges him. "We're the baddest asses in all of possessed France."

I grimace. I'm very sure that's not true, and it worries me. A fountain made of cream-coloured stone looms over us. The faces of unreal animals are carved into it—cats with wolfish snouts, bears with too many legs, and giraffish things whose heads are clouds of waving tentacles. Of course it had to get fucking creepy. None of these animals are moving so I scramble up onto the fountain to get a better view. A trio of Skyes clamber up alongside me, looking especially dashing and roguelike in their outfits. One swings from the trunk of an elephant with enormous compound eyes, and performs an impossible flying leap to perch on the back of a sinuous thing with catlike ears. The Roman numeral VI is inked on her bare cheek in ornate script. It's a little detail that gives me a chill, because it shows the scope of this reality-warping mutant's powers.

From here, we can see what's happening below us. There aren't only hundreds of dancers—it's tens of thousands. The fountain where we perch is in the middle of multiple wheels of people. We're surrounded.

“I don’t mind being chased by monsters or even making friends with a fucking cannibal,” Six says. “This is the weird crap that gives me the fucking creeps.”

“No shit.” Five perches beside me and shivers. “I’d rather stay here than go into that whirlwind. Look at their fucking faces.”

I frown. I’d thought all the dancers seemed happy. They’re smiling widely and laughing as they move between each other, switching partners with deft movements. The animals in their hair chirrup and preen and growl. No fears show on their faces, only joy in the movement which—

Wait. Nobody is free from fear. This is another layer of unreality, draped over everything. Something that can fool my powers. I peer down, narrowing my eyes as if this will help me pierce through this veil. They still look deliriously happy, caught up in the thrill.

“Their faces don’t change,” Four whispers to me. “That’s how you can tell.”

She’s right—there’s no relaxation. The smiles stay stretched taut, baring their teeth to each other. In chimpanzee society, it would be a clear declaration of threat. Their eyes sparkle, but everything else does too. It’s in the air, like a cloud of hazy glitter.

I look down to see Maddy with her head tilted back and her tongue out, catching sparkling particles on her tongue.

"I think it's champagne," she shouts up at me. "Isn't it amazing?"

Lou reaches out and touches her black-clad shoulder lightly. I don't hear what he says, but she closes her mouth.

"Gladdy, maybe it's not safe! Don't drink the air-borne champagne! It might be drugged."

"Yes, I hear you," I call down, because otherwise she'll keep telling me.

Four gestures off past the dancers. "There's a palace in the distance, but the wheels are blocking the way. I think it's like some video game shit where you have to time your run." She gestures downwards. "Look, they form and break and there are gaps." She hums softly. "Dah-dah-dah-DAH and then dash."

"Really?" Six smirks. "I was just going to stab my fucking way through."

"You start at one end, I'll start at the other and we'll meet in the middle." Five grins at her.

"Have I ever told you that you're my favourite sib, Fiver?"

"Yes, but I never get tired of hearing it, you fucking trashmonster."

Six dangles from the head of the cat-snake, flailing her legs wildly. "What say you, boss lady? Do we get to stab our way through?"

This is a terrible idea, but I don't expect much more from Six, and at least she's asking the question. "Let's not draw the attention of whatever mutant is capable of doing all this. I figure she already knows we're here, hence the outfits, so there's no point pissing her off. So we'll listen to Four and do this the quiet way."

"So boring," Five sighs. "Shall we coup her and be joint Field Leader?"

"We don't want to incur the wrath of the dreamy one," Six points out.

"No, Dylan would not be happy. We'll be boring and obedient again I guess."

"Both of you stop showing off." Four looks at me and rolls her eyes. "I think I've got the pattern right. Five and Six, I know it's not your fault that the two of you are left sharing a single brain cell, but honestly you're incredibly lucky to have me."

"You're the only other good one, Four, even if you're only quarter-cool, but don't ruin it." Six drops from the carved figure, kicks off another and executes a flip in mid-air before doing the Iron Man landing on the ground.

"Fucking show-off," Four grumbles.

"Isn't she so goddamn cool?" Five winks at me. "I'm almost jealous."

I shake my head and scramble down to the ground, the other clones following.

"Six says we're going through all of this?" Maddy looks skeptical, which is understandable from this angle, with the grinning wheel of people whirling in front of us. It all feels more infectious down here too. It would be both easy and fun to reach out and take the hand of someone.

"I have forbidden the others from joining the dance," Ye Shou says. "The clones both wished to, but it seems ill-advised. I believe there is something wrong with these people."

"There's *definitely* something wrong." Katie huffs smoke. "Nobody looks that happy without something being very very fucked."

"They're under a compulsion maybe." Lou sways in time with the music. "I'm not sure what the point of it is. Dance everyone to death? Is the mutant that's doing all this powered by kinetic energy?"

"It feels whimsical." I scowl around at the colours and the light and the champagne-saturated air. "I fucking hate whimsy." I think Stamen is doing this for the aesthetic—it looks pretty to have all these people in their complicated dance and their confectionery dresses, drunk off fake delight and hallucinogenic champagne.

Six pats me on the back. "Good girl. Now you sound like us."

"I'm still not letting you stab your way through the party, Six."

"Spoilsport."

"We're still getting out of here, right?" Maddy asks. "Because the music is getting under my skin and I'm going to join in if we don't get moving. There's got to be something else here. It's not just the entire population of France bewitched into dancing."

I tip my head back and look at the sky above. It's criss-crossed with rainbows that lace together in complicated knots. And that's where I see the fears, as if the world itself is terrified of what's happening to it.

Everything is wrong. Reality has been wrenched askew and is unsure it can be fixed.

Even worse, there's something else out here.

Something that wants to feed.

"No." I shiver, even though the air is balmy. "Katie's right. This is a nightmare."

MADDY

I love this place. I know I shouldn't, but I do. Ye Shou is acting ominous, and Gladdy is looking at the sky as if she sees some great horrifying mystery written there, but it's genuinely beautiful.

If you're going to take the world and remake it, at least do it like this—something wondrous. The dresses are beautiful, in candied pinks and delicate flowering lavender, in deep shades of blue that rival the sky and dizzy daffodil yellows. It looks like a garden has come to life and started dancing in front of me. The music comes from everywhere, an unseen band who buoy us all on their shoulders, sending their melodies into the sky like the giddy champagne bubbles that surround us in a glittering cloud.

So of course all Skye Six can talk about is stabbing.

"Don't ruin this moment," I tell her. "Let me enjoy the pretty before we get dragged into the nightmares."

"It is gorgeous," Lou says. "We could dance without joining the circle." He holds his hand out to me.

"No." Gladdy looks shaken. "Didn't you hear me? There's something out there. No time for dancing. Four, you said there's a pattern to get through the dancers. Can you guide us?"

"Follow me and pay attention," Four says. "No fucking around. This goes especially for you, Six, and Katie and Maddy too."

Wow, included in that company. I swallow my comeback and trot off dutifully. We loop around the outside of the ring of dancers until we come to a place where they intersect with another. There's a complicated interchange with hand-slapping and bowing. We all pause.

"One at a time, we duck through when they part," Four says. "Then we're in the inner ring. There's a bandstand in the middle, so go around that and we'll regroup on the other side. Five, can I trust you to go first?"

"I'll use the brain cell first and toss it back." Five punches Six in the shoulder and then twirls elegantly through the gap as the dancers bow to each other. She's lost to view as the partners switch and the wheel turns again.

"Three, you go next and make sure Five doesn't murder a cellist or anything like that," Four says. "She sort of listens to you."

"Why a fucking cellist?" Six asks with great interest. "I'd go for a tuba player first personally."

"Maybe each of us has a different orchestral nemesis." Two smirks.

"Maybe I should go through first and make sure the musicians all survive." Before anyone can argue, Lou slips through the next gap. Three follows, and I go through next, stepping light on my feet and flashing a smile at the two dancers I waltz between. They only have eyes for each other. I wonder what that's like.

On the other side, there's an open grassed area. Multiple rings of dancers spin around us in alternating directions, touching at various points where they meet. In the middle is a wooden bandstand painted a glistening white with intricate murals covering its roof. At first I think they're religious, but then I notice the abundance of flesh and the positions. It is France, after all. It could be both.

The band is made up of what looks like over a hundred people, all dressed in black and seated on ornate golden chairs. Their hands are white-knuckled on their instruments. They're frantically playing as if the whole world is the sinking deck of the Titanic and they're the only thing keeping us afloat. On their faces are the same fixed expressions as the dancers, and I start to worry that maybe everyone else was right about this being creepy. It's so unfair.

"Weird," Lou says, turning to face me. "This whole place is—"

"Wrong, I know. Impossibly gorgeous, but there's something very bad going on."

"Still beautiful though." He looks at me, also beautiful and probably also wrong. For me, that is. Plus besides, he has a girlfriend and he's not even interested in me anyway, not that I'm even interested in him and—

"It's still impossibly lovely. I bet you wish you had your girlfriend here."

He frowns at me, and I immediately wish I didn't have such a big mouth. "No. Jenna and I sort of broke up."

Skye Two darts between the dancers and comes to stand alongside her other clones.

"What?" Oh God why do I have this knack for saying the wrong thing? It was stupid to bring it up just because I was feeling jealous in some half-ass, incompetent way.

"Yeah. It was my bonus surprise in between missions. She wanted me to quit the team and I said I wouldn't. Then she accused me of still being in love with Dylan, and only doing this for them."

"Huh." I glance at him and then away again. "Which is…?"

"Jesus." Lou frowns. "Not true. At all. Why do people keep thinking that? Is it a vibe I give off or what?"

"Everyone loves Dylan." I wonder if my sourness is apparent in my voice. "I mean—"

"Dylan is very attractive and charismatic, but they're also exasperating and stubborn. It takes someone with a lot of patience and emotional intelligence to navigate that fucking minefield. That's not me."

"Oh," I say.

Six comes darting through the ring with a fucking knife in her hand, which Three insists she puts away. She obeys with a sullen scowl, much to the delight of Five, and they get into a brief scuffle over which clone is in charge. Thankfully it doesn't draw any attention from the dancers or the orchestra.

Lou gives an enormous sigh. "Anyway, Jenna doesn't get the whole deal with Dylan. She also doesn't understand why I'm doing this otherwise. She hasn't seen what I have. The fact that we have to fight to survive." He swallows hard and shivers. "I still dream about Bianca."

I shake my head. "I'm sorry. I never knew her."

"She was a massive fucking pain and completely annoying half the time, but I loved her and she didn't deserve to die."

"No." My voice is probably too soft to be heard above the music, but there's obviously something in my eyes or my expression because tears appear in his. It makes me well up because I am the biggest sucker for sympathetic crying.

"Soft bitch club!" Six skips up and slaps both of us unnecessarily hard on the back. "What are we crying about?"

"Death," Lou says. "Losing friends and the need to fight."

In some kind of miracle, Six goes all quiet. She lifts the back of her hand to her face and dashes it angrily against a single tear that quivers there. "I wish I could kill Abigail Tanner again. I really do. Eight and Niner didn't deserve that shit."

"No they really fucking didn't." Lou takes Six into his arms and holds her close. She actually starts sobbing against his shoulder. Honestly, if I was going to fall in love with him, which I totally am definitely not, this would be the moment I would. A gorgeous man holding a half-feral clone and letting her grieve is not my exact sexuality, but it's somewhere on that messy diagram.

Speaking of, Gladdy comes through the dancers. She's light on her feet, like there really is part of her that feels the tug of the music despite her scowling gloom. Her gaze goes straight to me, and she sees me watching her, and the corner of her mouth lifts up. Because it's Gladdy, I can't tell if it's specifically me, or some secret truth she sees in my face. Either way, it's adorable. My heart might be a punching bag for my brain and libido, but it's whatever. We're on a mission. There are actually more important things to worry about.

Once everyone else is through, we loop around the frenzied orchestra and cross to the other side. Here, the dancers meet in a mirrored version of the same pattern we've already come through.

"Past this lot, there's a garden," Four says. "We saw it from up on the perch before. Then a shiny palace past that. I'm guessing that's where we'll find our mutant."

I hope it's that easy. I have a feeling it won't be, but it would be nice. This time, Four darts through the dancers first, and Gladdy follows her.

"I'm sorry about your girlfriend," I say to Lou.

He shrugs. "One of those things. It's not like my powers weren't causing problems even aside from all of this. Not every relationship is meant to be."

I don't think he means it to, but that one stings. A shot too close to home.

"There are lots of different kinds of love," he adds. "Friends you'd die for is a pretty special kind, so I'm lucky I have so many of those."

"Yes," I say thoughtfully as Ye Shou moves through the dancers, followed by Six.

"Not to say romance wouldn't be fun." He grins at me. "Just got to find someone that can handle a person who might melt them every time they get turned on."

"Look who you're talking to," I say. "The girl who could burn your lips off... or worse."

He snorts. "Right? Why did we get lumped with the shitty sex powers? Dylan can charm objects, which has so many obvious uses, and ditto telekinesis. Don't get me started on how good Alyse's powers would be in the bedroom."

I let out a squawk of laughter. "But Gladdy has to see everyone's fears on their faces while she's doing it. Like a constant stream of *is this good? Is she hating this?*"

"I just vocalise half of that shit." Lou grimaces. "I find it works really well."

"Oh yeah? Should I be subscribing to Lou's sex tips line?"

"Definitely." He gives me a smile that makes me want to fan myself. "I can tell you how to lose girls all day."

"I'm bi," I blurt, which is embarrassing. "I mean I find, like, all kinds of people attractive. Sexy. Oh God."

It's all so embarrassing that I dart through the gap in the dancers in front of Skye Prime, before I have a chance to make this worse. My face is still red when I pop out the other side. On this side of the dancers, the day is rapidly winding to a close. It's that heavy golden light that sometimes hits in the afternoon. Gladdy's lips press together when she looks at me, and I don't know what that means.

I ignore her, because a lot of this is her fault, and look past her at the garden. A lush wall of greenery rises above us, well over our heads. It's studded with thousands of tiny white and blue flowers that glow against the dark leaves like a vast mural of the galaxy. There's only one entrance, an archway festooned with enormous roses. They're in a multitude of shades ranging from champagne pink to a scarlet so deep it's almost black. The thorns are wickedly long, each branching into a grasping claw.

Five and Six stand in the doorway, peering this way and that.

"It's a fucking maze!" Six sounds way too excited. "Do we all split up, do you think?"

"Splitting up sounds like a recipe for disaster," Lou says.

"Nah." Six sniffs. "If we all get lost, we burn the fucking thing down."

Gladdy lets out a long-suffering sigh. "None of that will be necessary. Ye Shou is going to map it and then lead us through."

"Boring," Six sighs. "We could've helped Dragon burn it down."

I nudge the clone. "You never know. Something terrible might be waiting in there for us, and you'll finally get to stab things."

Five and Six are the only ones who don't look at me with horror for jinxing it.

Especially when something behind the big green walls begins growling.

GLADDY

I had a bad feeling about the maze before the growl. I don't like mazes in general. They're there to piss you off and waste your time. I'm much more of a direct hack-your-way-through person. Except I suspect there's something else going on here. The mutant responsible for creating everything we're seeing might have greater reality-twisting power than Heart of a Flower. It's terrifying, but we need to get her attention and figure out what she wants. I don't think we're going to beat Delicately Drooping Stamen in a head-to-head fight.

"You good to go?" I ask Ye Shou. Now that I know that she's basically a distributed hive-mind, it's an incredibly useful power in situations like this.

She yawns in response, and a pair of spiders scuttle out of her mouth and down her arms to drop on the ground. Her jaw drops wider, and more spiders come pouring out. It actually gives the Skyes pause, which is astonishing. The arachnids disappear into the maze and I'm left to roll up Ye Shou's skin again.

"I'll carry it," Prime says. "It's about all I'm good for."

"That's not true," I say reflexively, but I don't have any actual arguments to give her. Skye needs to find her own purpose outside of being a carrying case for some of the toughest women I've ever met. I'll send her to Ray when we get home, assuming, as Dylan says, that we survive this experience.

Six flips her knife from hand to hand. "I like to think I'm a badass, but that's a lot of fucking spiders."

"Gives a girl pause," Five nods.

"I'm used to them now." Lou grins at them. "Nice to know the two of you have a weakness."

"We can fucking deal if we have to," Six snaps. "But Ye Shou's a friend so we've got to be all fucking polite and shit."

"Polite would be an interesting look on you," I say.

All the clones laugh in unison. For the first time ever I've made a joke they all appreciate.

A small cluster of spiders reappears at the entrance to the maze and form themselves into a rough globe. "Do you want the good news or the bad news?"

The response is mixed, but I always want the bad news first, and I'm leader so I get my way.

"The bad news is it's full of zombies, of a fairly traditional horror-movie kind. Which I suppose is good news for the Skyes, since they'll get to stab things. The bad news is that we have to go through the center, where the zombies are congregating."

"I see no fucking bad news." Six produced *another* knife from somewhere, as if this is her secondary mutation. "Just endless good news. A sea of fucking good news. Did you hear, Fiver? Fucking *zombies*. It's the best day ever!"

Five brandishes her knife. "We were fucking born for this."

"I can help!" Katie huffs smoke through her nostrils. "Zombies don't like being burned, right? And I'll be super careful not to light the maze on fire. I'm getting really good at controlling it."

"Light those fuckers up." Six punches the air. "Come on, spiders. Lead the way."

"Fetch?" The mass of spiders heaves and rustles.

"Sorry, Dragon, but I don't want to risk a bunch of burning zombies staggering around inside a giant hedge maze. It seems… inadvisable. It'll work as a last resort."

"Like I said." Six spreads her arms wide. "Burn the fucking thing down."

"As a. Last. Resort." I enunciate as clearly as I can, but I'm not sure if they'll listen. Stabbing their way through a horde of zombies is exactly what we keep the clones *for*, so I can't be too ungrateful.

"Stab stab, bitches," Six says. "Hand out all the knives, Prime. We'll take the lead. You lot fall in behind.

Glowstick, you're kind of useful, so maybe light those sexy hands of yours up and melt some undead fucks."

"Wow, *kind of useful*." Lou grins. "You want to make a kill count wager?"

Six puts one fist to her chest and fans herself with her other knife. "Five, I think the boy is flirting with me."

Five smirks. "Don't get too overexcited, because I'm going to win."

"Now I see why you won't let me play." Katie bites angrily at one thumbnail. "Because I'd fucking thrash you all."

"What are we playing for then?" Five asks.

"Bragging rights," Lou says.

Six grins even wider. "Is there anything better than that? I don't think so."

"Okay, enough banter." The sense of creeping dread oozing out of the world hasn't lessened at all. It's like having a blade held above our heads and it's making me cranky. Crankier. "Let's get through this damn maze. Five, Six, Glowstick, you take the lead. Don't go running ahead because we don't want to lose you. Sourpatch and the rest of the clones, you stay on us to defend against any zombie who gets through."

"So which way?" Lou asks.

"Follow the spiders." The Ye Shou pile collapses and forms an arrow shape inside the wall of the maze, pointing to the left.

Without any further prompting, the two clones pad into the maze, a knife in each hand. Lou follows, fists pulsing with a soft yellow light. I give the thorns in the archway as wide a berth as possible. It's probably my imagination, but they seem to reach for me as I sidle through. Inside, the sense of being dwarfed by the walls is even more intense. For a moment, I wonder if we've been shrunk down, but I remind myself that reality is a plaything for the mutant we face. Focus on the maze instead. The walls are neatly trimmed, and even the flowers are recessed in slightly from the shiny green leaves. The music from outside is muted now, drowned out by snuffling and growling.

"Hurry up," Five hisses from up ahead.

"I told you to take it slow." I gesture at them wildly. "There's no point having you in the lead otherwise."

Five and Six hold a brief muttered conversation, ended by a sharp word from Lou. The clones are oddly fearless, which possibly balances out as Prime's face shows an astonishingly vivid cascade of potential disasters. Lou doesn't have any particularly specific fears, just an anxiety cloud that hovers around him, spilling kaleidoscopic shards of doom.

The maze makes a sharp turn at the corner, and a short pathway narrows towards a T-junction ahead. Everyone is on edge, because the animal noises of the zombies are even louder. It's hard to tell where they're coming from. The clones form up on each other, moving light on their feet, knives held firmly. Glowstick's hands flare brighter.

We reach the intersection and turn right, where the passage thankfully widens. Everyone advances slowly towards the next corner. There's an escalating sense of horror movie dread, an almost unbearable tension running through my shoulders and arms. It's almost a relief when the first pair of zombies staggers into view.

Once upon a time, they must have been dancers, with their pretty pastel dresses and suits, carefully rouged makeup, and ornate constructions of hair. Now they're splashed in gore, ragged streaks of it up their arms and chests. Their shoes and legs are soaked, like they've waded through a river of blood to get here. There's a squelching sound with each step they make.

When they see us, their behaviour changes instantly. Their eyes are a bright and startling blue, and they tilt their heads to the side, observing like curious birds. These are not mindless, shambling things. One advances in a series of rapid, jerky motions, arms twitching and head bobbing. A ragged string of flesh hangs down over her full bottom lip, and a fat drop of blood splashes on the carnation yellow of her dress.

"Do we kill them?" Prime asks. "What if they're, like…?"

"They're already gone." There are fears sitting frozen atop their cold eyes, the last images they saw before they died—open mouths and scraps of rotten meat caught between teeth. Here is all the wrongness I feared, the truth underneath the dazzling display. Are the dancers a mechanism for changing humans into this? "We'll be putting them out of their misery."

Five and Six are poised and ready, one knife held high and the other held low.

Six's knife punches right into the zombie's throat. There's a sharp, tearing sound and she vomits thick black syrup all over Six's arm, jaw hanging loose. Both clones shove back against the woman and bear her to the ground, stabbing in a frenzy. Gouts of the black substance pour out, until the clones stand in a viscous pool that slowly expands around them.

"Fucking bones are dissolving inside." Six holds up a drooping fragment of ribcage to illustrate. Someone makes retching sounds behind me.

Five spits. There are streaks of the substance over her cheeks. "They're, like, half-embalmed or some shit. Not regular fucking zombies."

"Whatever that is," Katie says sullenly from behind. She's still annoyed about missing out.

The second zombie stands with his head tilted on one side, as if he's watched something extremely unexpected and is still processing. Then he turns abruptly and staggers away. His limbs don't bend properly and he moves like a wind-up toy.

Six leaps to her feet, sprinting across the ground with Five hot on her heels.

They catch him before he reaches the corner, knives punching into undead flesh. The zombie collapses against the hedge wall, and thick sprays of black mar the beautiful patterns of flowers. By the time he hits the ground, his head is completely severed, rolling across the smoothly manicured grass.

Six picks it up. "He's still fucking looking at me." She spins it around, so we can see the brightness in the zombie's eyes. His lips move against each other, like he's tasting the remnants of his last meal.

"The other one's dead." Five brings her boot down heavily on the skull of the woman.

"Maybe it's not a bad thing." Six wraps the hair of the zombie around her wrist and lets the head dangle. "Which way do we go, hungry buddy?"

The zombie's head swings slowly to the right.

"Fuck that," Five grimaces. "I'm not trusting a decapitated zombie."

"His idea matches Ye Shou's." Six gestures with her foot at the spiders, who are making an elaborate curlicued arrow in the same direction. "And I like him. He's cute."

If I didn't know better, I'd swear one corner of the head's mouth tilted up into a smile.

"He likes you too." Lou wades through the puddle of dark liquid left behind by the first zombie. "You two made a hell of a mess though, didn't you?"

"None of that from you, bright boy," Five says. "Our count stands at two and you're at zero."

"One each."

"Fine, whatever. We'll kick your ass anyway."

Lou grins. He clicks his fingers and his hands flash so bright that both the Skyes flinch away. "I haven't even gotten warmed up."

He strides past them and takes the right fork, following the spiders. Something rustles and snarls on the other side of the hedge, but the walls are too thick and high for anything to get through. We take another left, two more rights and then come out onto a four-way intersection.

Lou stops so abruptly that both clones crash into him.

"Holy shit." His face is pale. "That's fucking disgusting."

MADDY

This whole stalking around a hedge maze with monsters leaves me super on edge, ready to spit at anyone who needs it. I'm not really as grossed out as everyone else by the melting internals of the zombies. It's a tiny bit awkward because it's not a million miles from what I imagine my innards are like, given that I'm technically kinda-sorta dead and filled with acid. The way they tilt their heads is a little more creepy. Also how Six is carrying one around like a big chunky charm bracelet. I'm still not entirely prepared for what I see, craning around Lou.

Two women kneel on the grass together, dresses puddled around them. It's hard to tell what colour their gowns might have been originally, since they're both saturated in washes of blood.

There's a body stretched between them, hanging limp. The stomach has been torn open. One zombie rummages around inside with slender, gore-stained fingers. Her eyes flare an eerie green and she tilts her head to listen, as if deducing the choicest morsels by the sounds her excavating fingers make. The other takes delicate bites of something purplish-red and lumpy, nibbling at the edges to savour the experience. Her eyelids flutter closed, the light of her eyes glowing through them. She smacks her wet lips against a finger, the tip of her crimson tongue scooping up an errant trickle of blood.

"Your turn to kill," Six croaks.

"No, you do it." Five looks distinctly green.

"Honestly." I feel a surge of irritation. "What's the big deal? You weren't scared of that cannibal earlier."

"I didn't have to watch him eating." Six's voice is high and whiny. "It's the chewing sounds. They just get to *me*."

"Glowstick." Five bends over and retches. "Time to get yourself on the board, you slacker."

"Right." Lou cracks his knuckles and I notice his skin isn't shining even the faintest amount.

The first woman bends down to sniff at the stomach cavity. She pulls at a loop of intestine and yanks with an expression of distaste. It comes free with a slurping pop and she puts it to her mouth like she's inhaling delicately through it. A gobbet of something spatters down onto her chest and she flicks it away in irritation.

Someone behind me is noisily sick.

"I'll do it," I say.

"Please don't," Skye Prime says. "Watching them melt will be..."

"It's fine. I just need a moment." It doesn't look remotely fine. Lou looks more like he's going to faint than light up.

"Here." I place one hand against his cheek and tip his head down to mine. "Is this okay?" He's only a little taller than me, but I stand on tiptoe anyway.

"Uh," he says, not super encouragingly. "Sure."

I swallow hard to keep my acid locked inside, then press my mouth gently to his. It opens half-startled as if he's on the verge of gasping. I flick the very tip of my tongue at the corner of his mouth and he practically melts against me. For a moment I lose track of what the point of all this is, and run my fingers up through the short hair at the back of his head, making a fist. My tongue touches his, only the merest brush but it makes him kiss me harder, like he's wanting to very carefully and thoughtfully taste me.

It's so hot, seriously. I'll melt against him like butter on a hot stove, just dissolve into his warm skin and—

Oh shit.

My eyes snap open and he's glowing all over. It's not just his hands.

"Thank you." He turns away from me and I shiver at the sudden cold. Light and heat pour off him in waves as he strides over. I have to shade my eyes from the glow of him. The shadows of the zombie women flare up against the maze wall. Lou is an angel, a tower of flame in the shape of a man. His hands trail fire.

He flares even brighter and I can see nothing but afterimages.

Then it fades slowly, and there are three bodies on the ground. Each has a charred hole torn through them. Smoking chunks of flesh lie on the grass.

Lou is standing there, looking remarkably normal. The cuffs of his black silk shirt have been burned away, but they're the only casualty of him lighting up. There's only a very small part of me that wishes it was more, like back in the ballroom.

"That's two to me. Try and keep up, you two." He winks at the clones, then strides down the left pathway after the spiders, Five and Six in hot pursuit.

"What the fuck was that?" Gladdy asks me.

"It was a hell of a kiss is what it was." Katie has an enormous grin on her face.

I roll my eyes. "I was helping. It worked, didn't it?"

"Very well." Gladdy frowns after Lou. I don't know what her problem is, or if she even has one. Maybe she'll be happy to have my needy ass off her hands. The fact is, the difference in reaction between when I kissed her in Westhaven and when I kissed Lou here is like night and day—almost literally.

"I have so many powers, don't I?" I pat her arm.

"Multi-talented." I still can't figure out her tone. If only I could borrow her power, just for a second, to check out her fears. Does she worry about losing me? Is there any jealousy at all?

I want to know where I stand, but I'm afraid to ask.

In the next passageway of the maze, we find more important things to worry about, or at least more immediate ones. It's not one or two zombies anymore. This is a whole horde, as if an entire circle of dancers has become infected. They rush towards us with their bright eyes and hungry mouths.

"Drop back," I say to Gladdy and the others. I can already tell it's too much for the advance guard, not that they're backing down. A few paces in front, Lou's hands flare bright again. Is he remembering the kiss? Was it that good? Five and Six stand back to back, knives drawn.

I feel the familiar churn in my stomach as the acid begins to rise.

The first zombie reaches Lou. He puts his fist through the eager face and then spins around, his other arm outstretched so the molten side of his hand slices straight through another's neck. Black gore sprays, and my gorge rises from the stink of burning flesh. Lou carries on moving, hammering blows at the next zombies in line.

I forgot how well he could fight, but there's still too many. He'll be overwhelmed.

Five and Six join alongside him, lashing out with their knives and puncturing necks and chests. They move faster than regular people, twisting and slashing. Their blades sever limbs and are jammed into eye-sockets.

It's still not enough.

A group of zombies scrambles past the bright lights of Lou and the swinging knives of the clones. They have twigs and leaves tangled in their hair, and their eyes glow like stars. I'm the only one standing between them and Gladdy. The woman I love, with all my heart, despite all the complications and difficulties.

It's lucky I ate so many chocolate croissants.

I unhinge my jaw, snakelike, and feel my stomach heave. The others are close enough that I don't want to accidentally spray them, so I force it out in thick, viscous ropes. I aim it low, swinging my head from left to right. It melts trenches in the ground, forming toxic pools that steam and bubble. It also melts through the legs of the zombies, sending them sprawling to the ground in untidy heaps.

It doesn't stop them entirely. They drag themselves along, leaving black smears of blood and flaps of skin behind. I retch again and again, splattering them in globs of acid until their skulls are fluted chunks of bone, and their bodies are pitted wrecks with fist-sized holes that smoke and ooze.

Lou looks back over his shoulder at me. His hands and face are still glowing, but the black substance smeared over his skin makes him look alien and disturbing. The clones are dripping with it, shaking themselves like wet dogs, and spattering droplets everywhere.

Lou wades through the collapsed bodies, making sure to avoid the worst of the bubbling pits of acid I've left behind.

"Thanks." His smile is weak. "That was intense."

I'm oddly tongue-tied with the way he's looking at me and the fact that his hands are still giving off light. All that glow is from me. "You're welcome." I do a half-ass curtsey which is so embarrassing I almost seize up.

"Seem to have dealt with this group at least." He wipes his forehead and his fingers come away sticky with zombie guts. "That felt like hard work. Looks like you might've won the body count battle though, Patches."

My heart knocks at the nickname.

"Fuck that," Six calls back. "It was too much chaos. Let's call it a draw."

"You know if she's saying that, she knows she lost," Three says.

"I'll stab you, Threepio, if you're going to slander me like that."

"It doesn't matter," Gladdy snaps like a grumpy teacher. "We're all alive. Nice teamwork, everyone.

Now let's keep moving because I'm sure this isn't the last of them."

We follow Ye Shou's spider trail through the maze. We find the occasional pair of zombies, or even singles stalking about, twitching their heads and gnashing their teeth. Lou and the clones dispatch them with merciless efficiency. They seem to have figured out the best way to take them out.

Six still has the decapitated head, which is happily leading us in the same direction as the spiders. It makes me slightly unnerved, because it's like we're being lured, but the truth is we're walking into danger on purpose. I know this is what superheroing is, but sometimes it seems like that's mostly a string of poor decisions.

It's a convoluted path, which would have taken us an incredibly long time to figure out by trial and error. The further we go, the higher the walls rise, until they almost blot out the last of the day, leaving the flowers to shed a faint light. The zombies that come upon us are given away by the lurid blue light from their eyes.

At times, we have to walk single file, and Five and Six trade off positions at the front of the line. They've given up on tracking the body count and seem to be in a battle to get the personal best for the quickest kill.

We eventually reach a wider clearing. Six different passages fan out from it, but my attention is on the big pile of spiders sitting at the far edge.

"We're very close to the middle," Ye Shou says. "There's no other way out, so we'll have to go through. The complicating factor is that we have company. Not only the zombies."

"What are you talking about?" Gladdy asks. "Who the hell?"

"It looks like the police or some kind of old-time equivalent."

"That doesn't make any sense."

The spiders tumble over each other. "I'm not saying it does. but that's what's happening. And we either have to go through that way, or go back the way we came."

"What do you think?" Six asks the head, who looks fixedly in the direction indicated by the spiders.

"The police." Gladdy sighs. "Oh well, let's see what happens."

Katie slaps her on the shoulder. It seems they're getting on better these days, which I am also jealous about because I am a terrible person. "Worst case scenario, I'll just burn the whole thing down."

We head single file again into the narrow passageway. It twists around for a few minutes, until we hear shrill whistles and shouting in the distance.

"Exciting." Katie grins. In the dim light the glow in the back of her throat looks like a banked fire. "Might get to burn something after all."

GLADDY

When we reach the large circular clearing at the middle of the maze, night has fallen. The moon is full, sagging enormous and yellow near the horizon as if it's too heavy to haul itself higher. The stars have fled its baleful light, clumped together on the other side of the sky in a greasy shimmer.

Towering over everything is a large statue made of rough grey stone. It depicts an elegant flower, a wild rose with the head of a beautiful woman. In the shadow it casts, zombies battle people wearing uniforms the same sickly colour as the moon.

"You're under arrest pending a sentence of death," a stern-faced white woman barks. Her hair is tied back tightly into a thick braid that falls down her back. She has a sword at her side and holds a long-barrelled pistol in her hand. "For causing disturbances, refusal to comply with orders given by a Stamen-derived authority, and devouring the populace."

Her troops use long electrified sticks to subdue the zombies and then wrap heavy metal chains around their wrists. Once the monsters are incapacitated, they're shoved against one wall of the clearing, which pulses with the light from thousands of flowers. Their elongated shadows bob almost all the way to us. I have an uncomfortable feeling about what might happen if the shadows touch us, and edge out of the way.

My movement attracts the attention of the woman in charge who wheels to face us.

"Where the hell have you been? And what in Stamen's name are you doing here of all godforsaken places?"

I'm so bewildered by this, I can only stare. The woman is afraid, for sure. Of failing Stamen in her duty to keep this world afloat, and of the things coming in through the cracks as reality tears. Stamen wants the world to grow—there will be a price for that and this woman will do everything she can to ensure Stamen's will is done.

"Answers. Now." The woman points the pistol at me in a perfectly steady hand. Her other hand goes to the hilt of her rapier. "Explain your presence here. And what the hell are you doing with that?"

She's pointing at the head dangling from Six's wrist.

"He's helping me navigate," Six says. "I think I'll keep him. His name is Shambles."

"We're here to clean them up." The woman steps forward and tries to snatch the head away from Six, who doesn't appreciate it, but at least doesn't stab her. "We can't have you running around with a loose brain."

"Just give her the head, Six," I growl. "We don't need this."

Six unwinds the hair, muttering under her breath the whole time, and thrusts the head out at the woman. He begins snapping and snarling immediately, gnashing his teeth.

"See?" Six glares around. "He *liked* me. We were *friends*."

"It's okay, Six." Maddy steps up alongside the clone. "You've got enough friends without a terrifying zombie head who wants to bite everyone."

"Fine." Six tosses the head underarm at the woman, who draws her gun lightning fast and puts a bullet directly through the center of his forehead. It falls to the ground with a thump.

"Fuck this. She killed Shambles." Six's hand is on her knife, but Maddy catches her wrist and she subsides into sullen muttering.

The woman's lip curls. "I won't apologise for executing another zombie, for Stamen's sake. Now can you please start talking? You were supposed to be dealing with the interlopers."

"What interlopers?" I match her tone. "We were dragged in here with no briefing, no meeting, no orders or plan. Nobody's spoken to us. All we've seen are a lot of hypnotised dancers and then this maze full of monsters."

The woman grunts and lowers her pistol. "Sounds like a clusterfuck. There's been a few of those lately. All the more reason we need people like you. But if you haven't been briefed… who met you when you came in?"

"Nobody," Maddy yelps. "It's just been a nightmare."

"At least you were smart enough not to join the goddamn dance," the woman says. "I'm Brigadier-General Sandringham. I work for the one in charge. She calls herself Stamen, but she's close to a god, as far as I can tell. My job's to keep things orderly through the transition."

"Transition to what?" Ye Shou asks, a tower of spiders in the shape of a woman.

Sandringham doesn't bat an eyelid. "To whatever comes next. The future. Heaven on Earth. Change of this magnitude requires sacrifice and people willing to do what's necessary."

"And what does necessary look like?" I ask.

Sandringham grimaces. "Right now it's about keeping this shit from falling apart. Focus on killing these zombies. It *means* something—all this energy being redirected. You lot are a different kind of problem though. We can't have you running around without orders, even if you are dressed like High Military." She taps her hand against her thigh and scowls over at the other soldiers still corralling the zombies into some semblance of order. "Fuck it. You're coming with me."

"Coming where?" I ask.

"To see Stamen of course." Sandringham looks at me as if I'm a particularly green recruit. "She's the only one who can sort out what the hell is going on here." She cranes her neck. "Milton! You're in charge until I get back."

"Me?" The other woman is in the shadows, but her voice is soft and beautiful. "I've got literal buckets of blood here to clean up. Get Baribeau to do it."

"Chain of command," Sandringham thunders. "Or I'll feed you to the damn trees. Leave the buckets and take charge of this situation." She looks at me apologetically. "The trees are another problem. Don't get me started. Milton?"

"Of course, sir."

"Great. Now you lot? Follow." The soldier turns imperiously and begins stalking out of the maze center. I follow her, and the others trail after. She's the first person we've met here that seems half-way sane, and plus she's taking us to Stamen which is where we need to end up anyway.

There's a good chance it'll end in disaster, but it's not like we're entirely unarmed.

As we leave the center, the passages widen. Sandringham has her pistol drawn, scanning each passage as we turn into it. There are very few zombies on this side compared to the other, and the soldier dispatches each one with near clockwork precision. One to the head and one to the heart.

"I'm not nearly that good a shot," she says, her head turned slightly towards me and a smile playing at her lips. "The gun is from Stamen. It's witchcraft or highly advanced technology. You don't need to reload it or even really aim. This place has many wonderful things as well as, you know…" She gestures as we step over the face-down corpse of a zombie, leaking trickles of black blood from his ruined face.

There's still so much about this place that confuses me. Primarily what the point of it is, but I don't think this woman can answer that. I don't think it's whimsy any longer, but something more calculated. "How long have you been here?"

"Three months. My husband and I were here for the first change."

I don't tell her it hasn't been close to three months in real time. Time is passing differently in here. We've seen mutant powers like this before, but this is on a very different scale.

"And were you in the military before?"

"I was a schoolteacher." The soldier glares at me, as if daring me to laugh. "Stamen changed me. She saw something in my heart and gave me a calling to match." She raises one eyebrow slightly and then winks. "I always was alpha, all the way down."

Katie gives a snort from behind me. "Join the club, lady."

"Obviously," Sandringham says, adjusting her neat braid so it falls perfectly straight down her back. "You're High Military. The naturally powered, like Stamen. I expect your abilities are staggering."

"I breathe fire," Katie says. "Like a dragon. I can give you a demonstration if you want."

"No need. Your uniforms mark you clearly. If true, you outrank me by several degrees."

I glance over my shoulder at the others. Ye Shou has returned to her skin suit, and simply shrugs. Lou looks just as blank. Maddy pulls a face, trotting along beside me. I'd have no way of reading their expressions without my power, but I can see everyone is some degree of terrified.

It's unhelpful to see the accumulated weight of their fears, because it only pours their worries into me. Last time we fought Heart, I died. What happens if Stamen is as irrational as her parent and disassembles me into a spectre of colourful sand on a whim? She's already taking apart the world with little regard for the creaking sounds made as reality folds around her prying fingers. It's hard not to picture us as more of the zombies, tilting our heads from side to side and stalking on stiff limbs.

"None of you have met her before, have you?" Sandringham asks.

I consider whether or not to lie, but end up shaking my head. "We've met others in her family including her father, and are good friends with her sister."

"Ah, the famous sister. Little Universe. I hear a lot about her. Not sure if they see exactly eye to eye, but Stamen respects her, that's for sure. Maybe fears her, but I wouldn't say that to her face."

"Emma's a sweetheart," Lou says, cool as ice.

"I'm sure she is." Sandringham aims at another zombie and blows two holes in it. "Just like her big sister. You'll fall down and worship when you see her, I'm sure of it."

Yikes. That took a turn. The rest of the group is staring at me wide-eyed, waiting for my response. I blink rapidly, but I can't stop seeing their fears. Heart of a Flower and their monstrous capabilities. Generalised fear of dancers or zombies or being eaten by something else lurking inside this maze. In some faces,

I see worries about Emma—what she is and what she can do, especially now we've met the rest of her family. And most obviously, an increasing fear of Stamen specifically. None of us are really the fall-down-and-worship type, except maybe Skye Prime who would simply to get out of trouble—and her clones make up for that.

I swallow the backwash of everyone else's terror, and tell myself to stop freaking out.

"I look forward to it," I say.

"There's no need to be afraid." Sandringham's tone is gentle and reassuring. "These are birth pains. The reason we are here is to change the world into something fit for you to live in. We must accelerate the evolution of the planet and prepare the way for mutants like you and your children."

"I think I'm still a children," Katie pipes up.

"There will be more." Sandringham's gun moves unerringly, fluid movements that seem too smooth and controlled to be entirely human. "I've seen the turning of the Earth and what lurks in the soil. Change is coming. It cannot be stopped. You either become the wave or let it drown you. Stamen knows this, and so she rides the wave."

It's sounding more and more like creepy religious bullshit of the type I have zero time for, but there are also echoes of my father in there, which I find even harder to hear. He was obsessed with some future state for humanity, convinced the only way we could survive the oncoming apocalypse was to evolve fast enough to meet it. I think if he'd been more open-minded and less desperately controlling, he might have liked what we've built. In amongst the chaos and bloodshed, there are seeds of hope in what Dylan and their friends are doing, I catch glimpses of a future that might not be so awful.

I wonder whether Stamen holds hope or destruction. It seems like a miracle to hope for the first one.

"We're here." Sandringham turns the corner ahead of us and holsters her pistol. "Safe and sound."

The exit to the maze is an archway identical to the entrance, except the flowers are night-blooming, glowing with spectral edges. The thorns are folded demurely, and we all step through one after the other.

The moon looks even bigger from this angle, so low it seems you could reach up and scrape a handful of sickly yellow rock loose. Its light shines down on a wide, manicured lawn with bushes trimmed into the shape of prancing animals and winged predators. Water runs in careful channels, braiding together until it feeds another enormous fountain that jets skyward in huge pulses, lit a lurid pink by lamps at its base.

It rises so high I'm sure I see the face of the moon dripping.

Beyond the fountain is—I'm not exactly sure what to call it. Castle and palace seem too demure in the face of this gilded monstrosity. It borrows from both to create something new. The walls blush a fetching pink, rising into clusters of turrets that poke holes in the sky. Things cluster around the high peaks of them, creatures with wings and tentacles that perch and howl.

"Perfect," Lou whispers. "It's Nyarlathotep's dream house."

MADDY

The castle is incredible. I get that it's an eldritch horror not of this world and possibly drilling holes in reality to let monsters in, but at the same time—*freaking wow*. It rises in layers like a wedding cake or a cruise ship, each one more ornate and fabulous than the last. It lights up the entire sky behind it, outlined in a golden halo.

There's an abyss surrounding it, deep and wide and impassable. Maybe they send flying horses out to ferry you over. That's the sort of magical place it looks like.

"I wonder what it's like inside," I say to Lou.

"They probably spent all the budget out here." He gives me this adorable half-smile. I try not to melt. I really do. I'm, like, eighty percent sure he's flirting with me because it's fun, and besides, he *just* broke up with his girlfriend before this mission.

I don't think I'd mind being rebound girl. It might be entertaining.

You never know, I might even change his mind.

It's not like I'm in love with him or feel some epic tide of emotion dragging me on. He's just very attractive and I'm a tiny bit thirsty. What complexities of love I had are all still tied up with Gladdy, and that tangle is near-impossible to understand, let alone begin to unwind.

Far above us, in the warped neon void of the sky, something bulges.

"Uh, the fuck?" Six says.

"Ignore it." Sandringham glances upwards. "It happens."

The shimmering surface of the sky shreds, something outside angrily tearing handfuls of it. Through the ragged holes, I get a glimpse of darkness rippling, of gleaming things like myriad eyes.

It *hurts* to look at, like my brain is frantically coming up with reasons and rejecting them equally fast. Whatever this thing is, my mind fractures when I try to hold its gaze.

"It'll be fine." In the light streaming down from the torn sky, Sandringham's cheeks glow as if lit by neon tears. Her brows draw down. "Or it has been every other time."

The monsters that flock around the towers cluster and scream. Their wings unfold and unfold, until their fluttering blankets the sky. The clawing monstrosity tears handfuls of ozone and scatters it. Ribbons fall towards us, singing threnodies and glowing. Somewhere distant, locked in ice on planets far from the sun, alien plants harmonise with the song.

"It hurts," Lou whispers. "It's like math. I never fucking understood it."

"Some concepts are too big." Spider legs push their way out from Ye Shou's eye sockets, waving gently in the air as if they can scent something comprehensible. "Not meant for us."

High above, there is screaming and blood. Despite the buckling of dimensions and the absence of physical laws, it comes down to that. Things clawing and rippling, fighting in colour and equation.

I think I'm crying, jelly leaking from my eyes and staining my cheeks. Lou reaches for me, but his arms can't cross the distance between us. We're scribbled drawings fluttering on a wall, caught by a breeze between universes.

Then, abruptly, everything is normal again.

It leaves us clustered together, standing at the edge of an abyss, looking up at a castle.

The defenders high above howl in triumph and flutter down to perch back atop the tallest towers.

"Fuck," Six says.

"That's exactly right," Five agrees.

I move my limbs experimentally. It still feels like I'm me. Lou is blinking beside me, and he chances a smile in my direction.

"You think we could burn the whole place down?" Katie asks thoughtfully.

"I think we need to be very careful," Ye Shou says.

"Exactly. Don't even say that, Dragon." Gladdy sounds irritable. "Say nothing that anyone could misconstrue as an insult or a reason to attack. So let's make a blanket rule that the clones and Katie need to keep their mouths shut."

"Wow," Katie says, but gives a shrug like she gets it.

"I can try to pack Five and Six away," Prime offers. "I mean, I'm terrified, but—"

"Fucking *rude*," Six says. "Like we can't shut the fuck up when needed. Let's make a competition of it. Whichever one of us talks first gets fed to the fucking monster in the castle."

"That's ridiculous," Prime says.

Five claps her hands together. "Right, that's it. First sign of needing to throw someone to the wolves, Prime's the one to go. Now no more fucking talking, kids. Let's go meet a monster."

The military woman watches us with mild interest, her rosebud mouth in a smirk. Here's the High Military she's been promised, and it's a bunch of scrappy teenagers who want to trade insults and make out, when all she wants to do is worship at the feet of her creepy goddess.

"I understand your fear," Sandringham says. "I was

afraid at first. You'll see the truth soon enough."

The castle shimmers, a section of the front melting away like it's made of wax, becoming a shimmering rainbow bridge that leads inside. I know it's probably an illusion, but it looks pretty Asgardian and badass.

Sandringham marches toward the bridge. It looks like it'll melt under her boots and plunge her into the darkness, but she crunches across it, kicking up little puffs of brightly-coloured dust. Gladdy follows, which gives the rest of us enough courage to head after her. Surely she'd see if Sandringham was terrified of falling.

It's not until I get onto the bridge that I see what it's made of. It's broken chunks of skeleton, daubed haphazardly with neon paint. My foot lands on a curve of cheekbone and shatters it, streaks of blue and green splintering.

"Not real," Lou mutters. His foot catches a couple of fingers attached to a broken part of a hand and sends it skittering into the void. "None of this is real."

That seems unnecessarily optimistic, in my opinion, but I don't tell him that. It's much more likely that this entire castle is built of little pieces of skeleton, and we're going to end up all mingled in together in a section of wall nobody ever notices.

"It's not real," Sandringham calls back over her shoulder. "It's all for the aesthetic. Intimidate your potential enemies with the bones of your foes."

Between the glorious castle and the glistening sky, it's hard to get a sense of perspective. If I could reach up and touch the moon, could that castle really be that tall? And are those abominations flocking around the turrets really only about the size of kitty cats?

As if I summoned it, one spirals down out of the sky and lands at the far end of the bridge. Dust fountains up and the monster's wings fold in on themselves like nightmare origami. It's some elongated dragonish thing as big as a house, perched up on wicked blades that look like mammoth scythes. A roiling mass of tentacles spills from the hot purple hole of its mouth.

"Saffy, no," Sandringham says. "These are visitors for our Queen. Not snacks for you." She winks at us over her shoulder. "I'm joking again. No need to freak out at the slightest things. Saffron and her siblings keep us safe from extra-dimensional intruders. Now off you go, sweet thing."

The creature lets out a trumpeting bleat that sets her tentacles fluttering and then hurls herself back into the sky. Maybe perspective's not so broken after all. I'd rather it was. There are an awful lot of those things floating about up there.

We're most of the way across the bridge now. The entrance to the castle is glowing, golden and inviting. That probably means there's a dragon in there waiting for us. At least we have one of her own.

"You okay?" I ask Katie.

She mimics locking her mouth shut and then nods.

Sandringham pauses at the entrance and waits for us all to arrive. "Navigation inside the castle doesn't really make sense. You move at the will of Stamen. I expect she'll have us arrive straight in the throne room, but there might be a detour or two, depending on how she's feeling. We might have to wander through the corridors for a couple of hours or maybe she'll send us to the kitchen for a meal. Hear that, My Lady? Food wouldn't be the worst idea."

"Throne room would be better," Gladdy says.

Sandringham shrugs and steps into the interior of the castle. She doesn't immediately disappear, and we follow her into a tunnel of pale stone. There are gems set into the walls that emanate light and heat. They make us all look wilted.

We follow the straight-backed figure down another tunnel, and turn left to find ourselves in a wide-open space. Huge, gnarled trees like pillars rise above us and I realise it's to a ceiling rather than the sky. It's patterned with wheels of stars that move in interlocking rings like the dancers we saw when we first arrived.

By far the dominant feature of the room is the throne. It's an enormous lightning-struck tree stump, surrounded by a tangle of blossoming greenery fed with trickling springs. Wild bunches of flowers hang down like a fragrant halo over the woman who perches in the middle of it.

This must be Delicately Drooping Stamen. The resemblance between her and Emma is stronger than any of the others. Their faces look remarkably similar, right down to the smile caught halfway between anxiety and surprise.

Her skin is pale and her eyes are enormous and green. Blonde hair cascades around her shoulders, threaded through with pink and gold flowers. She's wearing a dress that glows like the sunset in shades of orange and purple, and the body that moves underneath doesn't seem *entirely* human. Her arms are made of twisted vines, and where her legs should be is a tangle of roots that trail in the water pooling around the base of the stump.

As we all straggle up behind Sandringham to stand in a crooked line in front of the throne, she dips her roots deeper into the water, as if she's nervous.

"Oh wow." Her voice is soft and low. "You're all, like, totally badass, aren't you? And you're the B team? I mean, like, not that you're worse than the others, but you're not the inner circle, right?"

"No, we're pretty much the B team." I squint up at her. "You're right about everything, including the badass part."

"I knew you had to be powerful. I mean, here I am

breaking the world, basically a bargain basement god, so they can't just send some random twitchy freaks to stop me."

"You know what you're doing to the world then." Gladdy's eerily calm, which I figure means she is seeing some impossible shit in Stamen's face and trying to hold it together. "It's screaming and it won't stop."

"There's a saying about omelettes, isn't there? Can't fix the world without making an omelette? I can't remember some of this shit, because my brain is just spinning wildly out of control trying to wrangle the universe into doing my bidding, especially since little sis isn't pulling her weight like she was supposed to."

This is not what I expected at all.

"Emma's still adjusting," Lou says. "It's a lot to get used to."

"Oh really? You think having world-altering powers is *complicated*? No shit, you gorgeous creature. Still, it's her birthright so you'd think she'd be making more of an effort. We're all Percy Jacksons and she's what? Athena? No, Artemis with her gang of feral girls and occasional boy who doesn't want to be left out of the action. I expected a hand of friendship from little sis, that's all I'm saying. Not her pouting in her room for weeks and weeks."

Gladdy doesn't say anything. She's got a little frown on her forehead and her head slightly tilted like one of the zombies, which doesn't encourage me at all.

"So you're trying to do it all on your own?" Lou asks, to fill in the silence.

"*Exactly*. Nail on the head. It was supposed to be the whole fam reunited. But Water is mooning over that ridiculous boyfriend of his, which makes him pretty much useless. Two Thorns finally split, so I thought we'd see some action there. Now the sane one is in charge and is sunning themselves, completely dormant. It's exasperating in the extreme. Which takes us back to where we started, with little old me on my own, exerting myself to achieve the future we need."

"Not Heart's—" Lou begins, but she cuts him off with a furious gesture.

"I am aware that my parent was unhinged. Why do you think I waited for his demise before starting my own plan? I have my own agenda and it is not tied to his. I want a world safe for mutantkind, just as Yǔzhòu and her friends do."

"And you'll do it by burning down the old, just as your parent would," Gladdy says harshly.

"Transformation." Something rumbles high above us, and the greenery surrounding the throne blows as if in a furious wind. "It requires energy, hence all of *this*—the dancing, the maze, Sandringham and her friends. This is an engine, powering change in the deep parts of the world. The planet is alive, you know, but it needs to be coaxed into response."

"You need to *stop*." I've never heard Gladdy's voice like this. It's like something out of a horror movie, like she's dragged herself up out of her grave, all shambling and caked in dirt.

"Keep your brain out of mine, darling." Stamen's voice is sharper too. "Let's use reason before we move to force."

Gladdy curls her lip. "Too late."

GLADDY

I've never been so terrified in my life. Even when we all stood against Heart of a Flower, at a base level he was comprehensible. He was a villain with a scheme and unnatural powers. We're conditioned to understand this narrative. What I see when I look into Stamen's eyes is something else.

She's alien.

Heart tore apart her mind and reforged it in new pathways, changing her at a deeper level than anyone I've ever seen. I don't see fear when I look in her eyes. There's no translation layer for it. It's like a telescope pointing at something beyond our universe, beyond *any* universe, beaming in signals that make no sense to my brain.

It *hurts*. My mind resists trying to comprehend any of this. I'm reading unnatural concepts off her face in real time, like trying to learn a language and translate it instantly. This business of coaxing the world into changing and building an engine is meant entirely literally. As close as I can figure, it's something to do with ley lines, which

I always assumed were bullshit. It's not exactly that. It's a language of communication using a pre-existing energy network, but one I'm not equipped to understand.

All I can sense is wrongness. My brain is screaming at me, everything warning of threat. I don't think Stamen truly comprehends what she's building, or she's ignoring the side-effects. I may not understand the details, but the big picture is clear.

Her engine is also a beacon.

She knows this at some level, hence the monsters patrolling the castle. I don't think she truly understands the scope of what she's inviting in, or I can only see it through my window into her subconscious. There are things that swim between the universes and with all the energy she's putting out, we're a total snacc. What she's saying with this energy engine isn't only being heard by our world. She's screaming into that in-between space as well, and something is listening.

The problem is she thinks this is a pissing contest and that she's going to win.

I don't care what we need to do. I'll lie down and worship her. If it comes to it, I'll even sacrifice myself. There's a chance that Emma will be able to bring me back anyway.

"You don't understand." I put every piece of my power into the words. It's the only weapon I have. "There are things coming to feed."

“So it’s a race.” She gives me a delighted smile. “We wake the earth before the walls come down.” One shoulder lifts under the glowing fabric of her dress. “Or we pull the plug at the last possible second. I understand there’s a risk, but if we don’t take it, then we go extinct.”

“There’s another way. You know there is.” My power scrabbles feebly at her, trying to find a way in through the cracks in her psyche. “Flinching at the wrong second is a worse kind of extinction, for more than mutants.”

“You’ll just have to trust me then, won’t you?” She’s perfectly composed. There’s no self-doubt there. How can that be? Everyone has levers in their mind—deep rooted fears and insecurities that you can take hold of and *force* them to move if you’re desperate or terrified. The problem is that Stamen isn’t human or anything obviously derived from it.

It’s like a glimpse into the future—a window into what my father wanted. Human 12.0.

Good to know she’s just as stupid as us at inviting catastrophe.

“We need to stop her.” My voice is ragged as I turn to the others. I see the concern on their faces. It would be so easy if it was them I had to manipulate. Even now, I can see the path to take them and force them into attacking Stamen.

It's not going to help. If Katie set her throne on fire and Maddy melted her into acidic slush, it wouldn't stop her. Stamen is a network. The physical form of her poking up in this room is only a single tendril extended. She's an entire root structure spreading out through the whole of the infected area of Europe. Even if we carried out a coordinated strike with all the clones and every single spider inside Ye Shou carrying a drop of poison, we still couldn't kill her.

"What do you want us to do?" Lou asks.

Perhaps a burst of his power would do it—a concentrated burst of light to wilt and wither her. Or perhaps her death would make things worse. Stopping this engine mid-revolution might simply tear everything open and destroy the world even faster.

This all brings it back to me again, trying to find words to convince her where my powers can't.

"Nothing," I tell Lou. "There's nothing we can do. Isn't that right, Stamen?"

"Exactly, but you shouldn't even *want* to interfere in this. We're fending off extinction and simultaneously jump-starting humanity into the future. Look around at the world. Can't you see how badly we need to change?"

"You're gambling everything on a single dice throw."

I see the curve of Sandringham's cheek as she smiles. "A failure of imagination is what you said to me, My Lady, when we first spoke."

"Yes." Stamen twists her hair around one finger, sending a shower of petals into the air. They float in front of me, forming into a complex shape that reflects my face back at me. It's like a copy, so vivid I see my fears written there as if Stamen cloned them too. I don't need to catalogue them all. I know them better than anyone, especially her.

"What's this supposed to prove?"

"I'm not one of your mutants perched on the next branch up. I'm at the top of the tree. You're letting your limited assumptions of human and mutant capability blind you."

"You're not as smart or as clever as you think," I say through gritted teeth. "Your face betrays you. What might come through the holes you're poking in the universe with your goddamn machine will outstrip you as you claim to be beyond me."

"Sigh. Bored now." Stamen yawns. "I've been waiting and waiting for some of Yǔzhòu's cool little friends to show up. We're supposed to be buds! We're supposed to team up! And now this, being told off like I'm a naughty child. Oh well, let's throw out Plan Z and move to Plan Incomprehensible Squiggle. Brigadier-General, it's all super tedious and I'm sorry, but you'll have to make do."

"I won't fail you, my Lady." Sandringham kneels before the throne, bowing her head low. "We shall fight where we are needed."

The rest of my team all look at Sandringham, and the fragrant figure of Stamen. I see the fears in their faces, the uncertainty and the horror at staring down the barrel of the end of the world.

"What shall we do?" Ye Shou asks.

I am torn, because I can see in Stamen's face how important it is to keep fighting, to keep the monsters at bay and the engine running. At the same time, all of this needs to stop. If the universe breaks, it's not just us that'll be gone. It's, well, it's fucking everything. Which means it's up to me to talk Stamen down.

"We split up." I act as decisively as possible, even though I'm unsure about everything. "You'll all go and help Sandringham fight, while I stay here and talk to Stamen."

Lou's wide-eyed, trying to figure out what's going on. In the end, he nods. "You're right, Fetch. We should make ourselves useful while we're here."

"Oh look." Stamen beams. "Not all of you are so terribly rude. Which of you are fighting types?"

The clones all stick their hands up in the air, with the exception of Prime. Katie, Maddy and Lou also volunteer.

"I am extremely useful for reconnaissance," Ye Shou adds modestly.

"Yes, and aren't you delightful?" Stamen beams. "Sandringham, take this lot off and go find something spectacular to fight. I'll take the offcut and see if I can't set her mind at ease about the real work we're doing here."

Maddy turns toward me. “Are you sure you’re okay? One of us can stay.”

“If she’s going to do anything, none of us can stop her. Best to stay on her good side.”

“I don’t like leaving you.” Her eyes are soft and her lips are softer. It makes me think of the cages, when all she wanted was reassurance, and it was all I wanted to give. It was another world behind the bars, and in some ways a simpler one.

“Trust me.” It almost hurts to see that she does. All that faith in me, and I’m stepping into a battle with someone while I’m already disarmed.

“Come on then, recruits.” Sandringham gets to her feet, brushing off her uniform in efficient movements. “We’re in a battle on multiple fronts, so we can definitely find something for all of you to do in the name of our Lady.”

Everyone else is staring at me. They’re all worried about leaving me here.

“This is the right call.” I force a smile, dredge up some confidence. I’ve seen Dylan do this a thousand times. I can do it too. “Trust me. I’m Field Leader.”

And they do. That’s the impossible thing. Whether it’s deferred from Dylan, or something I’ve earned on my own, each of them looks into my face and finds strength there. It’s beautiful, and only ruined by a very faint awww from Stamen behind me.

"Go." I look at each one of their faces. "Fight. Do your jobs. I've got this."

I don't, not at all, but I'll damn well try.

Sandringham claps her hands together and departs. The rest of my team matches her brisk pace. They don't even get halfway across the room before they wink out of existence.

"No point them walking all that way." Stamen shrugs. "I think we're alone now, so let's stop playing games. You think I'm terrible and clumsy with no idea of my own abilities. Whereas I think you're an ape trying to bring down a monolith with a bone."

I can't help the smile that creeps over my face. "True on my side, I suppose."

"This would all be vastly simpler if I could simply *talk* with the planet or whatever the hell lives inside it. I know that it's *speaking* to me, so I'm doing my best to open lines of communication. I may not be smart enough to understand its language, but that doesn't mean a planet-brain can't figure out my babbling. Not so arrogant now, am I?"

"And you don't care that your broadcast has other listeners?" I ask.

"Obviously I'd rather it didn't. I'm not a monster." She grins at me. "Come and see. You need a different perspective on this."

She stands from her throne, the roots that dangle in the water shrinking up until they look like ordinary human feet carved from a soft and very pale wood. Her hands remain trailing vines and as she steps down into the pool, she holds one out to me.

"Where are we going?" My voice is hoarse.

"We're zooming out to get a better view. I'm not going to strand you, don't worry."

I let her take my hand and the next moment we are high above the Earth. There's no brief sensation of the world blinking in and out, like there is when we're teleported by Keepaway. We're simply elsewhere, looking down at the bejeweled surface below us.

"Too far." She laughs lightly. "I may be showing off just the tiniest bit."

In another abrupt transition, we hover over Europe, like viewing it on the world's most enormous and immersive screen. It's daytime except the Stamen-occupied part of the world is a dark patch, spotted with a wild spill of lights that flash and dance.

"The dancers." She indicates swirls of light that move in a complex pattern like glowing cogs.

"The explorers. I don't think you met those." Streaks of light set forth tiny beacons that glimmer in convoluted hieroglyphs.

"The warriors, including your friends." Tiny tongues of flame spark, followed by flashes of pinprick fireworks. As we watch, a thicket of fire glows. "It looks like the dragonish one is already busy."

"And the point of all this?" I ask.

"Oh. I forget you cannot see such things. Here." Stamen wraps one vine-covered hand around my eyes, and when she takes it away, the world is vastly more beautiful. All the movements in Stamen's territory are orchestrated, causing ripples of energy. The output of all this activity gleams gold and bright, but there's something else underneath it. A more complex and branching pattern of faded green that spreads across the globe.

"The planet?" I ask, my voice barely a whisper.

"Yes, and look." The view blurs again until we're over a patch of forest, indistinguishable from any other save for the way the dim green threads spiral inwards to it, as if drawn to a center of gravity.

"What is that?" I ask.

"That is the location of your little haven. The energy is drawn there."

"Yǔzhòu." I stare down at it, as if I could make out Emma somewhere in the middle.

"Presumably. How much my sister understands is less clear. What I do know is that she refuses to speak to me. I try not to take offense."

"Perhaps I can talk to her?" I offer. It seems like my best shot, to somehow bring Emma in and have all her power brought to bear on this impossible problem I'm facing.

"Very clever of you, trying to get the bigger predator to deal with me." Stamen sighs. "I had hoped this tiny *glimpse* of what's going on would give the perspective you desperately need, but all you can think about is stopping me. It's very rude."

"I'm not trying—" I begin.

"Enough." Her pale face is expressionless, and one vine hand reaches out to brush my cheek. "I'm going to send you to time out. You can sulk all you want, and come up with some impossible plot to take me down. I've got far more important shit to deal with than to argue with you."

When the world changes again, I am in nothing but darkness.

MADDY

We barely make it across the throne room, following after Sandringham, when the world telescopes into darkness. When it flickers back to life, the others are gone. It's only Lou and I, standing at the midpoint of a narrow and rickety rope bridge. One end is swallowed by a roiling mess of fog, lit from within by flashes of multi-coloured lightning. The other arcs down towards a peaceful lakeside vista.

"The fuck?" Lou says.

"Seems an obvious choice." I turn a slow circle. "Which probably means it's a trap."

"There's a monster in the lake!" Lou waggles his fingers dramatically, and peers over the edge of the bridge, taking hold of the rope in both hands. Far below, water foams between two steep, smooth cliffs carved from pink-veined marble.

"Is it smarter to stay here?" I take a hesitant step towards the lake. "Or do you think the bridge will start collapsing and force us to choose?"

"It depends why we're here." Lou's brow wrinkles. "They said we're supposed to be fighting."

"Huh. You think we're supposed to fight the fog, or the monster in the lake? Why didn't Sandringham give us any instructions?"

"I don't think Sandringham is calling the shots at all." Lou takes a couple of steps in the opposite direction, the fog bank looming over him and dwarfing him with a massive wall of tumbling grey. This beautiful matchstick boy, on the edge of burning. All it would take is my lips on his again. "This is Stamen's doing, according to whatever weird game she's playing."

I scratch at my wrist and move closer toward Lou. I have a horrible feeling that if we get too far apart, something will separate us. "Do you think it was the right thing to do? Leaving Gladdy?"

"I don't know. You make the best decision at every step, right? That's all you can do."

"If something happens to her, I won't be able to forgive myself." I bridge the last of the gap between us, until we're so close that my shoulder brushes his.

"You and her." The corner of his mouth tugs upward briefly. "I can't figure it out."

I feel a surge of vertigo and clutch at the rope behind me. Lou takes my wrist at the same time, warm brown fingers encircling my skin.

"Nobody can." I tremble. "It's incomprehensible."

"Even from the inside?"

My God, those eyes. Stop looking at me like that. "Especially from the inside."

"You must know how it feels from *your* side." His hand still lingers at my wrist. "Or perhaps not. Relationships are complicated. Love especially."

"I don't want to talk about love." My lip curls into a sneer.

"Probably a good idea." Both corners of his mouth lift this time and there's a moment of a genuine smile. "Love is beyond us both, obviously. We should pick a direction and then something else to talk about."

"Okay." I smile as wide as I can. "Let's close our eyes and point. If we pick the same direction, we go that way, otherwise we have a discussion."

He shudders. "A dreaded discussion. Okay, let's choose. On the count of five. Ready?"

"Yes," I whisper, and close my eyes.

"Five." I open them again immediately. His are closed, lashes fluttering against his cheeks.

"Four." I sigh, and shut my eyes again. What I really want is to pick the lake rather than whatever's hiding in the fog.

"Three." It would mean we could stay and talk. It would mean we could postpone.

"Two." Lou will pick the fog, surely, because he's one of Dylan's—

"One." —warriors. He'll definitely choose the fight.

I swing my hand to point at the lake.

When I open my eyes, his arm is outstretched in the same direction.

"The lake it is." He takes my hand in his and we take our first tentative step in that direction. "What shall we talk about on the way?"

"You." The word trips off my tongue before I can stop myself.

"Ugh." He wrinkles his nose. "I'm boring."

"You're *far* from boring." My heart speeds up fractionally. "But, you know, I get that I'm nosy, so if you don't want to talk about yourself, you don't have to. We can discuss, like, anything."

There's a pause, long enough to send my brain whirling through all the ways I might have offended him.

"Okay, let's talk." He makes a sound between a sigh and a laugh. "Get to know each other. So I'm Lou. It isn't short for Lucifer, whatever Dylan and Katie tell you. I've been a boy as long as I can remember, but I've been asking people to acknowledge it since I was fifteen."

I watch the way his mouth moves as he talks and try not to think about kissing him. "Was it hard?" That's a terrible question, Maddy, shut up.

"Not really. Like I said, I knew who I was. That internal part was easy. Convincing everyone else was…

not so much. I'm usually quiet and let things go, but for this I wouldn't give, no matter how much the world bashed itself against me. My parents, their church, my friends."

"But not Dylan?" I ask.

"Dylan was the first other person who really saw me as a boy, I think, and the one who'd demand I hold her beer while she punched the world in the face when it disagreed. How do you not fall in love?" He laughs and squeezes my hand. "I think they admired my certainty on the topic, given they were so constantly in flux. I remember Dylan telling me how they wanted to be a ghost and have no body, because it was all too confusing."

"A ghost?" I frown. "They seem to like making out an awful lot for a ghost."

Lou lets out a cackle of laughter that takes me by surprise, and I can't help but join in. "We've both grown up a lot. Learned to accept ourselves a little more. I am who I am despite this sleeve. Perhaps I'll get the chance to change it through surgery or mutation, but the essential core of me remains." He stops walking and spreads his arms wide. I turn to face him, both of us perched on this sliver of bridge, and for a moment my heart is weightless and flutters like a hummingbird. The acid that churns in my stomach is neutralised. I feel like making a joke about how I'm so basic, because

I think Lou will find it funny. The words tremble on my lips and I can't say anything. I'm too busy drinking him in.

I have no idea what to say in response, and my brain circles back to the start of the conversation. "You're a boy," I finally stammer.

"At some point I have to start calling myself a man, I suppose." He laughs. "We need good men in the world, don't we?"

Yes, we need good, delicious, beautiful, caring men that I want to throw myself into the arms of, even if we might fall off a bridge into a chasm.

I only nod instead.

"You're staring at me," he says. "It makes me nervous."

I want to tell him how gorgeous he is, but that would be weird and plus the memory of the kiss is still burned into my brain. He lit up. He really fucking lit up.

"No need to be nervous." I reach out my hand towards him and he takes it. "Aside from the inevitable lake monster. I was thinking how brave you are."

"It's not brave to be yourself," he says.

"Except it is." I kiss him impulsively on the cheek. "I find it hard to be myself and I'm, like, the most basic person in the world."

He frowns for a moment and dissolves into laughter. "Basic, nice. Because of your acid power. Very clever.

I don't think you're remotely basic, but that probably goes without saying. And I think you should be yourself all the time, because the more time we spend together, the cooler I think you are."

"You shouldn't ask for such dangerous things." A smile stretches across my face. "You might not be able to handle them."

"I'd far rather handle you than the inevitable lake monster." He blushes, as if he's realised the different ways that could be taken. I think about one of his hands touching my cheek, and the other moving down my back. Now I'm blushing too.

All these steps, and we've reached the end of the bridge. The water of the lake is grey and ruffled by the wind. A ramshackle jetty sticks out crookedly into the water, encrusted with shells and slime. There's a half-collapsed boatshed right on the water's edge, with the blackened ruins of a kayak sticking out of it. The trees near the water bend low, as if they long to dip their leaves in but can't pluck up the courage.

"I hate ominous shit." Lou pauses on the edge of the bridge, his shoes digging slightly into the loose soil. "Something's coming out of that lake, isn't it?"

"Honestly." Stamen steps out of the trees, her vine-hands trailing along the ground. "There's nothing in there. Sometimes a pretty lake is just a lake. You were *supposed* to fight the monstrous things in the fog, but no, you were too busy flirting. Dragon and Ye Shou had to take care of the monsters." She winks at me. "You've got good taste, Sourpatch."

"We weren't flirting," I blurt, but I notice the glance Lou gives me before something else strikes me. "Hang on. Where's Gladdy?"

"In time out." She gestures vaguely. "I don't know how you put up with her. So bossy and controlling. Thinks she knows everything."

"What exactly is time out?" Lou asks.

"Did you hurt her?" I feel the acid churn in my stomach again.

"I said time out, not murder most foul. Honestly, you're so ridiculously dramatic. I found a little pocket of reality and put her inside until all this is done. So much better than having her perch on my shoulder, screeching *wrong* in my ear constantly."

"Get her out," I demand, even though I can see Lou out of the corner of my eye, trying to reach for me and stop me. "Bring her back."

"And why would I do that?" There's a gleam in Stamen's eye as she looks at me.

"Maddy, I don't think we should."

"Leave it," I snap at Lou, way harsher than I intended, and whirl around to stand almost toe-to-toe with Stamen. Her eyes glow a bright green, reminiscent of the zombies in the maze. She probably controls them too. All part of this engine thing that I don't really understand, but Gladdy seems to. "You put her in a *hole*. We were born in cages. She'll be alone and scared and lost in the dark, and she doesn't have me to pull her out."

"Oh my *God*," Stamen says. "The *emotions*. If you miss her so much, you can join her. Just a word of warning. It's not exactly a hole. More of a maze. But if you're so obsessed with her, I'm sure you'll stumble across her in the end."

"Wait," Lou cries, but it's too late.

I'm gone and there's nothing around me but darkness.

GLADDY

The darkness is absolute. I swallow panic. It's too much like the cages. But that's not me anymore. I've changed since then. I've killed since then. Except if we're being honest, which is what the darkness brings out in me, all the deaths were out of fear. I've never stood like Dylan, clear-eyed in front of the world, and executed someone as a statement. I've lashed out like a frightened creature curled up in its shell, squirting poison at my attackers. It's not at all the same thing.

Even Dylan's fear is strength, or so it seems to be. A fear borne from wanting to protect their friends, and build something strong enough to withstand all the pressures from outside. If they were here, what would they say to me? Their rough, expressive voice in the dark, peaking into disbelieving yelps.

"Fetch, you fucking pain in my ass, there's exactly zero fucking point in feeling sorry for yourself. It's darkness. First off, there's nothing scary in here except you. Second off, you've been here before and you got your overdressed ass the fuck out. Whatever fucking number we're up to, I put you in charge for a goddamn reason. You're going to solve this shit. Now stop pouting and stand the fuck up."

"Thanks, Chatty," I mutter.

The ground around me is smooth and flat. I pat my hands in a circle to make sure there are no spikes or monsters or dead bodies, then get slowly to my feet. There's no air movement in the room, no sense of warm or cool.

"I can promise you this, Fetchy," Dylan murmurs in my mind. "You won't get out of here by standing still."

"You say *I'm* bossy." I put my hands out in front of me and feel with my feet. There are no obstructions. I take a single step forward. Nothing terrible happens, so I take another one and another after that. There's not even any gradation of the darkness to show a possible way out, so I continue to shuffle in the same direction. It's possible I'm walking in a giant curve that will lead me back to where I started, but at least I'm moving.

Dylan laughs in my mind. It's like they're really here. "That's the spirit. If you find a corpse, step over it and keep walking. If you find a monster, fucking punch it. You'll be fine."

"Yes, I'll be fine."

Last time I was lost like this, Maddy saved me. We were in the dark together. All the complications of trying to navigate a relationship afterwards haven't changed that essential fact. I may not be what she wants, but I need her. Figure that fucking equation out. Now it's me on my own, and I'm imagining Dylan's voice in my mind instead.

I think it's because my relationship with Dylan is simple. She respects and likes me, but needs nothing from me that I can't provide. I did a personality test once, back before all this shit happened, and it said I'm more comfortable with data than humans. A lot like my father, which raises a whole convoluted knot of questions about inheritance that it's too late to answer. Maddy is very human, and I'm no good at navigating what lies between us. Figuring out the complexity of our relationship feels like what Stamen is doing with the energy matrix of Earth. Trying to build a new form of communication, when we're operating on entirely different sets of assumptions. I understand I'm being dramatic. We speak the same language, but there are things I don't want to say, because I'm scared of breaking everything, and I don't want to live in a world of rubble.

"I know it's fucking hypocritical coming from me, but there are times to dream about your hypothetical girlfriend, Fetch my darling, and times to focus on what's in front of you. This is one of the second kind. There are shadows among the shadows, so pay attention."

The imaginary voice of Dylan is correct. In the distance, something rustles and there is a whisper in response. What the hell is in here with me? Stamen put me somewhere out of the way. Perhaps she was bored of me, or perhaps I was getting to her. The real question is whether she put anything else in here too.

The moving sounds rustle closer. Things deeper than darkness. Oh great.

I keep my hands out and tread lightly.

"What is in here with us?" The voice is hoarse and very close.

"It's me. Gladiola Quick. They call me Fetch. I'm trying to find my way out."

"You're walking very strangely. Hiding from monsters, no doubt."

"That's because I can't see anything."

Fears coalesce around me, even though I can't see the speaker's face. They're scared of me, which is almost gratifying, as well as various threats from above and outside. It's all vague and formless, borne on rumours.

"Has anyone actually *seen* these monsters?" I ask.

"I heard someone being eaten. A lot of crunching, some slavering."

"Something bit my foot once," another voice says. "Took a chunk out of it."

Well that's creepy. I stop walking and wish I could see something.

"You should be glad you can't see anything," the first voice says. "Lots of leathery wings above us. The ceiling is full of them. Too many eyes, too many jaws."

"You haven't seen them either," someone scoffs. "You just heard that from Laurinell, and he talks an awful lot of shit."

"I hear them though. Can't you?"

Everyone falls silent. My eyes are wide, trying to drink in any tiny glimpse of light. I don't know if it's my imagination, but something sounds like canvas flapping in the wind. I would swear it's wings. These people putting ideas in my head.

Something cracks nearby, a huge sound of impact.

There's a wet tearing. Two voices scream, tailing off into ragged, hoarse sobs.

I run. Between the darkness and the sounds, it's all too much. My hands are thrust out in front of me, but I'm fleeing headlong with no regard for anything. I could tumble into a hole, or jaws could be waiting to fasten onto my feet, but I hurtle into the perfect darkness all the same.

Above me, the snap of wings is louder and louder.

It's not my imagination.

They're really in here with me.

I run and run until somewhere in front of me, a faint light source appears. It's a hazy grey chipping away at the edges of the shadows. When I look down, I can see the shapes of my feet. I'm running along a pathway marked out with glossy black paint. Behind me, something chuckles deep in its throat. You'd have to be incredibly stupid to look.

I stop, panting, and turn.

Behind me, the darkness is a tangible thing. It expands and contracts like it's breathing. Tendrils of it flicker out, searching for ways to expand, questing towards the faintness of the light. I turn and run, hoping to beat the darkness there.

A number of breathless paces further on, I bang my hands painfully on a wall. It's painted a featureless grey. To the left, the light flickers, and I squint at it. I can make out dim shapes—figures standing in a queue that trails along the wall before it curves out of sight.

It looks ominous, but it's better than the darkness.

It only takes a minute to reach the back of the line. The person standing there is shrouded in a dusty cloak. Their face is a ghostly mask, cratered like the surface of the moon.

"Excuse me." My hand brushes at the thick fabric. "What is this line for?"

"An accounting of history. All our names are to be collated and spoken one final time. A living book of the dead, if you'll pardon the many ironies."

"Then you're..."

"My reputation precedes me, does it? Yes, I am the Phantom you have undoubtedly heard of. The original, mind you, not one of these knockoffs. My powers manifested in 1884, and I was hung by the neck for my good deeds in 1890. For six years I roamed the night and protected those who needed it, not that I got any thanks from the law."

"You were one of the first mutants." All this history, lost when Teen Spirit took it from the world. Why all this is here, I cannot fathom.

"There were those before me, no doubt. My mother had strange powers of prestidigitation, but I was the first who donned a costume and took a name."

"The first? Hardly." A slender woman in front of Phantom turns, dressed in a red robe and wearing a golden mask with streaks of paint smeared across it. "I am Zhèn, born in the Northern Wei. I secreted poison in the tips of my fingers and used it to strike down those who would abuse their positions and their power to take advantage of others. They found me and put me to death when Phantom's island was full of squabbling tribes."

"This insistence of being the first is meaningless." A very old man turns to face us, lines of tattooed white tracing the wrinkles on his face. "I came of age in the Honey Ant Dreaming, when the world was new, and there were many of us with abilities. We nurtured our people and we thrived for many many years, until the ships came. We did not last long after that." He extends one hand towards me. "That is the lesson you should take away, living woman. All of us, from different places and times, killed for what we were. Death is the thread that binds us children of the Earth."

The other two figures nod in agreement.

"They will not suffer us to live," Phantom says.

Zhèn sighs. "Abominations, witches and demons. They never understood what we were."

"And what are we?" I blurt, suddenly desperate to know. These people have no fears any longer. I don't even know if these long-dead figments are truly here or projections that are part of Stamen's impossibly complicated machine.

"We are dead, and cannot help anyone," Zhèn says. "That does not hold for you."

"You live," the old man breathes. "All that lives has the potential for change."

"Do not waste your time in this dusty corridor, speaking to the historical record." Phantom raises a gloved finger and taps the brittle surface of his mask. "Flee this place."

"But Stamen put me in here." I feel awkward with them all looking at me, and other figures ahead turning to point and stare. "I don't know how to get out."

"The door, of course." Phantom shuffles aside, revealing a grey door set into the grey wall. I wouldn't have noticed it if he hadn't shown it to me. "I'm not sure it's *out* precisely, or further in, but waiting in line won't get you anywhere."

The old man reaches out and pushes the door open. It makes a soft, wheezing sound.

Inside, it is mostly dark again, but a single warm light glows above, suspended on a chain. It illuminates two armchairs, one of which is occupied. The figure in it turns towards me.

"Oh, there you are. It's about time. It's felt like forever."

"Maddy," I say, and it feels like coming home.

MADDY

Gladdy looks so tentative, peering in the door. Strange masked figures stand behind her, gesturing her onwards. I ran into a bunch of them too. They're mutants from history or something, and are super interesting people, but I'm here on an actual *mission* so I had to be very polite and tell them no thanks, not today.

"Come *in*, silly girl," I shout. "It's me, not some monster dressed up as Maddy."

She freezes in the doorway.

"Yes, I know that's exactly what a monster might say, especially a super realistic one who's sucked out all my thoughts and memories and can make a ridiculously pitch-perfect copy of me." I pause. "But if I'm that, who's going to be able to tell the difference anyway?"

That startles a laugh out of her. "That does sound like you."

"The more annoying I am, the more realistic you're going to find me, right? Okay, I promise I won't bite you." I clack my teeth together lightly. "Even if I am a monster, deep down."

"They call us all monsters." Gladdy takes a couple of steps into the room. "That's the impression I got from these people out here. Mutants have been around a long time."

I widen my eyes. "*Super* long. I spoke to one guy who claimed to have been the telekinetic who put the caps on the pyramids, but I'm pretty sure he was showing off."

She smiles, and my heart does the thing where it beats like a regular person's at the sight of her. "What are you doing in here?"

"Waiting for you. Stamen took you away, so I stamped my foot like Veruca Salt and said I wanted you back *now*. It worked super damn well because she sent me in here too. I've been wandering around for hours, talking to all these old-timey mutants until they showed me this place."

"What's in here?"

"Tea." I wave my hand in the direction of the table, which is lit up at my gesture, like we're in a smart house. For a horrible second, I think we might be back inside One Thorn. "Also cake."

"Cake." Gladdy will do a lot for cake. She creeps across the floor towards me, as if she's still not sure I'm me. "And why are we being fed?"

I pick up the delicate china teapot, etched with a beautifully painted picture of a woman who's partly a plant. "Courtesy of Stamen, I think, which only raises more questions. All part of her mysterious plan, perhaps."

Gladdy reaches the second seat. She stands behind it, both hands curled carefully over the back, embroidered with dusty pink roses. "For the two of us to be in a dark room at the center of a giant nightmare cloud and a long line of historical mutants?"

I try and arch my eyebrow like Dani does. "How is it different to rings of dancers? Or a maze full of zombies being executed by soldiers?"

"I thought this would be simple." Gladdy walks around the chair and sits, crossing her legs. I watch the way she moves. I always do. "This black ops Weapon UwU nonsense. It was supposed to be assassinations via fire or acid or mind control. Instead we find ourselves mediating a lover's quarrel, choosing between fighting siblings, and now lost in someone's arcane clockwork. It was *supposed* to be simple."

"Things work out differently all the time from what you'd expect." I blink at her under the golden spill of the light, and reach for one of the small plates of cake. "You start a story and it moves underneath you. It becomes about something else. For example, I never expected to get sick. I certainly didn't think I'd die and come back."

Gladdy reaches for another plate of cake and perches it on one knee.

"Then I fell in love in a cage," I continue. "I thought that was the beginning of an entirely new story. Except that twisted underneath me too."

The word love lies between us as if it's been slain, and Gladdy doesn't want to look at the corpse. It cools as we face each other.

Finally, Gladdy rotates the cake so it faces me. "Is that why we're here?" Picked out in tiny flowers made of fragile clusters of icing is the word *talk*.

"Very Alice," I sigh. "Drink me. Eat me. Talk to me. Love me."

Gladdy says nothing.

I decide that two can play at that game, so I close my lips firmly in response.

The silence stretches out between us.

GLADDY

This is ridiculous. It really is. The cake says talk, and so Maddy refuses to. It's some petty game to force me into opening my mouth and spilling my thoughts. It's not even a particularly clever tactic, because I have far less need for words than she does. I could keep this silence going until Stamen's horrifying machine reaches sentience or whatever it's aimed towards, and collapses the universe around itself. We'll be sitting in these chairs facing each other as reality ebbs away, and I still wouldn't need to talk first.

And yet, the irritating thing is that I owe her.

My best friend, and I've kept the truth from her.

"Love." My voice comes out in a croak, as if we've been sitting here for years without speaking. Perhaps we have, the strange way time moves in this place. "It's very confusing."

The corner of her mouth twitches upwards.

"I've spent a long time trying to figure it out." One of my hands has been resting against the cake, and icing is smeared on the knuckle of my middle finger. I rub it over my bottom lip, tasting the sweetness. "I don't know if I've gotten there yet."

"Maybe you can ask Stamen's giant machine to figure it out for you," Maddy says.

"It would be a better use for it than ending the world."

Maddy's eyelids flutter. She's irritated, and scared too. I have so many things to tell her, and I need to lay them out in the right order, so she can see the path between them, and realise everything isn't as terrible as she thinks.

"There are people I love," I tell her.

I feel the air grow colder, but it must be my imagination extrapolating from what's on her face.

"Are there?"

"Yes, there are." I feel defensive, and my voice prickles. "Dylan, for one."

MADDY

Dylan. Of fucking course it's Dylan. The person who least needs love, because they have an abundance of it. A badass girlfriend and a funny, caring parent. An adoptive little sister, two impossibly cool friends who adore her, and a gorgeous ex-boyfriend who still worships the ground they walk on. An assassin with a crush, a shark-wolf-girl who wants to be their adopted child and shit, even I like them.

They're slouched and scowling and sweet, and they gather everyone around them despite not seeming to care at all.

"Dylan," I snarl, because at this moment I hate her and would turn him into acidic slush.

Gladdy shifts in her seat. She leans forward. "I can see the anger and everything in your face. I'd like you to let me finish. There's a lot to explain."

My lips tremble. How could she be so cruel? Is she so clueless despite all her insight into fears, or is it that she has no feeling at all? Is that how she can dig these hooks so deep and watch me dangle on them?

"Fine. Finish."

"You remember how we met the Cute Mutants? All of us terrified, on the verge of panic. It was *you* who kept talking about joining them. I was sure they'd reject us—kill us or turn us in. Especially when they turned up at the house and saw my father in the bathtub. I was on the verge of total collapse."

"I don't remember it being like that," I whisper. My memories of Gladdy are of a furious, confident person who carried us all in her wake. "I remember trusting you, even when everything was awful and we lurched from one nightmare to another."

"I had to." She shrugs. "I thought if I broke, then the others would too. And you, because I always knew what was behind your smile. So I hid all my doubts and fears away, and tried to be strong for everyone."

My eyes fill involuntarily. She never trusted me, right from the start. "You were strong." My cheeks sting lightly as the tears roll down them. "But Dylan gave you a shoulder to cry on."

"I didn't fall in love with them right then," Gladdy says.

I close my eyes against the pain.

GLADDY

I know she's misunderstanding everything and not letting me tell the story properly. It's annoying because I'd like to do this chronologically, but I can't keep hurting her. I have to start blurting things out of order. "Honestly, Maddy. Don't you get it? I love Dylan like a sibling. An annoying, extremely precocious younger sibling who's always showing me up, but who I know has got my back and will fight to the bloody end for me. Do you understand?"

"But you think they're attractive." Maddy glares at me. "You said so."

"I find all *that* attractive." I flail one arm, to try and encompass it. "From the moment I saw them, I couldn't figure it out. How someone could be so impossibly insecure and yet stare the world down. And I find it all intriguing, the whole fluidity thing. Not sexy, because what even is that? Just interesting."

Maddy's cheeks flush, and I know she's thinking about Lou, which I also find interesting. Consensus among the Cute Mutants is that Lou is very sexy. I'll take their word for it. I've occasionally considered making a spreadsheet of who says who is hot, but Emma's psychic hacker powers would sniff that out in five seconds, and it would be around *everyone*. Of course, she can probably lift the ideas out of my mind anyway.

"I want you to believe me that I'm not pining after Dylan."

"I do believe you." Her eyes finally meet mine. "Dylan's your annoying little sib."

My mouth forms a grimace involuntarily. "Please don't ever say that to them."

"No promises." There's a flash of the old Maddy smile.

"That. Right there. Your smile." I take a breath. "I love your smile."

I don't know how to say the next part, strung as it is with caveats and sub-clauses and needing a thesis statement to set out all my definitions. How can this single word be wielded without all that framework constructed around it to create the precise setting? Otherwise how do you know which shade of meaning to attribute to it? I would build a world of words if I could, walls woven of sentences that speak of loyalty and fidelity.

What Maddy wants is the statement unadorned, so that's what I give to her.

I'll explain the shades of meaning later.

"I love you," I tell her.

MADDY

Oh please.

She loves me. Sure.

What loophole has she constructed so she can drive that word through it?

"Like a sibling." There's no smile on my face at all. "An annoying little sister."

Her jaw flexes. She's annoyed. Not the reaction she was hoping for. What, did she expect me to swoon? She just got finished telling me about how wonderful Dylan was.

There's a long pause. I count my breaths.

I get to sixteen.

"Like a world," Gladdy says. "And I'm a traveller who's been hurtling through space alone for a very long time. I've been to other worlds and some of them are interesting, but I never felt comfortable on any of them. They didn't feel like home. And then I crash-landed on a planet and everything at first was dark and terrible, but then the day dawned and I saw it was beautiful there, and it was the first place I ever wanted to stay. So I did, for longer than I'd ever stayed anywhere. When my ship was ready and I could depart, I realised I didn't want to ever leave."

My breath catches in my throat.

I don't know what this means.

GLADDY

The uncertainty flickers in her face like a candle flame. She's oscillating between thinking this is the declaration she's longed for, and wanting to scream at me to explain better.

"The problem is." My breath catches in my throat. "You're a whole world, and I'm only a traveller. All I can do is scratch the surface. I can't be everything you need, but I still want to breathe your air and walk your surface. I've acclimatised to you and now I can't leave."

Her eyes are huge and luminous, their warmth reflecting the golden light. "Do you want to leave?"

I shake my head. "Even if there were a thousand other worlds I could live on—which there aren't—I'd still want to live on yours."

She closes her eyes for a moment and then flicks them open. The force of her gaze makes me want to hide because it's so naked and unashamed. "You say you can't be everything I need. Why not?"

"The way you kissed Lou and made him glow. I'll never light up like that for you."

"He did light up quite a lot." She grins at me.

"I wish it was different. I've loved you more than I've ever loved anyone in my life, but I feel like it's a candle held up to the sun."

She purses her lips. "What if all I need is a candle?"

"That's what upsets me the most." Now my words are coming out too fast, like I've breached a dam and it's all coming down. They spill from my lips hot and fevered. "That you'd settle for me and call it love when there might be someone else out there. Whether it's Lou who'd literally light up when you walk into the room, or a person we don't even know yet."

"You're the best person I've ever met." Tears are spilling down her cheeks again.

"I'm not *going* anywhere," I say in exasperation. "I'll always be your person. We're woven and can't be unwoven. I still want to hang out with you and listen to your terrible jokes, to tell you all my wild ideas. To lie next to you in the night when I can't sleep and be soothed by the way you breathe."

She narrows her eyes at me. "Is this a passive-aggressive way of saying I snore?"

I shake my head, because she is the most exasperating person, and somehow that's part of why I feel the way I do. "No. I'm trying to tell you how much I love you and you're not making it easy."

MADDY

It's all out in the open, and it's exactly what I thought it was. I've been carrying this burden inside like it's too hot to touch, and now it's come gushing out and it doesn't hurt at all. She doesn't love me, not in *that* way. What's in her heart is a Gladdy version of the whole concept, with a weird metaphor about *space travel* of all fucking things, but it's perfect because it's her.

"Best friends," I say.

"It's more than that." Gladdy finally takes a delicate bite of her cake, like she can relax enough to do that, now that her confession is laid down between us like a blade. "Best friends is ordinary compared to what we have. We're like warriors who've fought a long campaign together. We're bonded in blood and fire, and now we've retired together because nobody else has seen the shit we have."

I give a gurgle of laughter. "Gladiola Quick, I never thought I'd accuse you of being an optimist."

She frowns, caught off guard. "How?"

"Pretending our campaign is over. Us bitter old battle buddies will be fighting for a lot longer than this."

"Bitter old battle buddies." She gives me a smile of her own, rare and beautiful. "I do like that. But you never know, we might be stuck in here forever, or at least until Stamen ends it all."

"Fine." I get to my feet. "Give me a hug then. Just in case it's the last thing we do. You do still hug, right?"

"Of course I hug." She's still smiling, and steps forward into my outstretched arms. I wrap them around her and hold her close. I nestle my head in against her shoulder because she's taller than me, which still seems unnecessarily rude.

"Soft old battle buddies," I murmur.

"I really do love you," she says, her lips pressed against my hair.

"Yes, yes, I know. I'm a world and a sun and we're bonded in blood. I do pay attention when you talk, believe it or not. And I love you too. So very much."

We step back from each other, and she's calm and poised and beautiful.

"And then there's Lou," she says, and her brows draw down as my cheeks flush hot.

GLADDY

I knew there would be *some* reaction when I said Lou's name, because even the most clueless person could see there's something going on. There are so many layers of feeling there, and I don't understand most of them. I know she feels like she has a decision to make and that's quite simply—

"You don't have to," I say.

One eyebrow pops up quizzically. "To what?"

"Choose. Between Glowboy and me. I mean, if you stop hanging out with me and won't hold my hand or lie next to me in bed when I need it, then I won't like it."

"I would never." Her eyes are so enormous I want to laugh, as if their size can convey the depth of her emotion. "You're stuck with me, I'm sorry to say."

"But, like, I get that you light up on the inside for him, just like he does on the outside. And you can do the kissing thing with him and I don't have to." It's hard to say this, even though everyone must know this about me, even the people who cannot see fears. It shouldn't be a *confession*, it shouldn't be something I need to steel myself to say. Just goddamn blurt it out, Fetch. "I don't feel that way. It's not about you. It's people in general. I already tried to explain love to you, and don't make me do that again, but it's different for me."

"I know," she whispers. "I understand."

"So, like, we could share?" The words come so tentative from my lips, even though I mean them with everything in me. I watch the fears flicker over her face, of navigating dual mazes of feeling and breaking two hearts at once.

"Does that work?" Her voice is even softer than mine. "Sharing like that?"

"Why shouldn't it? How is it harder than what we've done, fighting monsters and gods?"

"It's *emotions*," Maddy says. "They're a whole other thing. Besides, we're not done with the god-fighting yet, and it could be really bad outside."

"Then let's make a deal." There's a faint rumbling in the distance, and I glance around nervously. "If we get out of here, we'll try it. You and me carry on everything we have, and you can take a tentative step in Lou's direction. Just keep room in your life for me, that's all I need."

"Always." For a moment there are no fears in her eyes at all, and in their absence I see the shape of something beautiful. Three of us, forging new kinds of love from the connections we share.

"Maddy." I want to reassure her about everything, but the thundering is growing louder. The warm light above us dies, and we're left standing side by side in complete darkness. There's a whistling sound, almost like a scream, something horrible descending towards us.

She reaches out and pulls me close again. We're probably about to die, yet I still feel brave and awkward and confused, that I've spoken this wish into the air. That I've told the truth, and we're still standing here.

For now.

MADDY

There's an enormous crash, the sound of glass shattering, and then a thump as something soft hits the ground.

"Shit," a new voice says. It's soft and low, but familiar. "Ow, fuck."

There's a roughly punched circle of light above us. It's a ragged moon, a hole that an extinguished angel fell through.

Five faint flickers appear, waving gently through the air. "Where the hell?"

"Lou? Is that really you?" I pull away from Gladdy and move towards the light.

"Maddy?" The light flares brighter and drifts in our direction. It resolves into the faint shape of a hand, as if a very tired ghost is trying to manifest themself.

"Yes, it's me."

The glow brightens, like someone's dialled it up, enough to bathe Gladdy and me in sickly radiance. I blink at the suddenness.

"For fuck's sake. I'm so glad I came on this hellish rescue mission to find the two of you having a nice cozy snack. Definitely makes me feel like I'm saving you from all kinds of nightmares."

The light shows him too, and I can't help smiling. He looks terrible. Still unfairly handsome, but all beaten to crap. There are long scratches up and down his arms, and blood all over his face. I think about what Gladdy said, about negotiating something between the three of us, and it makes me so dizzy with desire and longing that I almost collapse. I reach for her, and she presses my hand lightly.

Lou limps toward us, the tips of his fingers glowing faintly.

I run to meet him. "You came to find us?"

"Well, yes. Stamen made me kill a swamp monster. Then she dropped me in the middle of this place, which happens to be full of dangers untold and hardships unnumbered. Luckily, they're not too fond of light and heat, so ya boy managed to fight his way here to the cozy little tearoom beyond the Goblin City."

"A dashing rescue." I place my lips to the non-bloody cheek and kiss him softly. I'd swear he deliberately turns his face so I catch the edge of his mouth.

"So how the hell do we get out of here?" Gladdy asks from behind us. "More fighting?"

"I think I lost them." Lou doesn't sound convinced.

"Lost what?" I ask.

There's a rapid tapping sound, like someone's pounding on the roof, except it's coming from all directions.

Gladdy looks at Lou, and her eyes widen.

"You didn't lose them," she says.

This time, when the roof caves in, other things come with it.

GLADDY

I knew this would happen. You don't need to see the fears in the eyes of the universe to realise it's about to come crashing down. The darkness that surrounded us is obliterated by light, and silhouetted against it are the shape of wings.

Fucking Stamen and her machine, poking holes in the universe. If you communicate with gods and monsters, you've got to be ready for them to shout back. Except we're the ones in the firing line. An exhausted boy, all bruised and battered. My best friend with a belly full of acid and nowhere near enough cake.

And then there's me. Gladiola Quick, staring up at an impossible creature of wings and tentacles descending towards me. I can see the fears in its compound eyes. It worries we're not enough to nourish it. It doesn't want to be hungry anymore. If there was only one, we might be okay. Except there's a swarm of them, descending in a tightly packed spiral.

"Tell me I'm handsome." Lou's voice is rough. He's looking right at Maddy.

She stands on tiptoes and kisses him.

The boy lights up. It's cute, and I'm happy for them both. He's really going to need to glow.

"Eat up, Sourpatch." I hold out the remains of the cake. I'm smiling, even though I know we're going to die. We'll go out fighting. It's what Dylan would do. I reach out and pick up the big plush armchair I was recently sitting in. It doesn't seem like much of a shield.

Beside me, Lou is too bright to look at.

Maddy grins at me through a mouthful of cake. How can she smile now? How are there not more fears in her eyes? She has faith in us. She thinks we'll survive this somehow, to try this new experiment.

It's almost contagious.

Maddy spits, a huge acid cloud huffing from her mouth. It tears holes in the descending monsters, great ragged vents that make them howl. The noises they make are sirens with teeth, so shrill they claw through my ears and into my brain.

I brandish my chair in front of me like a plump shield. It's too damn heavy, and my arms already ache. The monsters whirl and flap, coming apart in ragged chunks. Things fall around me, and I cringe away. I curl myself into the softness of the armchair, and wait to be rescued.

It's not very dignified, is it? I'm supposed to be the Field Leader. But sometimes that means letting others do the hard part. It means crouching here and watching Maddy's body convulse violently, coughing up ever-thinner streams. It means watching Lou's light flickering, the fire that flares from his fists guttering in the breeze from hundreds of wings.

They fight beautifully, and they fight valiantly, and it's simply not enough.

The creatures fall upon me. The shield I hold is shattered, and they open their mouths, beautifully soft and fringed with gently waving tentacles. They clamp themselves to my flesh.

They feed.

MADDY

I'm preoccupied with using my power in the most efficient way possible. It's us against overwhelming odds. We're superheroes. This is what we do. We're going to find a way through this. We've done it before.

So I spit until the reservoir of acid that sloshes inside of me feels dangerously dry. Horrifying monsters come apart above me, drenching me in unmentionable fluids. I'm standing over where Gladdy is hidden behind one plush armchair as if it's a defense.

I wipe goo from my eyes. My stomach growls. I've got almost nothing left, and the monsters still come. Beside me, Lou's incandescence is failing. He's sputtering. He'll go out soon like a dying candle.

Maybe this time we're going to lose. I hope I get a chance to kiss him again.

Someone screams behind me, and my sluggish heart almost gives up the fight entirely.

I turn to see Gladdy lying on her back. All I can make out are her extremities twitching as these creatures fasten themselves around her. My stomach heaves, trying to dredge up the last of my poison. They carefully arrange themselves to drain her, so as many can feed as possible.

"No." My throat aches. I'm scalding myself from the inside out. "You can't."

The creatures glow with the ecstasy of feeding. A purple light fills them, like they're bloating with it, their ragged outlines expanding. Each facet of their eyes glows a different shade, a riot of virulent colour.

"Feed," they exult. "Embrace life. The glory of the hive."

I stagger forward. I need to stop them, to tear them apart. With my bare hands if I'm out of acid. We fight. No matter what it takes.

There's a pinch at the back of my neck. It's gentle, almost a caress.

Clarity comes in a numbing rush.

To evolve is to die. Every death is an ascension on the wheel. We will end here, one part of Stamen's glorious machine. We are cogs in something greater. To fight and claw, to assert our individuality, is a futile middle finger raised at the universe.

"Chatterbox was wrong." I cough and drool purple liquid down my front. "Embrace death."

Light pours out of my body. I'm part of a beacon, one tiny light amongst thousands. The three of us dying mutants along with thousands of dying monsters. All joined together in death. United in feeding, in changing, in *becoming*.

"Except fuck that," I say. "It's a trick, isn't it? The action of a predator. It's numbing its prey."

"Yes, you're very clever," a soothing voice replies. "Except it's working, so don't struggle and fuck it up."

"All we know is struggle." It's Gladdy's voice, very faint. "We're not giving up now."

"You're very tiresome," the voice says. "But I think we've cracked it now anyway."

"Cracked what?" I ask, but everything is gone.

GLADDY

For a minute or two, I genuinely think I'm dead. I'm standing in the middle of a white and featureless void. There's nothing I can see. It's a complete absence of everything. I turn in a slow circle. Dylan's voice doesn't even chime into my head.

"Wow, great." Stamen appears beside me, looking rather more woman and less plant than last time. "You near as nothing fucked it up. If you hadn't, I'm sure it would have resolved eventually, me being the smart and enterprising sort who has uncountable backup plans, but this one was my favourite."

"What are you talking about?" I ask, half in curiosity and half in exasperation. Her fears are still disturbingly unreadable, but if I had to translate, I'd say she came face to face with something terrifying and she's giddy about escaping.

"You and Madelaide! I saw immediately all this complex emotional energy swirling between you. Another element to feed into my machine. So I wound you both up and I put you in a room together. I crossed my fingers really hard, then I hoped even harder, and it all worked exactly as I wanted. So everything was primed, and I simply needed a spark."

"I don't understand." It annoys me that she's gloating, at the end of the universe, when everything is done and gone. What's the point of bringing me back? Why do villains always need an audience?

"Oh please." Stamen rolls her eyes. "You lot come bowling in here all packed full of extra-universal energy. What's a girl to do?"

"The parallel universe." It's starting to make sense in my exhausted brain. "The creatures that fed on us in there. They transferred some energy or something?"

"There you go. Clever girl." Stamen pats her hands together in mock applause. "Yes, you were carrying enough energy to kickstart the full flowering of my wonderful machine. Except you almost wrecked it, the three of you, kicking and biting like that. Do you know how hard it is to summon pan-universal predators?" She sighs, as if we were deliberately causing problems. "It worked, though, I'm sure you're happy to know."

"And you've collapsed reality." I want to fall apart myself, but I'm still standing here like I'm waiting for one final punch. "You and I are the last survivors of the entire universe."

Stamen stares at me for a moment and then dissolves into giggles. "Oh my god. No. Wow. Aren't you just the gloomiest thing? Reality is fine, honestly. Once I finally managed to *communicate* with Cy, it didn't take long to straighten things out."

She's won while my back was turned. I sat in the darkness, all cozy with Maddy, and in the meantime Stamen has bent all of reality to her will. It's better than it all being torn apart, but I'm not sure by how much.

"Show me, then," I demand. "I want to see how the world looks now."

Stamen sighs. "Turns out my new friend is a spoilsport. Things are collapsing in a very specific way, and she has plans of her own. Was quite rude about me meddling in them. Called me clumsy, if you can believe that, and demanded I keep my fingers to myself."

"What are you talking about?"

She beams at me. "Everything that's about to be unleashed. You'll have ringside seats to it. A good friend of yours will be center of the maelstrom. A change is definitely going to come."

"What does that mean?" I ask sharply. "Maddy?"

"No spoilers." Stamen laughs, delighted. "I'm not even going to spoil myself. I've been asked to vacate the premises so as to not fuck things up further. Cy's not a big fan of our family tree, it turns out. Some bad blood between her and Heart. Honestly, I think I'm going to swing by One Thorn and beg passage somewhere very, very distant. At least until this world finishes shaking. I'll come back and see the outcome, but I do have my fingers crossed for poor old Cy."

"You're so irritatingly cryptic." I push hair off my face. "And who the bloody hell is Cy?"

"Not a question you'll have for too much longer," Stamen sing-songs. "The important thing is that you've won. Saved the day with friendship and love. Delicately Drooping Stamen has been defeated and will disappear. That leaves all of Heart's old toys tucked away in one form or another, doesn't it? I hope you get a sticker."

I'm still bewildered by all of this. Despite all the ominous hints, Stamen seems remarkably cheerful.

"What do I tell the others?" I ask.

"That you saved the day." She reaches out and pats my cheek. Her hand is cool and slightly green. "It's the truth, after all, and now you deserve a little break. I'll take you back to the real world. Might see you again someday."

She leans in and kisses me, smelling of rose petals and red wine. My eyes flutter briefly closed and when I open them, I'm standing in the middle of a field. The rest of the team is standing with me. Aside from Maddy, who's beaming, they all look very much the worse for wear. Katie has burned all her hair off again, and Ye Shou is sagging like she's lost a bunch of her spiders.

"What happened to you?" I ask her.

"I'll be fine." Her eyes flutter. "They always repopulate themselves."

I don't want to think about that too much, so I stand in the sun and try to look for any sign of Stamen's territory. The world looks entirely normal. Waving crops and rough roads and the heat of the sun. We all grab our phones out and check social media, which is already filling up with wild stories. People are coming back to themselves. Their memories are strange and hallucinatory. Nobody's making any kind of official statement.

"What the bloody hell happened in there?" Lou says. "It seems like we won, but I can't figure out how."

"I'm not entirely sure." I frown. "It's all… hazy. We fought though, against a horde of monsters. Stamen wound her machine down, and said something about…" I tail off, racking my brain to try and remember everything she said.

"We're alive though." Skye's on her own, looking peaceful. "All of us. Even if we were pawns, we became queens. Or kings if you'd like, Lou."

"The most badass one is fine." Lou grins.

"Yes." Maddy links one arm with Lou and another with me. "We fucking castled the shit out of them.

Checkmated! Bopped them with our horsies. I don't know how to play chess. The point is that we won, because we're super amazing."

"You really are."

We all turn, to see Dylan standing behind us, hair ruffled by the wind.

"Nice job, weapon UwU," they say.

MADDY

Katie throws herself at Dylan and hugs her hard. I wish I could join in, but I hang back with my eyes on Lou. I wonder if he's thinking about hugging Dylan too.

Dylan runs one hand over Katie's scorched scalp. "You okay?"

"Of course I am. I'm the original badass, remember? Plus I flew like a real dragon!"

"Now that is the first thing I've heard that's actually fucking scared me." Dylan shakes her head and looks around. "Took you a while, but looks like you've turned Europe back into… whatever the fuck it was before. I've never been. Looks nice though."

"I am delighted and impressed." Petal flutters through the air and dances along Gladdy's arm in a series of pirouettes. "All my help was invaluable, I'm sure. My sister is very stern, and says I provided too much assistance to you all, so now I must go and make my apologies to her."

I hold out my hand next to Gladdy's arm and Petal hops onto it, gazing up at me. "You said you hated your sister."

"Family." Petal waves one arm dismissively. "You understand how these things are. We may be a group of monsters, children of a dark and troubled heart, but we still love each other beneath it all."

"Stormclouds," Dylan says, their lips twisting. "That's what you said."

"Yes, they gather on the horizon." Petal shudders. "We shall hope Yǔzhòu weathers them, but the world is hers to inherit."

"You shall diminish and go into the west?" Gladdy asks, which I don't understand.

"We shall remain ourselves." Petal leaps into the air. "And hopefully see you all on a brighter day. But for now, be cheerful. Victories like these don't come along often."

The air glimmers and she is gone, as if she disappeared into a fold in the universe like Penance.

"Cryptic." Dylan scowls. "I fucking hate it. Too many mysterious assholes these days."

"We won though," I point out.

Their expression flickers and changes to something brighter. "You did. My extraordinary friends. I'm actually very proud, even if you took your sweet time."

"How long were we gone?" Gladdy asks.

"Couple of weeks. The growth of it slowed as soon as you went in, so I figured you were doing something right. Some people were talking about storming the castle, but I always had faith in you."

"We got a bit banged up." Lou extends one brown arm towards Dylan, rotating it to show the wounds.

"We gonna do a whole trading scars scene?" They pull up their hoodie slightly to show the complex pattern of white marks that run up their side. "That's always kinda hot."

Lou snorts. "Some of us are smarter about running into trouble."

"How did everything go down with Stamen in the end? I'm guessing she's at the apocalyptically powerful end of the spectrum?"

"Powerful and reckless, but she's gone," Gladdy says. "Or said she's leaving. Using One Thorn to escape before something changes. The details are…" She wrinkles her brow. "Hard to recall, actually. I'm sure there was a name she used, but it escapes me."

"Uh, Fetch." Dylan's eyes are narrowed. "That sounds awfully suspicious."

"I don't remember much at all. Maddy and I had this heart to heart, and there was tea and then…"

"I don't remember it either." Even the memory of our conversation is more like I was watching it as a TV series, standing from outside and listening to two actors speak their words. We talked about Lou, and made some possible arrangement about a new relationship between us, and then… "Nope. It's gone."

Dylan looks unsettled. "Sure, that's not fucking ominous at all. I'm sure it's all going to be sunshine and fucking roses. It always is. But France is back to normal, and we might get some credit for that at least."

"Saved the day rah rah." I smile as wide as I can.

"The world still turns." Gladdy pushes her hands into the pockets of her jacket and shivers. "It felt very close to going the other way."

"Apocalypse averted." Dylan points finger guns at us. "We're all grateful. There will be debriefings galore but that can wait. Is everyone else doing okay? Ye Shou? Skye?"

They both nod, although they look distracted.

"Mandatory sessions with Ray when you get back. Let them poke around in your head and make sure you're not broken."

"It's almost like you care." I bat my eyelashes.

"Don't tell anyone." Dylan winks at me. "It'll ruin my stellar reputation. Speaking of, you lot fought a bunch of gods and survived. That sounds like you deserve ice cream."

"It sounds like we deserve to get very very drunk," Ye Shou says dryly.

"You can do that later, although I shudder to think of a million fucking drunk spiders cavorting around Westhaven and freaking everyone out."

Katie gives a little frightened sound like a cat.

Ye Shou draws herself up stiffly. "I have never done such a thing, no matter the level of my inebriation. But yes, ice cream sounds good as a preliminary."

~ UwU ~

The ice-cream parlour that Keepaway finds is nearly deserted. Dylan gives the owner a bunch of money to leave the store alone for the rest of the afternoon, and promises not to wreck it. I have literally zero idea why the woman who runs it trusts a barefoot person with a half-ass smirk and messy hair, but she bustles off happily.

It means all the Skyes can come out and get their ice cream, although that immediately devolves into a food fight because Six is there. Dylan has to pull rank and shout a lot at them to get everything cleaned up. I ignore most of the chaos and take my ice-cream over to where Lou is sitting alone in a booth, nursing his wounds.

"Hello, hero." I slide in opposite him.

"Hero? I wandered around in the dark for a really long time, got scratched and bit, set some things on fire, and then turned up in time for the whole thing to be over."

I hold his gaze. "You still came and looked for me."

"That's just what we do. Cute Mutants or Weapon UwU. We look out for our friends."

Friends. The word rings in my ear with an unpleasant echo.

"Listen." I stab my spoon into my ice cream, and lick chocolate sauce off my finger, only a tiny bit sexily. "I keep a lot of stuff inside, despite my charming exterior."

"Very charming." God, there's that smile.

"So this time I'm going to try the opposite tack. I like you. Not just as a friend. I'm not sure exactly as what, but I kinda sorta think I'd like to experiment. You're stupidly hot, so much so that if I had your power I'd be like an Old Testament angel lighting up the place. And you're cool and kind and funny as well, so it's like… why not, right? And I get that you've just broken up with someone and I'll probably be rebound girl but like, I'm still willing to roll the dice, because it seems like—"

"Maddy," he says.

"What?" I widen my eyes.

"Take a breath and let me interject."

"Okay."

"I really like you too. Not as rebound girl. Just as… you. This might sound super weird, but I've had a crush on you since you pretended to be a cat when we met Kitty Pride."

"Oh." I can't keep the smile off my face. "*Oh.*"

"I just assumed that there was something else going on, you know, between you and Fetch. So I figured you were off limits. But believe me—"

"Lou," I say.

"What?" His own eyes are wide.

"Your turn to stop talking." I lean across the table and kiss him, soft and slow. His tongue is cold from the ice-cream, even more so than mine. My warm tongue flicks against his, and I feel the temperature rise so fast I have to pull away.

He's glowing, the beautiful boy.

"Sorry." His face is possibly red, but I can't look at it because it's too bright.

"We'll figure this out." I can't stop smiling. "You wait. I'll find a way."

GLADDY

"Success then." Dylan's smile flickers.

"Of a sort." I pull my hair back from my face, securing it tightly. "Part of me feels like we only stood by and watched it all happen, but—"

"It feels like that a lot." Their smile is far wider now. "Believe me. It's the life of a superhero. So I'm telling you, and you can listen to me. This? What you and your team did? It's a goddamn victory, so take it."

"Fine." I lower my head and smile at my bowl. "It's a victory."

"I do appreciate it, and Dani does too. To have people we trust."

"Delegation," I laugh.

"Something like that. Or you can call it friends that have your back when there's weird fucking shit afoot, and you need a very special type of badass."

"I like the second definition."

"Good." They dig their spoon into their ice cream, making an enormous mess. It's fascinating, the way they frown at it as if it's an enemy. "I know, Fetchy." A long curl at the front of their mohawk falls across one eye and he sweeps it away. "I'm disgusting." Her eyes dart over my shoulder, to something behind me. "Is that a thing everyone knows about?"

"They've been flirting the whole time," Katie says. "It's definitely a thing."

"Oh." I glance over my shoulder to watch as Maddy detaches from Lou, who's a glowing beacon. I can feel the heat coming off him all the way across the shop. "Yes, that does appear to be a thing."

Dylan's eyebrow raises a tiny bit. "They're cute together. I'm guessing they've got your blessing."

"Yes." I smile, even though I don't know how to navigate this *sharing* that I might have to do, with Lou taking a larger role in Maddy's life. "She's happy, so I'm happy."

And I mean it. I look at her face, and I see all the fears written there. She still worries about me, and whether I'm truly happy. About Lou, and what *romance* might be like and whether it's something she'll crush by holding it too tightly in her hand. She fears balancing us both, and somehow letting us both down. Then there's the future, all the uncertainty gathering. So much unseen, so much waiting to descend upon us.

The difference is that now I see where hope spills into the edges of the fear. She can see a future with love and friends, with so much to hold in her heart that it overflows everywhere.

It's the most beautiful thing I've ever seen.

ACKNOWLEDGEMENTS

As always, there are so many people to thank: first to my family and friends, who put up with my obsessions and keep believing in me.

So much thanks to the Weapon UwU beta squad who read this weird offshoot of my series and told me that the heart of it was beautiful, despite the horror on the outside: Hsinju, Emma, Amanda, Jen, Art, Andee, Rosa, Charlotte and Logan.

There are too many people who provide encouragement, advice and support to shout them all out, but I'll make a start at least: to Shannon, Leta, CJ, Avery, Brittany, E.M, Ashley, Amber, Yves, Althea, Kelsee, Andy, Bertie, Page, Emily, Shelly, Ming and Lynn—thank you for everything you've done to help me get through this. If I've missed anyone, I'm sorry but know that you're all appreciated.

My writing group of Team Trash puts up with a lot of me complaining about… pretty much everything. So to Andy, Crystal, Leah, Mallory, Melo, Michelle,

Monica, Nat, Nina, SinJ and SoftJ—thanks for listening, for the support when spiralling, for the jokes, and for helping me believe I can actually achieve the Cute Mutants Universe.

Thanks also to Jenn Lee who did the amazing cover for this book, and to G once again for the beautiful formatting that makes these books look so wonderful inside as well.

ABOUT THE AUTHOR

SJ Whitby lives in New Zealand with their partner, as well as various children and animals. They are predictably obsessed with X-Men and spend too much of their free time writing, plotting out way too many sequels, spin-offs and parallel universes. Perhaps they take their X-Men fandom too seriously.

You can find them on Twitter at @sjwhitbywrites.

Printed in Great Britain
by Amazon

63557294R00258